# HECTOR'S WAR

a novel by

# GEORGE WING

**RIVER BOOKS**
an imprint of The Books Collective
214 - 21 10405 Jasper Ave.
Edmonton, Alberta, Canada
T5J 3S2

Copyright © George Wing 1999

All rights reserved. No part of this book may be reproduced or transmitted in any form or by any means, electronic or mechanical, including photocopying, recording, or by any information storage and retrieval system, without permission in writing from the author and publisher, except by a reviewer or academic who may quote brief passages in a review or critical study.

All characters in this story are fictitious.

River Books and The Books Collective acknowledge the ongoing support of the Canada Council for the Arts and the Alberta Foundation for the Arts for our publishing program. We also acknowledge the support of the City of Edmonton and the Edmonton Arts Council. We would also like to thank David Macpherson of Ingénieuse Productions.

Editors for Press:
Candas J. Dorsey, Paula Johanson
Cover design by Gerry Dotto

Inside layout and design by Dianne J. Cooper at The Books Collective
in Impact, Arial and Century Schoolbook (True-Type Font)
in Windows Quark XPress 4.0.
Printed at Convention Graphics

Published in Canada by River Books, a member of:
The Books Collective,
214-21 10405 Jasper Avenue,
Edmonton, Alberta, T5J 3S2.
Telephone (780) 448 0590

## Canadian Cataloguing in Publishing Data

Wing, George, 1921–
    Hector's War

    ISBN: 1-895836-68-9
    I. Title.
PS8595.1595H42 1999    C813'.54    C99-911173-6
PR9199.3.W499H42 1999

Dedicated to
Joan, Marje and Daff

Art has rightly nothing to do with the history of war; it should be concerned only with its anecdotes. Art should go into the byways of battle. It must move the soldier and love him individually, not in battalions.

Alice Meynell, Magazine of Art, 1879, p.209

# ONE

As the two boys huddled at the base of the trench, tin hats cold on their heads, boots and puttees soaked through, they knew dread in their battle-hardened bones. If he hadn't volunteered for the army, Hector Plouvier would have been on the family farm in the foothills of Alberta and perhaps still in a crazy and furtively exciting relationship with his Aunt Sammy. Bob, his buddy, was from Quebec, and so far as Hector was aware had not had carnal knowledge of any of his aunts.

"Mam'selle from Armeteers parly-voo…" Hector sang the first line of the ballad in a monotone of disgust. He could speak fluent French when he wished.

"So?" Bob asked.

"Inky-pinky parly-voo! Them two women!"

"What's the problem, old buddy?"

"They are all the same."

The boys heard the crack of the enemy mortar bomb as it started on its trajectory towards the stars above a typically doomed stretch of the Western Front near C\*\*\*\*. The blasted landscape was seared on their lives like a cattle brand. The bomb must rise one heck of a height before swooshing down and exploding among them, two hundred yards from where it started.

"I bet they're full of pox, them two at the estaminet. Tyler should never have risked it. The dummy!"

Hector could speak grammatical English, too, even though he was a farm boy. Lousy English and execrable French were part of his psychological armour, part of his army swagger, though as the trench-bound years dragged on, he was beginning to care less and less.

The bomb burst into lethal fragments somewhere to their right. Brutalized as they had become, they still hoped it would be an isolated one, that there would not, despite the clear sky, be many more like that tonight. The two soldiers and their comrades leaned against the wall of the trench to try to catch some sleep. Damp from the clay sweated through the timber revetment.

"Hi fellers. Listen up to this hick from the prairies. Knows it all, don't ya, Hec?"

"For Chrissake knock it off, Jake, you bastard. Just leave my buddy alone. You want to get some service in, you do. You don't know shit."

"Only fuckin' kiddin'. Can't you guys take…"

He was interrupted by shouts and screams further down the trench, past the zig-zag. A slim figure, hatless, in khaki service dress, Sam Browne belt, pistol with a cord attached in a leather holster, came from behind the blanket that screened the company headquarters and officers' mess, just as though he were in a play.

"Any of you men hit?" the boy subaltern asked. Silky down on his upper lip, he had not long to live. He was a statistic already, a Great War cliché in this primeval sludge. Just one more Killed in Action.

"I think it landed in D Company, sir."

"Poor devils."

"Yes sir."

03 ❀ 80

There was not much to do on the ranch in winter other than watch the snow fall and the cattle fart and belch and the prairie harden into iron. From time to time the chinook winds would come and melt some of the snow, but their warmth could not reach far into the deep frozen earth, and when they stopped blowing they left a surface of treacherous ice. Hector and his father would bring the cattle and their smell nearer the ranch-house. His father would have cut Hector's liver out if he'd discovered there was anything shameful going on between him and Aunt Sammy. When he told the family he was going into Calgary to enlist he'd intended to join the local regiment, but by some quirk of military bureaucracy he and half a dozen other volunteers were put on a train and sent east. They had a brutal infantry training, largely under the sadistic rule of a Neanderthal sergeant-major from Glasgow who had served in the Boer War.

"Some of the guys'll tear the balls off that Scotch jerk when this shit's over—which won't be long. I sure hope that we get out to France before it's all over," Bob said to Hector.

"He's a big brute, though," Hector said. "We had a Clydesdale like him once. On the ranch."

Bob and he had clung together through shot and shell since. Bob once asked how come Hector spoke French. "Plouvier. That's a French name, ain't it, but you sure as hell don't look like a Frog."

"My mom's from Montreal. She learned us French at home."

"Is that right?" Bob was polishing his boots so that that Scotch fucker could see his ugly face mirrored in them. In the trenches, their boots were caked with mud.

Hector Plouvier had explained to Bob that his dad wasn't French, despite the name. The paternal grandfather had come from south Wales in fact. His dad's dad.

"Really!"

In Hector's tunic pocket with his paybook was a brown and white photo of Bob and him at the infantry training depot. Bob had his cap at a rakish angle over hair shaven high up the back and sides. In real life he was ginger with bigger freckles than Hector's. Friendly eyes. Faint eyebrows. An incipient ginger moustache. Though they were same age, Bob looked older than Hector, whose prairie blond hair looked white in the creased photo and whose features were still plastic and adolescent.

☙❀❧

Some unlucky soldier had been hit by a jagged piece of mortar casing, and they were carrying him on a stretcher to the regimental aid post. He was sobbing and asking the bearers, "Why me? Why have the cunts got me?" Hector and his mates stood up and flattened themselves against the trench wall to let them pass. "He's got one in the belly," a bearer said. The officer smoothed down his soft moustache and gazed mutely, soulfully on them.

But the lone mortar bomb which tore into the guts of the infantryman from Sault Sainte Marie proved to be the deadly herald of what the boys feared. Far from being a solitary burp in the night, it was the premature shot of one of the bloodiest and noisiest battles that Hector had ever been in. He and Bob had endured many battles and neither had gotten so much as a scratch, not even trench feet or fever so that they could be evacuated to Blighty, or even, mirabile dictu, Canada. They never got much further than a local estaminet like that one where they'd seen those two girls in their black stockings, smelling of cheap perfume and dried cattle dung. Hector had been there a couple of nights ago with Tyler Brown who would fuck the ass off anything female, a mangy alley cat if push came to shove. Not all of the boys in khaki were like Tyler Brown, who would risk getting a dose at the estaminet. Many of them were still moral and religious, brought up in pioneering rectitude and despite repression and temptation keeping themselves wholesome for their sweethearts back home. Not many had scored with an Aunt Sammy either.

"It's all right for some guys," Tyler said. "But if a feller needs to get the dirty water off of his chest then he needs to get it off. You following me, Hec?"

"You bet."

Their brigade had been in a reserve area, not far from the front line where they were now, but far enough to get rid of some of the lice and not live all the time in their sodden boots. The authorities did precious little in the way of welfare for the men in or out of the line other than put bromide in their tea in the vain belief that it dulled their sexual appetite. A padré was attached nominally to each battalion, but the officers of the Lord, the God-botherers, were like the rest of the canon fodder—some good apples, some rotten.

Hector and Tyler had walked across the pocked fields and rutted lanes, hardening now like the winter prairies. Bob had not been able to come; he'd copped a couple of nights' jankers from an asshole of a new sergeant from Hamilton. He would learn, the sergeant would, as time went by. The boys were indifferent to petty authority and endured it as they did the rats and the lice. The estaminet was out of bounds to other ranks, but no one gave a shit about that, not even the Military Police.

"Jeez! Am I ever horny," Tyler said as they opened the bar door.

The village had been battered, but still some of the inhabitants, old women mostly, clung to their wrecked houses—some still standing where all the trees and hedgerows had been flattened—and went to the village pump, which was still working, and cooked scraps over what little wood they could forage at the back of the battlefield.

"Just you leave this to me, Hec."

Tyler was older than most of the other soldiers, brought up in Toronto, city smart. He had never experienced the sod houses of the prairies, but he had huddled on icy street corners, stamping his feet, swinging his arms, blowing on his hands.

"Bonsoyer, Henree. How's aboot a pettee drinkee-poo for starters? For moy and this monsoor." He turned to Hector. "You gotta know the lingo, Hector my lad. The Froggies respects you for it."

Winter had left a permanent pallor on his face which the hot humid summers of Toronto served only to intensify. The subterranean existence of the trenches seemed the natural habitat for him. Dapper, black moustache, tended and clipped even in the worst of trench living, bristlier than his lieutenant's, his pale face seamed with memories of cheap boarding houses, one night stands, struggles for a living in a raw city, for a respectability. Squandered, misdirected talent.

The bald head of the man behind the bar glistened in the lantern light.

He sported a Kaiser Bill moustache, stained by nicotine and brandy and home-made soups, and his patriarchal belly was wrapped around with a blue apron. He placed a couple of small glasses on the bar. As he poured a miserly measure of viscous liquid into each glass he muttered something sardonic without opening his mouth and the two women laughed. Hector knew what he said even though it was in patois, but he never let on about his French. Bob was the only one in the platoon who was privy to his bilingual gift.

"They're fucking glad to see us, Hec. You can tell, can't you?"

"Why isn't this place packed out?" Hector asked. "Why aren't the squaddies lining up for a piece of tail?"

If Hector had not become so cynically passive, his heart would have sunk as they went in. He and Bob had been in many a broken down French bar where they'd got as drunk as they could on what little money they had, but the sight of these two women, faces bravely painted, did nothing to give him an erotic charge. The dead white skin and the disillusionment still showed through the cosmetics. Tyler the irrepressible was already kneading the breasts of one of them at the rickety round table they sat at. Celine. Literally a sad sack with uncorseted body and bosom flopping about like giant dumplings. She was younger than the other, Suzette, but the years didn't matter here. Hector shook his head and thought of Aunt Sammy. Memories of her invariably carried a mixture of guilt and delight, though over time the lousy war cauterized his conscience and made him believe there was no darned use being sorry for anything.

"How much moolah you got, old buddy? She wants it on the table before she'll lift her flippin' skirt."

Celine gave Hector an indifferent, sickly smirk.

As the stretcher bearers carried their latest burden away, Hector told Bob that no fucking way had he lent Tyler one centime, but somehow he'd managed to persuade Celine to let him rattle away on her spongy body. In a recess by the bar a mattress with the feathers bursting out of it lay on an iron bedstead with three of its four brass knobs missing. It was partly screened by a curtain of heart-sinking browns hanging from a rod fixed between the top of the bar and the wall.

"I wouldn't touch either of them with a broomstick. Jesus! You shoulda seen them two, Bob. Tyler never took his cap off. And heard them. There was nobody to listen, mind, except the barman and an old bozo with one of them big red boil things on his neck. Musta had two pints of matter in it. Where's Tyler, anyways?"

"He got sent on a detail. To brigade H.Q."

"No kidding. Some guys get dead lucky, eh?"

# TWO

Aunt Sammy's name was Bridget Donnelly before she married Sam Plouvier, Hector's uncle. As little kids, Hector and his sister Michelle couldn't pronounce "Bridget" and so she became Auntie Sammy to them and the childish sobriquet stuck right through to the time of Hector's mounting her in the Sick Barn early in the summer he enlisted to go and fight the Hun in France. It just so happened there was a sick steer in the barn that day in a makeshift corral, munching at dried grass and from time to time looking over at them through moist, sad eyes.

"That creature seems to know we are doing something naughty."

Aunt Sammy giggled. In her superior voice mode she was too refined to call it a "critter", but did not appear to think it unladylike to have the long skirt of her summer dress with the little roses on it hoisted way above her waist nor the grey stockings on her long legs covered in bits of straw.

"No, not like that, Hector, you silly boy. You've got to come down a bit. It won't bite, you know."

Hector was delirious that day, flying high as a kite above the barn, and although it was not the only time he dipped his wick into his aunt it was this first ecstatically perilous bout that he remembered in the long months in the trenches when the shells and the bombs were bursting and his comrades were being picked off by German snipers and the poison gas came creeping like a prairie mist through the barbed wire.

"Oh dear. Now you are hurt and it's gone all soft. You mustn't mind my teasing, dear, dear boy."

Hector jumped off his prostrate aunt and rushed to the barn door. The steer made a noise, resonant and deep like a foghorn at sea.

"What is the matter, Hector?"

"I thought I heard a horse. I though it was me dad come back."

Aunt Sammy looked fondly at her open-faced nephew, not yet seventeen, quick to blush, freckled, glowing with prairie health. Virile as only a teenage boy can be. Big man, collarless flannel shirt tight across his shoulders, screwing his aunt. His cock showing in his unbuttoned trousers had now shrivelled into derisory flaccidity. Bridget shouldn't be messing like this. She was fond of her brother-in-law, Nick, for all his furtive lechery, and knew he would be appalled at her seducing his son. Appalled at least. Maddened, stark staring crazy more like. Perhaps he would think it was some form of revenge. What the heck. She sat up in the hay and smoothed down her skirt.

"Come back here," she commanded in her beautifully superior voice. Aunt Sammy had two vocal registers, one the socially arrogant which she'd copied from the Lady Icen and which she was using now as she debauched her nephew, the other the common Irish brogue of her slum childhood.

"They've all gone to the Elkingtons' picnic. They'll be away for ages yet. Come back and sit down. Put your arm round me, and we'll start all over again. Unless you don't want to do it and you can be damned and go and frig yourself in the outhouse…"

"Oh no."

"…as you've been doing up to now."

Her husband, Sam, had been killed in the cruellest of accidents. He'd been skating alone on a frozen slough shortly after Christmas years ago already, it seemed like for ever, and been found dead on the middle of the ice with his skull split open. He was an expert skater and it was never discovered what had caused him to fall—perhaps the sudden appearance of a bear or even a jackrabbit in its winter white. No one really knew. He and Bridget had no children, which folks around at the time said was a blessing. Neither of the two women who married the Plouvier brothers were exactly what one might expect to open the door of a foothills ranch house.

"That's better, Hector. Now just relax. You're getting the hang of it."

The top of Aunt Sammy's dress was undone and Hector was breathing heavily and salivating on her breasts. A splattery noise came from the steer's pen—there must be something badly wrong with its innards.

Hector's mother had brought with her to the western prairies not only her language but also the little bourgeois manners and certitudes of provincial Quebec, some of which were dainty and attractive if at first laughably out of place in a cowboy home. Bridge, as Sam called his wife, brought to her new marriage a disturbing sense of English "class", an attitude largely mimicked by a street smart draggle-tail who had graduated from the Dublin slums to the prestige of a lady's companion in a grand house in the English shires. Not only the hired hands but the ranch owning neighbours suspected that she looked down on them. Her hoity toity ways did not seem to bother either Sam or his brother, Nicholas, Hector's dad. "Don't you listen to any of the gossip about your auntie, son. She's a good woman, that one, for all she behaves like Lady Muck at times. It's mostly an act. She's having them on. She's all right, believe me, and I'd trust her anywheres."

"Push harder, Hector," gasped Aunt Sammy, gazing up to the roof of the barn. "You won't hurt me. But for heavens sake don't get too excited yet. Try to contain yourself, dear lad."

Aunt Sammy's rose-strewn dress had been both pulled down and hitched up and was bunched unceremoniously around her slim waist. When he thought about it later, going over the details both joyously and guiltily in his recollection, Hector was puzzled about her comparative lack of underclothes. After all, though he hadn't until now taken much notice of them, he couldn't help seeing his mother's stays and other underthings and those of his sister Michelle lying around the house on wash days and later flying on the line in the back yard.

Sam Plouvier had met his wife-to-be at Higgins Bend Park races and had immediately fallen in love as he'd never done before. Bridget was travelling with the Lady Icen from Gloucestershire whose companion she was and from whom she'd learned her Victorian propriety. A real lady would never do a thing like that or this or that, she'd say to Hector and Michelle—pick her nose, put her elbows on the table, talk with her mouth full. Both children simply adored her and would spend many hours at the neighbouring ranch house where she lived with Uncle Sam. As a child, Hector could not put his finger on it exactly nor could he notice much the difference between the civilizing domesticity of his mother's and his Aunt Sammy's establishments compared with the homes of his friends which he visited, basic and rough, functionally pioneer, however warm the hospitality may be in them. In Aunt Sammy's home there were lacy things, cushions, bright colours, prints of celebrated paintings, lots of books, pictures of royalty and of Lady Icen in high society. They became, however hazily, an integral part of his aunt.

"Tell us again about them balls in London," Michelle would ask.

"Those balls, darling."

Sam Plouvier had broken a few hearts before he married Bridget, but in a rural community like theirs, where everyone knew everyone else and their most insignificant goings on, there was little opportunity for extramarital shenanigans without risking your head being blown off by an outraged shotgun. It was rumoured that he made regular trips to the bawdy houses in Calgary. "What Sam does is his own business," his brother said. Then Sam set his sights on Bridge and with flashing eyes she appeared to return his ardour. You could not put anything across the Lady Icen, not when it was happening under her beautiful aristocratic nose, and she remonstrated with her companion. "You are not, I hope, going to throw yourself away on a"—in her hedged-in stridency she sought the just word—"a worthless cowboy? A provincial oaf? Just pull yourself together and think of all the nice fellows, gentlemen of good breeding you know in England, my dear."

If Bridget's marriage to the rancher, Sam Plouvier, had not been bracketed by fatal accidents, there's no telling how she would have reacted to her lady's opposition to Sam's advances, but that resistance was destroyed as the Lady Icen was when she slipped under the wheels of a runaway wagon on Higgins Bend Hill. She was killed instantly, and at great expense her remains were transported back to her estates in Gloucestershire.

She is a beauty, Hector thought, clumsily atop his aunt in the musty scented hay of the barn, or rather, later in the trenches, he believed he thought about her beauty. Once or twice his fevered mind betrayed him and he imagined his father rushing into the barn with a horse-whip and he nearly lost his erection. He tried to allay his fear, pumping harder and deeper, marvelling that such a woman would lie beneath him sharing his lust. At the sharp end of a ghastly war he would recollect how she never seemed coarse like the estaminet whores, no matter how gross her position. She never lost her cool attractiveness, her charm and seeming innocence.

"Anyone at home?" she inquired, breathing hard underneath him. "You haven't gone to sleep, dearest Hector? Not a very nice compliment to a lady."

Hector had his eyes closed tight and was not really listening, and if he was thinking anything at all he was drifting through a process of primal concepts, floating in a fantastic joy. He gave a compulsive final push and moaned. Unexpectedly the earth moved and he came and Aunt Sammy was indignant and said he was a selfish fellow and couldn't control himself.

෮৩৫

The big pushes Hector had been in, either going over the top with his buddies or waiting for the enemy to attack, had followed set patterns. First the horrendous noise of the artillery bombardments hurtling at them from both sides before the dawn, enough to drive you to distraction, shredding the wire, making it more fearsome. You had a dry mouth and you worried you were going to shit yourself in front of the guys. And then some officious time-keeper would blow a whistle as though he were refereeing a hockey game, and the young officers would climb up them ladders, pistol in one hand, waving the other and shouting "Come on men, follow me." And you would all scramble up after them making damn sure that you did not stick your bayonet up the asshole of the feller in front of you. Some of you would fall, mortally twitching, before you'd gone more than five yards.

"We'd best keep a long ways from each other," Hector had said to Bob on their first assault. "We don't want the same fucking shell to get us both."

After the war, Hector rarely spoke about those things and it was only partly because of his desertion. In any case it was impossible to describe to anyone else what it was really like out there on a modern battlefield where the ploughshares were turned into bursting star shells, whizz-bangs and spitting machine gun bullets. Back in the chateaux the moronic generals, minds pickled with brandy and fine wines, could devise no way of winning other than committing waves of obedient men to a ruined piece of earth where the air was thick with speeding bits of lethal steel. And yet as Hector and Bob had proved, you could survive out there on the lonely battlefield. It would be unwise to stand and stare, but you could jump into a shell hole, being careful not to drown in it in winter, and listen to the din above you and the quieter cries of mortal men. You could think in there what the fucking hell am I doing here. You could have a quick piss. Or a crap, and you sometimes needed that, fear having moved your bowels. You could try to dream of your Aunt Sammy and the barn but most likely the erotic images would not come. You could escape all the hissing fragments, perhaps because your number was not yet on one of them, and come back, one of the few unscathed. Yet you could not get the uninitiated to appreciate this. How could they? And you rarely mentioned any of it even to your surviving comrades or they to you except to mutter a few referential obscenities.

"It's too ruddy quiet tonight," Bob said. "The fucking Hun is up to fucking something."

"Put that goddamn fag out," the Hamilton sergeant screamed from along the trench. He had a high pitched voice, bleating like a tethered goat.

"You don't want to let yourself think about nothing," Hector said. He ran his hand down the stock of his rifle. "I wonder how Tyler's weaseled his way out of this one."

The two boys had once been in the line where the enemy trench was so close that, as Tyler put it, you could hear Jerry jerking off. No Man's Land this night was about two hundred yards deep.

"I wouldn't trust Tyler as far as I could throw him," Bob said. "He would cheat his own grandmother. But I gotta say I like the guy."

Hector too had now got a queasiness beginning to churn his gut and could smell the impending slaughter. At two ack emma that night, two o'clock in the morning, the world exploded. Bob was killed instantly, and Hector and Tyler deserted from the Canadian Expeditionary Force.

☙❦❧

"I'm not sure how Grandad Plouvier got these sections, Hec. But I'm sure gladder than hell he did. Feels good to be alive when you looks around. The mountains. Them stands of trees. Big Hill country."

Nick Plouvier let the reins drop, and his horse ambled to a halt and bent its head to graze. Hector dismounted from his brown mare and watched his father take out a plug of chewing tobacco and stick it inside his cheek. They had stopped on a knoll on the boundary of the ranch. To the west, the foothills ran up to the Rockies still glistening with winter snow. Behind them, the land ran down to Calgary and the prairies. Further east was the unbelievably broad North American continent and then the Atlantic and across that Europe, which had been ablaze since August 1914.

"Where'd he get the money from? Was the family rich?"

"I've never figured that out. Course they was giving the land away in them days. Handed it to you if you managed to stagger here with a wagon and a hoss."

"How long before you was born? Did he get here I mean."

"I don't rightly know. He wasn't married when he come. Gramma Plouvier was raised hereabouts."

The father too got down from his horse. He squirted a brown stream of tobacco juice in the direction of a gopher hole. Nick was a tall man, thin to the point of gauntness, had a sharp face, could have a sharp tongue with the help but was often soft and awkward with his kids, hard eyes, rarely missed a trick. He wore a floppy broad brimmed hat with a dome shaped crown like most of the hired hands wore. A serviceable but a tad clownish head-dress for tough men.

"I thought your Auntie was looking broody when I sees her yesterday...sad like, not quite with us, like. You or Michelle knows about anything bothering her?"

"No, dad."

Hector was sick to his stomach. He was getting deeper into a morass of deceit, sneaking over to Aunt Sammy's for a quick lay because he couldn't help it and feeling as though he were cheating on his family, and all this because she guessed what he had been doing in the outhouse. And that was only natural, wasn't it? His dad had never discussed things like that with him. But that wasn't all, his jerking off on the wooden box with a hole in the top, far from it. There was something so irresistible about her, demonic, he would risk any disgrace going to her and he would refuse to think about any future. Once or twice he'd considered confiding in his sister Michelle and then stopped himself from being such a blazing idiot.

"Mind Bridget's up and down. The other morning when I was over at her place she was singing away as happy as a lark. As though she had come into a fortune. Good to see her like that, cheerful like. For a couple of year after, we all thought she'd never get over Samuel getting himself killed the way he did."

He stressed all three syllables of his late brother's name, Sam-you-ell. A grating voice when he talked about death.

"Do you think Aunt Sammy'll ever marry again?"

"Not now, son. Mebbe a few year back she would of. There was that feller from Medicine Hat come by, but she wouldn't have nothing to do with him it seemed."

Hector was fond of his sister and they did not keep many secrets from each other, but this present one was such a God Almighty one, screwing your own aunt, an enormity. They were close, thrown together in the human sparsity of their country, they'd seen each other naked, examined the differences with curious giggles, slept innocently in the same bed a couple of times, yet however mutually warm and affectionate, she'd always been his sister, part of himself somehow. On one occasion when he was thirteen he'd got horny and tried to push his prick at her bum and Michelle had been so outraged he'd never done anything like that again. "We are the same flesh, Tor," she said, wise beyond her years. Hector was not quite sure what she meant at the time and later wondered where she'd picked up the phrase. Sunday school perhaps, but religious instruction was sporadic and often ambiguous in the Plouvier family since their Quebecoise mother was a Catholic and Dad, if anything, was a half-assed non-conformist of one stripe or another who went to the Anglican church in Higgins Bend, All Saints, at Christmas and Easter. Neither parent pushed their doctrines hard, but being in the Bible belt they all mostly went along with conventional morality until the day in the barn when Hector broke the code with Aunt Sammy who was fortunately not of the same flesh.

"But if she did, Aunt Sammy, get married I mean, what would happen to the ranch?"

"You mean Sam's half?"

"Sure."

"Well, we took it over to manage with ours. You know that. Ever since Samuel passed away. But legally it's hers and if she...What's all this about anyways? You and Michelle learned something I don't knows about?"

He looked sternly at his son.

"No, Dad. Honest."

"Well let's get outa here. There's them fences by Beaver Slough we got to get us fixed this morning."

As they rode, a wind got up from the west with the smell of dust. A chinook arch framed the mountains. Hector wondered whether his father was beginning to suspect something, whether he, Hector, was looking guilty as hell, giving everything away. Despite the beauty of the morning and the freshness of the air blowing into his face as he rode, he felt sicker than ever. How could a kid like himself, barely out of school, be such a damn fool as to get hogtied like this with a woman more than twice his age. And his uncle's wife at that. Well if you want to know, Hector argued, it was simple. You had only to look at Aunt Sammy and her soft clothes, listen to her voice which could tear a guy in half, smell her, her perfume, her female smell which was different from his mom's and his sister's, and feel her, her hips brushing against his and her fingers sweeping back his tangled hair.

"You all right, son?"

His father looked across at him with hard eyes and Hector felt as sick as a dog.

"You bet, dad."

## MARIE

My name is Marie Louise Plouvier, and I have a flint-faced cowboy whose eyes can pierce granite at twenty paces for a husband and two lovely children, Hector and Michelle, born a year apart. What is a gracious lady like me doing on a raw piece of earth like this, you may well ask. Literate, fond of decent music other than the jig and its accompanying screech of western fiddles, used to a certain degree of civilized comfort and nicety, appreciative of the gentler arts of life, though I allow that some of the peasants in parts of Quebec live more squalid lives than the good folk here in Big Hill country. What am I doing in this isolated ranch house where you have to go outside in the foulest, iciest weather to la chose? Where practically all the males chew tobacco and hawk and spit and have atrocious table manners? Where life revolves entirely around horses and cattle, and their pungency and excrement percolate into every nook and cranny of the yard and house, where miserable roads are either covered in impassable snow or full of rutted mud or choking dust. And all they lead to is Higgins Bend, which is a collection of wooden shacks and drunken Indians. Higgins Bend is named for an English gentleman speculator, Sir Henry Higgins, who owned shares in the railway. Well I'll tell ya what I'm doing, as they say here in their quaint English, in the back of beyond. (I do my best to get Tor and Michie to speak slightly less like prairie hinds and to me they do sometimes).

My ancestors came over from France in the same way as the British piratical adventurers did to grab as much of the New World as possible when the getting was good, although some of my hypocritical compatriots would say that our voyageurs came in the spirit of pure exploration and that any exploitation of the native Indians was fortuitous and unintended. After much heroism and endurance, raping and pillaging, and then war and monumental upheaval to the south, we came together under Confederation of 1867 and, according to the politiques maudits, the French and English were to live harmoniously together ever after. Poppycock, or to paraphrase what they they would say here, male bovine excrement! The French and the English in Canada will never accommodate each other, will always be jealous of each other, just mark my words.

I met gimlet eyes on a chance visit to Winnipeg, and one of the reasons I was interested in him was his name, Nicholas Plouvier, which naturally I assumed to be French. There were other reasons, spontaneous, uncontrollably personal. He could never be accused of trop d'embonpoint, but was even slimmer all those years ago, debonair. The girls would talk about all sorts of men at Madame Chevrier's, my finishing school in Montreal, sons of wealthy bankers, diplomats, sophisticated Europeans, milords. One of our young ladies said she'd like to meet a real man from the wild west, virile; she'd read of the great cattle round-ups. We laughed her to scorn, as though she were slightly touched. I was one of the most contemptuous and so it served me right, I suppose, that I should be the one to marry a cattleman.

The circumstances were decidedly unromantic. The middle of a Manitoban winter, a blizzard howling across Portage and Main, the hotel full of damp smelling fur coats, both men's and women's.

"Excuse me, miss."

I was standing, rather lost, peering around, outside a large room where a fur auctioneer was chanting his inanities when Nicholas came up to me. I am not short, au contraire, but he towered over me. A sleeveless leather jacket, plaid shirt fastened at the neck with what looked like a bootlace, a line across his forehead separating the white skin from the tanned, black hair like mine and Michelle's, but not so thick as ours, plastered back. Even then hard eyes but young and challenging.

"Yes?"

I put on my unpropitious face. He was unfazed.

"The name's Nicholas Plouvier."

It was then that I thought he was French and I softened a little.

"Enchantée," I said and continued in my native tongue. "I am arrived here from Montreal to find a French family but alas it appears that the address has changed. I wonder, monsieur, if you know Winnipeg? But forgive me. My name is...."

He was grinning at me like a stupid jackass.

"Me no comprenee, missy."

With his forefingers he pointed to his lips and his ears and shrugged. Over the years I've never known Nicholas to grin so much as he did that day. His lips are normally set in a severe masculine line. A ghastly silence between us was broken only by the unintelligible monotone of the auctioneer as his assistant held up the pelts—silver fox, beaver and so on.

"Sorry, lady. No offence. But you might be talking double Dutch so far's I'm concerned."

In those days people, once they'd settled, did not travel much across continental Canada. So we rarely stirred from our regional enclaves and it was unusual to say the least that an eastern woman of marriageable age, especially French, should meet a young man from the west. These new-fangled psychologists claim that l'amour is as much a matter of chemical and electrical activity as anything else, but whatever it was and given the disparity in our backgrounds, way of life, practically everything, the unlikelihood of Nicholas and me falling in love was high. Nevertheless something old and primitive flashed between us and was sustained.

I prefer not to go into embarrassing detail—I've assimilated from Nick an anglo-reticence in matters of the heart and sexual activity—but the next few days were full of bursting delight and incredulous happiness. We did not notice the wretched winter. We made furtive assignations like naughty children. No one who knows him would believe Nicholas could loosen up in such a way, and in our life together he never has again except in the privacy of our bedroom. That is part of old stone-face's secret attraction.

I eventually found the family I was supposed to meet. Nick and I stayed over our allotted time. He was there on some arcane breeding business, allegedly to do with cows, but I do believe that our son Hector was conceived in Winnipeg.

On the morning after, Nick had had to scurry to his own bedroom in the wee hours, and we met at breakfast. It was blizzarding, a white-out, the thick shaggy hair of the horses driven or ridden up to the hotel covered in snow, moustaches of the men frozen with rime. I was shy and could not look him in the face but sat deliriously enchained.

"Well, missy, that sure puts the tin lid on it."

I'd never heard the phrase before but I knew what he meant. His face was wonderful to behold. The hard eyes, the flinty features softening into loving light and affectionate creases—I'm getting carried away with myself here. Over that western breakfast of revolting steak and eggs and some indescribable hash he said he supposed he ought to make an honest woman of me although I could not feel the slightest twinge of dishonesty. According to ancient tribal and redneck custom the woman must follow her mate, and so I ended up on this ranch in the boonies.

CB❧EO

Hector was born towards the end of the hot dry summer of 1898. There was no hospital in Higgins Bend but in any case, even in Montreal, I should have had my accouchement at home in the marital bed. No one except his father guessed that our son was not conceived there.

"He's got good feisty lungs on him thet one, Mrs. Plouvier, I'll say that," the nurse said.

Dorothy Howard was an excellent midwife, but according to law she could not, except in the direst emergency, assist at a delivery without a qualified medical doctor. These were few and far between in the foothills. I remember the sot we were saddled with. With unhurried energy Dot was cleaning up the general mess, getting rid of the afterbirth, slopping out the vase de nuit, giving me clean towels, powdering Hector.

"It's hotter than the dickens in here. Goodness, you was sweatin' like a pig, missus. Just before the little guy poked his head out into the big world."

Dot bent over the crib in passing and made clucking noises at Hector, who had the faintest blond fuzz over his bald head. She never stopped, not jerky or jumpy but smooth efficient movement from one task to the next. I watched her as she scrubbed fiercely at the footprints of our doctor, who had arrived wild-eyed, breath smelling of whisky and dirt all over his boots. She was a dynamic scrap of a creature, bony, angular features with a faint moustache and hair going grey though she can't have been more than forty or so. She'd been married to a homesteader who'd walked out on her when she was eight months pregnant. She told me this in bits over the months she came to see me. I was fortunate in having an easy pregnancy, no early sickness and then fat and content, Hector behaving as he should inside. Of course there is always some discomfort. I told

Nick once when he complained about his dinner being late that he should try being enceinte himself like one of his fat cows, and his poker face cracked into a rare grin. "No can do, missy." He was very considerate after that, for a cowboy.

"My baby was still-born, Mrs. Plouvier," Dot told me. "You see I don't come from round here like and I didn't know which way to turn. When my Herb took off, for Montana I finds out after, I was on my own and I cried my eyes out, like."

"It must have been terrible for you, Dottie."

I remember so clearly the day she told me this part of her story. Mid-July. There'd been a thunderstorm in the morning crashing about the mountains and the lightning slashing the dark sky. In the afternoon, when Dot came, the sun shone and it was humid and calm. She was wearing a summer frock, which hid her boots, and brought me a basket of petits fours which she'd baked and put a white cloth over to keep the dust off. Despite her homely, leathery face she looked as pretty as a picture when she came into our living room.

"You can say that again. I loved that guy even if he turned out to be a useless gopher-head. A real jerk. You see we only had an acre 'n a bit and a shack rented from the Ranche Company and practically no stock to speak of."

She started to make me some tea—to go with the cakes she said.

"You have two to feed now, don't forget."

"You don't have to do this, Dot."

"I know. Where's the kettle gone and hid her?"

I never have got used to tea. Hector and Michie like it, they got the taste from Bridge, but Nick always drinks black coffee like tar which has been simmering on the stove all day. A man's drink.

"So what did you do, Dot?"

"Them at the Ranche was good to me, they sure was. They let me off of the rent and give me a couple of dollars."

She brought the tea over to me. I was sitting in what was to become the nursing chair by the window. I looked out onto the vegetable garden. There was not much space for flowers, but Nick had set aside a small lawn and one of the hands who had the most appalling limp, it made you cringe to see him walk, had sown some poppies along one end of it.

"I pulls myself together as best I can. I packs up our few scraps, gives the cat to the neighbour in the next shack and takes off for Calgary. I goes to the hospital and says I want to be a nurse. They dipsy doodles for a day or two, they wonder whether I got enough learning and then they takes me on."

During the latter months of pregnancy I grew inordinately fond of Dorothy Howard. To my surprise I found when I arrived at Higgins Bend a social division, a truly laughable snobbery in this small community, as sharp as anything in Montreal, and though I suppose I'm a bit of a snob myself I thought it preposterous in Higgins Bend of all places. Those of us living out here, pioneers struggling continually with the natural and mostly hostile elements for a living, are on the edge of civilization. You'd think that would be enough and we'd be beyond the scourge of spite and envy. I mean, much to my regret, I can't ride in fine carriages to theatres and soirées and wear dainty clothes. How often in dark, raw winter, when I've made a necessary excursion to the frozen outhouse, have I wished for those things. For a little witty conversation, for after dinner subjects beyond the cow and the hoss. Whatever my own case I discovered an absurd class consciousness in these pristine foothills. The ranch owners were contemptuous of the new arrivals, those would-be homesteaders who had no land or property and came with what they stood up in. They lived in unsanitary shacks or even tents of rags, some of them, and were considered so much scum. Things are better now but Dot must have had a hard time.

And then she qualified as a nurse and returned to Higgins Bend. But she'd had to endure long months of doing the dirtiest work in the hospital before she was allowed to start her training. She was so selfless and devoted and competent that when anyone was sick or hurt in the community, wealthy or poor, the wretched labourers or fairly well to do landowners like us, we sent for Dorothy, not that drunken doctor. As you can see she did not restrict herself to midwifery. She came for Michelle's birthing too. She got a bigger and better shack but not another husband.

Dot eventually got the doctor's filth off the bedroom floor and sweat glistened among the fine hairs on her upper lip. She walked over to the crib and looked down at Hector.

"Yes, Mrs. Plouvier. You've got yourself a bonny fighter there. What are you going to call him?"

ଓଷ୍ଠଃ

Hector found himself outside the estaminet, but how or why he'd got there he could not remember.

"It's Plouvier for Chrissake."

The soldier who had been hitting the door with his fists, rattling the latch, turned round in alarm as Hector slunk up looking over his shoulder like a sneaky coyote. It was Tyler. Not far away the battle still thundered, its fiendish noise making the village ground shake as though some apocalyptic stampede of monstrous beasts were approaching. Yet it was eerily inactive on its western perimeter, with only occasional files of men trudging to their deaths as into some grinding mill.

"You are one hell of a mess, boy. Where are the rest of the outfit?"

"They're all dead."

Hector was sobbing violently inside his gut, his face stunned into passivity. His eyes were large, about to burst out of their sockets, he couldn't seem to bring them back or close the lids. If he ever got out of this slaughter he would be pop-eyed for the rest of his life, the pitiable lunatic of Higgins Bend. Folks would tap their foreheads and turn away from him as he walked down the street. Tyler stared at him fearfully.

"Your eyebrows is burnt off."

"You ought to see the company, Tyler. They is all laid out in a row. The fellers. Bob had half his head blown off. That new sergeant got one right in his fat mouth. They never got out of the trench."

Tyler hammered on the door again.

"Jerry's got through to Brigade headquarters," he said. "They all run like hot shit. Me included. Lotsa the guys got mowed down."

"What we gonna do now, Tyle?"

"What we gonna do, Hec? Me? I've had this stinking load of crap right up to here. We either gets out or we gets ours next time. Do you follow what I'm telling you, Hector? This is our big chance. I'm going over the wall, old buddy. Too fucking right I am."

"They'll shoot you if they catch you. And they'll catch you, Tyler. You bet your goddamn boots they will."

"Don't give me that bull, Hec. Where's your rifle anyways?"

"Where's yourn?"

"It fell clean outa my hands."

The estaminet door opened and Celine was in the doorway swaddled from head to foot in an old cloak. Her lips were encrusted with cold sores.

"You'd best come in," she said, expression blank, unsurprised. "We're not staying for those Boches pigs again. We're going. Finally, dad's agreed. We've got a cart, but all our horses have been stolen." She spoke in a monotone, her grievance impersonal.

The mutilated horses sickened Hector almost as much as the torn and bleeding men. They would never believe such butchery on the ranch where hosses were kings. Here their legs stuck up stiff in the air, their lips drawn back in an eternal snarl.

"What's she fucking well sounding off about?"

Hector translated for him. Both soldiers were now trembling as though with ague. Celine's face was so drained of blood that she looked like a corpse, her eyes half closed, as if her cynicism sustained what little will was left, letting the terrible events wash over her.

"How do you know that? What she's saying?"

"Never mind that right now, Tyle. What we gonna do? Us two?"

"Listen, boy. If a couple of whores can scoot, we can. We can go with them. Easy as shooting fish in a barrel."

An errant shell burst in the street and made them fling themselves to the ground.

"You got any Frenchy clothes?" Tyler asked Celine when he got up. "Pantsy-poo? Shappoo?"

He plucked at his filthy trousers, touched his cap. His face too was ashen, drawn, but his moustache was still neatly trimmed.

"You ask her Hec. You seem to know the fucking lingo. We gotta get us out of these uniforms for starters."

"You keep some scissors with you Tyler then? For your 'tache?" Hector's voice still had a croak and a tremble to it.

"Piss off, will you. Ask her the fucking question and then pay attention. You gotta get rid of anything personal. Letters. Pictures of your sweetheart. Don't leave nothing in your uniform pockets which we gonna stuff down the well."

"Which well?"

"Any goddamn well, dummy. And your identity discs. Lose them. We gotta disappear off of the face of the earth, see."

"I done it," Hector said. "They've gone the same way as my rifle."

03 ❀ 80

A weird group moved with the straggling half-starved refugees as they fled once again before a German advance. A farm wagon with two wheels and one centre shaft was covered with a tarpaulin affording some protection against the driving rain. Under the cover Celine and Suzette were dressed in all the clothes they possessed, swelling their substantial figures even more, and about them pitiful remnants of their household, pots and pans, a smoothing iron, the large feather mattress they were sitting on. An oil painting of a hauntingly beautiful woman in a chipped frame. A big meat cleaver. No furniture, that had to be left behind. The family bible. Crushed between the two whores was a girl of about six or seven called Tina who had appeared from nowhere. Taking turns in pushing the cart or trudging behind it were Hector, Tyler, the bald headed barman, his imperial moustache glistening with raindrops, and the customer with the large growth on his neck. Sometimes all four had to strain their shoulders and backs and guts to bursting on a particularly bad patch of road.

"We gotta get right down to our long johns and undershirt," Tyler had said.

Suzette had pulled out some peasants' clothing from a wooden chest, coarse stuff, smock-frocks, pantaloons, berets, belonging to brothers, uncles, long gone to the war, God alone knew, long dead. The two women stood around by the bar as the soldiers shucked their country's dirty uniforms and dressed in French farm clothes. Celine gave Tyler's balls a languid squeeze as she helped him tuck in an oversized grey flannel shirt.

"Don't do that!"

"Tell you what, Tyle, you wouldn't get yourself a job on our farm, for sure. Not fucking well dressed like that."

"You ought to take a look at yourself, smart ass."

But their hearts were not in fooling around. Becoming a deserter was no joke and under the latest shock, the continuous strain, Hector had to suppress a protesting conscience, a disturbing loyalty. To what, though? How sweet it is to die for your country. To lose your reproductive organs, your eyes, your legs. Like hell it is. And now they were going to get out of hell in a handcart. But it was niggling and unsettling, a real shitter either way.

"This is my father," Celine had said. "Monsieur Trou."

The barman passed his hand over his huge moustache, drawing the grey bristles down, and bowed his head about one centimetre.

"He doesn't talk much, our dad. And this is Uncle Joseph."

The carbuncle seemed to keep Joseph's head permanently inclined. He burbled something at them good naturedly enough, but he seemed to have a speech affliction too.

"Pleased to meet you, gentlemen," Tyler said.

They got the cart loaded after much heart searching about what they had to leave behind. Although she was seven, Tina was sucking her thumb and clutching a rag doll with one button eye hanging by a thread and the stuffing coming out of one leg. The little girl was wearing a long woollen dress which must have belonged to someone else as she kept tripping over the skirt. On her head was a knitted hat with a huge red pompom. Her small hands were red and raw like a washerwoman's. Joseph lifted her up onto the cart and they pushed off with the heavy artillery booming in the distance. An emaciated dog ran after them, and Celine's father shooed it away.

"Where we goin', Tyle?"

"Christ knows. We just goes with these folks."

"Tyle."

"Yes?"

"If anyone stops us. Asks questions, like. You'd best let me do the talking."

As he bent and heaved, Hector thought of his first journey up to the front line with Bob. They had been as excited as two kids, singing all the fighting men's songs, "Pack up your troubles," "Tipperary" and some with dirty words like "I don't want a bayonet up my a**ehole / I don't want my b*ll*cks shot away." Betcha I kill me a Jerry before you do, Bob had said. Hector recalled waving goodbye to Canada from the troopship as it left Halifax. Some of the guys' sweethearts were on the dockside but of course there was nobody from the new province of Alberta. He was as sick as a dog on the Atlantic and thought nothing to come in the war could be worse than that.

With his shoulder to the wheel of the Trous' cart his memory surged back and forth as the shock of the last enemy assault began to ease slightly—from that achingly beautiful view of the Bow Valley from the top of Higgins Bend Hill when he'd gone riding with Aunt Sammy the day before enlisting in Calgary—to the disgraceful, treacherous throwing away of his rifle. In his brutalized psyche the images merged sardonically in recollection, the natural joy of the silver river and hills and morning, the old leather smell of the saddles and the movement of their horses, the external femininity of Aunt Sammy. He'd oughta call her something else, but what? Bridgie? Christ no. Her rounded flushed face, the graceful fall of her bosom. She was elegant on a horse, schooled in the English way on an English saddle, not born to it as the rest of his family were. All that together with the furtive underside of love making, the hairs, the cunt, the juices, her cry of satisfaction, black forbidden ecstasies. He looked up at Celine, a few feet in front of his nose, her face a pale mask. She would be the same down there too, presumably, under all those clothes, and the cow Suzette. Sickening even to contemplate, yet he felt a quick surge of lust. What did it look like when it was diseased? He tried to wash all such thoughts from his mind.

An artillery spotter plane buzzed over the column like a pesky skeeter, and many of the refugees cowered in the ditch, the old women too beat even to cross themselves, the old men too dispirited to shake a stick at the infernal thing. Tina was staring at Hector with the fixity of a child's gaze, his musty blue clothes, the prairie freshness long gone from his looks, his eyebrows missing.

"Hi," he said to her.

She hid her face in Suzette's thigh not far from her crotch. He never looked at Aunt Sammy's. Always kept his eyes averted.

As he'd scrambled away from his dead and dying comrades, he didn't know how, blasted by exploding shells, tripping over the second lieutenant whose unblemished face held a fixed seraphic smile. It was Bob's copping it which had thrown him for a loop, made him lose it for a time; he was just getting it back again now as he pushed Celine and Suzette, a blind flight from that trench of corpses, grasping his rifle, hanging onto his helmet.

"This is fucking it," he'd shouted to himself as he ran. "This is the goddamn end. Oh you Jerry bastards! Oh Bob, old buddy, they got you in the end, did they, the stinking shitfaces."

Nobody stopped him.

He'd scrambled out of the trench, which was a fucking dangerous thing to do, but again no one stopped him. He went sprawling over a couple of bodies and lay panting on the ground. Someone shot a Very light into the air and the scene was frozen in ghastly whiteness. One of the prostrate soldiers was only half a corpse, and without any thought or compunction Hector threw his discs on the military remains. Plouvier H.H. The second aitch stood for Henri after his maternal grandfather. R.C. on the second line, not because his mother was a practising Catholic, she wasn't, but because he heard Catholics were excused church parade. He placed his rifle reverently across the chest of the other soldier. Then he ran, screaming at the stars, as though he were rounding up some stray steer. This corner of the battlefield was now eerily quiet and still no one stopped him or herded him back.

Tyler Brown and old man Trou took over the pushing, and Hector walked side by side with Uncle Joseph, whose ripe red monstrosity of a boil Hector kept glimpsing in his peripheral vision. What they needed here was a pair of strong draught horses from the ranch, Clydesdales with their big solid hooves. It would not be so bad if it were not pelting with rain and if they could keep the cart balanced on its axis, but the road was so uneven.

"A moment, if you please."

M. Trou stopped and they lowered the shaft to the ground.

"Some fire?"

Before bolting from the deserted Brigade H.Q. Tyler, ever resourceful, had scrounged around the store area and to his great joy had happened across a cache of tobacco, twist, coiled like a black snake, evil smelling stuff that the troops would carve with hasp knives and then rub in the palms of their hands. He'd filled his haversack with rolls of it and given a liberal portion to M. Trou who smoked the same kind of clay pipe, yellowed with nicotine, as Tyler did. Hector had tried a pipe once and nearly thrown up and so contented himself with fags. He didn't like those much but they steadied the nerves, broke perfunctorily the long hours of trench boredom.

"You can't keep it going in the rain, Pops," Tyler said as the old man struck a Lucifer and sucked at the damp tobacco.

Trou grunted and turned the burning bowl upside down.

☙❀❧

Bridget Plouvier got out of bed and threw a shawl around her shoulders. She unfastened her hair and it cascaded down her back, thick, with the sheen of a raven's wing, black as a drunken Irishman's soul. She swore with a vocabulary which would have made the hired hands in the bunkhouse sit up in wonder, used cuss words from Dublin they'd never heard of.

"That stupid, stupid boy," she ended after rehearsing her litany of foul oaths and throwing her pillows on the floor and jamming her comb savagely into her silver backed hair brush, "and isn't he going off to France, the idjit, and himself only seventeen."

She paced about her bedroom barefoot, more anger and frustration in her movement than dismay. Her nightdress was full and white with lace trim at the cuffs and the neckline, her shawl, a gift from the Lady Icen, was open work, mauve mostly with flashes of gold thread. Too good for a bed jacket really. More suitable for a sophisticated reception, a musical evening in high society, a fat lot of those around Higgins Bend. She pulled back the drapes and scarcely heeded the late summer morning, the mountains sullen in the distance, just a suggestion of turn in the leaves.

"And me, Bridget Donnelly, the biggest fool that iver they was. Daft as a brush! Getting myself pregnant indeed. At my age. And niver before in all my born days."

In her soliloquies, which had become more frequent in her lonely widowhood, she dispensed with the overlay of elegant speech she'd assimilated to perfection from Lady Icen and her upper-crust friends, mimicking their nasal inflections, their supercilious drawl, and reverted to the dialogue of her native city. She still retained the lightness of tread of her girlhood, its grace and erect carriage. She ran down the stairs and let out the cat. As soon as she opened the back door her dog, Mike, half golden retriever, came bounding in smelling of the stable and jumped up and licked her as she held him by his front paws. He was named after her father, Michael Donnelly, the feckless drunk, idle sponger, mostly out of work, who had impregnated her mother with eight daughters and a final son who was afflicted with a monstrously shaped forehead and uncoordinated limbs. He was Nature's signal to Mike to lay off his wife.

"I towld him," her mother revealed to Bridget in a burst of maternal confidence over the Monday morning wash tub, "Michael Donnelly, I said, you're not to come near me iver again, neither drunk nor sober."

"And did he, our mam?"

"Wunst. And wunst only."

"Ee! What did you do, our mam?"

"I sets up a foin screeching, that's what I did. And punched him in his fat mouth where the beer fumes was coming out like smoke out of a chimbly. He jumped clane out of bed he did. I nearly gave in to him at that very moment—he looked such a daft specimen of a man standing there in his nightshirt."

Bridget was still holding her dog by his front paws and he was looking at her with devoted, affectionate eyes. She thought back to her father without any love in her memory. Her mother had told her this story when she was about fourteen and getting ripe herself for impregnation. She'd had to wait a long time for that, dear God. She was the fourth child, one sister had already died of scarlet fever, another of whooping cough, and later on little Theresa who was always poorly passed away in the diphtheria epidemic.

"He tried to soft soap me," her mother said, "like he always did. 'Hush, Mary, me darling,' he says, 'You'll wake the bairns.' The bairns, I yells at him. And who's responsible for all the bairns? That's what I'd like to know. Who is it that comes home dead drunk full of the devil's lust ivery Friday night? Don't talk to me about waking the bairns." Her mother put the heavy, dripping clothes at a furious pace through the mangle. Outside over the little yard the Irish sky was raw.

Bridget looked through the kitchen window at the smoke rising over a knoll which concealed her sister-in-law's house. She wondered whether she could possibly discuss this latest irony of focking fate with Marie Louise. Oh Lord! She had only to go along the stone road which connected the two ranch houses, easily and pleasantly walkable in summer, through the coulee which bent round the hill, no more than a mile at the most. And when she got face to face with Marie it would be simple—all she had to say was I am expecting a baby and the father is your son, my nephew, who has gone off to the wars to fight for his country and who right now is training somewhere in Ontario or maybe on his way to France. Dead easy. Through the open door she could hear the robins and sparrows twittering in the spruce by the barn, the sick barn, dear God. And what about Nick? What would she say to him? He had not yet been over this morning. She dropped her dog's feet gently to the floor and patted his side vigorously.

"Micky, old boy, Micky, Micky, Micky! What am I going to do?"

She gave him his food, put milk in the cat's saucer and boiled water on the wood stove, which had not quite gone out overnight. She climbed back up the stairs, carrying the pail past the pictures and prints over the hand rail. Both ranch houses were luxuriously appointed by Higgins Bend standards, but Lady Icen would have considered them little better than pig sties and their furniture laughably crude. And yet the cottages on her Gloucester estates were nothing to write home about, leaky roofs, damp walls; some of the shacks in Higgins Bend were better. Bridget looked into her bedroom at the bright curtains, the rumpled quilt, the clean sheets, pillows on the floor, and smiled grimly and thought how palatial this was compared with the Dublin shithouse she and her sisters had been brought up in. Nick's and Marie's house had been built by Grandfather Plouvier but had been much added onto and improved since. Sam's, now hers, had been erected only after Marie had come, the blushing bride to be, from Winnipeg.

She was subdued by her morning's thoughts, by the process of coming to terms with the inescapable fact of her condition which she was now certain about. But make no mistake, Aunt Sammy was one tough lady. She was aware and proud of that. She'd had to brazen things out all her life. Pregnancy had been around her throughout her childhood, and not only her mother's. There was the case of her second cousin, Lizzie Golightly, who had found herself in the family way at fifteen and was shipped off to be looked after by the nuns and never seen again. She poured the hot water from the pail into a large white basin.

"Them Donnelly girls'll come to a bad end, you just mark my words," Mrs. O'Reilly had shouted over the back wall.

"Withered old cow," her mother had replied. "She's only jealous."

Her father had wanted to fight Mr. O'Reilly, who had a bad back and had been laid off work for years. He was a great one for the family honour was Mike Donnelly. He was the dear old da who had tried to sell her years later to an English lord, what he thought was an English lord, the drunken old bastard.

"And a lovely girl she is that, sor, though I says it myself. And very accommodating, your warship. Very obedient and all."

The unspeakable dirty old swine. Bridget took off her nightdress, stood on a large towel and soaped a flannel. She began to wash herself. A lady must ensure that she never smells, the Lady Icen said, not anywhere. And her mother had said that a good scrubbing never did anyone any harm. But in her family it was only once a week, sometimes not so often, in the back kitchen. Her father said only dirty people wash. Bridget was a little suspicious about Marie Louise in this respect. Frenchwomen were notorious for using perfume instead of soap, her lady said.

Her bedroom window overlooked the road to the older ranch house. As she soaped herself Bridget saw a horse with a girl rider, Michelle, galloping up. She heard a clatter at the back door.

"Aunt Sammy."

"I'm just bathing, Michie. I'll be down in a minute. Put the kettle on, will you." The Lady Icen voice was back.

"Aunt Sammy." Michelle was halfway up the stairs. She loved the way her aunt spoke. "There's a letter come from Hector. Isn't that something? He says he's got a rifle and bayonet."

It was not so long ago that she'd waited up in this room for Hector to appear on the same road, to come to this very bed. Maybe that's where the conception had happened. It had to be here or the sick barn, or even by the slough.

# THREE

After a time, some of the refugees simply gave up and lay in the ditch in the rain. The roads became more crowded as the Allies tried to plug the immense hole punched out of the flesh and steel line by the Germans. There was a new factor which saved a disastrous rout, the arrival of American forces. Time and again the Trou cart had to be pushed to the side of the road as regiments of doughboys came squelching along the muddy road, imbued with a New World idealism, the new crusaders, singing "Marching through Georgia."

"Full of piss and wind," Tyler said, "them are. They'll get that malarkey knocked out of them soon enough, Hec. I can tell ya."

Even so the two deserters kept their heads well down whenever any military personnel appeared.

"It's the French police we have to worry about, though," Hector said. "We just spouts French, I do I mean, at the Yanks and the Brits. They don't know nothing. But them Frogs is the danger. They'll want to find out what a couple of young jerks like us is doing pushing a cart. If we're not careful. And who's to say any of this lot won't tell on us."

He nodded questioningly at the Trou family.

"We don't know them from a bar of soap."

It was the second day since leaving the estaminet and they had still not reached any village or town unshattered by high explosive. Meantime the daily necessities had to be coped with. Both ex-soldiers were practised enough in moving their bowels under primitive circumstances and so were the Trous, though the women and Tina managed a feminine delicacy in concealing themselves. Uncle Joseph, head tilted awkwardly away from his carbuncle, pissed uninhibitedly in the middle of the road, much to Tina's amusement. Their little store of food began to run out.

"Leave it to me, Pops," said Tyler. "Leave the mangee-poo to yours truly."

Many of the army dumps were thinly protected. The cooks, Ally Sloper's cavalry, the pioneers had been rushed up to the front as stop-gap cannon fodder. Foraging was a joke for a man of Tyler's talent.

"Here you goes, mez amee-poo. Help yourselves."

He returned from his forays laden with tins of plum and apple jam, "hard tack" biscuits, large cheeses, and once a bottle of rum which M. Trou uncorked expertly and sniffed appreciatively.

About this time, the second or third day of desertion, a profound sadness settled over Hector, a heavy gloom which was evident even in the texture of his skin, overlaying the pallor of dugout existence. He had inherited the sinewy fortitude, the sense of rightness of his father, which had sustained him as a boy thrown into the appalling circumstances of trench warfare, tested to the limits as has long been the fate of young warriors. Theirs was an uncomplicated morality. It was the young squire's burden to go to battle, the maiden's to wait and weep. And stoicism and courage of that kind were natural in Hector; he did not think of himself as heroic from the time of his breaking in an ornery bronco as a kid to advancing with fixed bayonet behind an artillery barrage when he was not much older.

"Cheer up, old buddy. You've a face like a hoss's ass."

"Piss off, Tyle."

They were bent over the shaft, heads close together. Under the draining fatigue, Tyler's urban knowingness still prevailed, the foxy features, the sardonically neat and debonair moustache, his eyes forever darting like an animal's, his lips drawn across his teeth, the thin muscular body under the ill-fitting farm clothes. Once street wise, now army wise. The rounded innocence of Hector's face was disappearing, his eyes were narrowing like a slum child's, the cheek bones showing, denying his youth. The war had disfigured and dehumanized both of them. Disguised in borrowed clothes, they pushed a couple of fat whores through the French mud, united in a common desperation to get as far from the front as possible. They had been so dissimilar when they enlisted. Now they were on the lam and the kinship of outlawry brought them closer to each other even in physical appearance.

That night they found a barn to sleep in instead of huddling by the cart in drenching rain. Père Trou guided them off on a side lane then up a track where the going was hard and the ruts deep to a cluster of farm buildings mostly destroyed, but the barn had miraculously kept its roof. Heaps of rotting hay were strewn along one side as though a lost platoon had bivouacked there, but despite its being fusty and congealed in layers it seemed not too repulsive. On the contrary, it was a heavenly refuge for the bone weary travellers. To the not too distant rumble of the great battle they ate some of Tyler's stolen food and drank some of the rum. Tyler and Trou lit their pipes and the acrid smoke hung peacefully, domestically in the humid air. After necessary trips out into the rain they all collapsed on the hay, Hector removing himself as far as he could into a corner. He woke in the night after an uneasy sleep of physical exhaustion plagued by weird and unaccountable dreams. The night sky had cleared temporarily and a watery moon shone through a shell hole in the roof, lighting him up like a spotlight in a theatre. He started to weep silently.

An amorphous bundle detached itself from the others and moved over to him like a porpoise propelled by invisible flippers.

"Don't cry, mon cheri, I entreat you."

Hector blinked through his tears at the flat face of Celine, her bloodless complexion made paler, more deathly, in the moonlight. Her fat arm, swollen by the many clothes she wore, lay across his chest and a mittened hand caressed his cheek. Christ, he thought as he narrowed his eyes to squeeze out the tears, not her of all people. Not this baby. I need her like a hole in the head. A few nights previously Tyler had been on the top of this woman, shagging her determinedly as she had lain as unresponsive as an inert jelly fish. Diseased probably.

"I'm all right, mam'selle." What the hell should he call her? "Celine." He whispered to her in French. "You go back to sleep. Back to Tina."

But she had her arm firmly about him, the damp wool of her mitten scratching his face. That squalid night at the estaminet with Tyler he had been a serving soldier in a war which was shitty and horrible but which he could tolerate. Just. The comradely reciprocity with Bob kept them both from slipping over the edge. They were each stretched taut, at the limits of endurance but hanging in there. The shell that blew Bob away destroyed the fundamentals of Hector's existence, too fucking right it did.

"Tell me about your family," Celine said in a low caressing murmur. It was wonderful that such a—what? debased, cruddy?—woman should have so attractive a voice. "You are from a farm, no? In the wild west."

Tyler must have told her. He was shouting in his sleep, mimicking the sergeant-major, giving drill orders. The rest were breathing deeply, snoring. Hector tried not to be repulsed by this shapeless mound of flesh, most likely disgustingly infected.

"Yes. My father has a ranch near the Rocky Mountains. And my aunt, she owns half," he added and started sobbing uncontrollably again.

Goddammit to hell and back. Fuckit up and down a rat's ass. Celine pulled at his shoulder so that he lay on his side staring at the moonlit garishness of her face. The stale smell.

"And many horses, cheri? You have?"

"Lots. Big heavy hosses for ploughing and hauling loads. And hosses for riding, for chores on the ranch like."

"You have a horse, 'Ector?"

"I had one when I left home, a brown mare."

"And many cows?"

"Hundreds of cattle on the range. We have to round them up and brand them."

"C'est vrai? I wish I had a horse. Women here are not permitted to ride horses. Even when we could afford one."

Between fits of uncontrollable silent sobbing, shit, he found himself opening up to her, describing the ranch, telling about the long winters, about his mother from Quebec. Celine did not know they spoke French in Quebec.

"And you have a girl?" Celine whispered. "You are affianced? A prairie flower?"

Holy moly, you sure as hell caught me there, sister. He'd known a couple of girls in Higgins Bend half-serious like, and there had been moments when he'd felt a certain heartache, but then that had all gone up the creek when the Aunt Sammy thing hit him like a ton of bricks. He learned more of the relationships between men and women since joining the army than he'd ever imagined in his wildest fantasies. Of course many of the young single men made most of it up, he was sure, bragging, exaggerating their exploits, telling how irresistible they were, how many girls they'd made. Yet some of the older men, married, who were quieter, talking among themselves and Hector listening all ears, came out with stories that made his hair curl.

"No, Celine. Not what you'd call a proper girl friend."

"A big strong boy like you! Quel dommage!"

She stroked his cheek, and he did not flinch.

"What a waste!"

Tyler Brown was screaming in a half-throttled voice as though he were bayonetting the guts out of some poor devil.

Hector had walked by the Bow River with one of the girls, the one who had given him a temporary heartache and also, from time to time, an embarrassing hard-on. On one occasion he'd had to move along with a kind of sideways skip and hope she hadn't noticed. Angela had a firm chin, he recalled, not grotesquely elongated but noticeably firm, like herself. She could be real obstinate, that one. She lived in a shack in Higgins Bend and was ashamed to go out much because she had only one half-decent dress.

"She's not your sort, son. Not really," his father had said. "Nothing against her personally, mind. That whole family works their butts off." Hector started sobbing again and Celine patted him on the chest, on the heart. He cursed quietly in English between the sobs until he got control of himself.

"Just as well though, Celine, eh? As things have turned out? A lot of the guys have got sweethearts or just got married before they left..."

But the guys were no more. He squeezed his eyelids tight and hard together. What was he doing exposing himself like this to a fat harlot anyways?

"Sump'n the matter with your leg, Hector?" Angela had asked as he walked grotesquely by the river. "Fall off your hoss, did you? Sump'n like that?"

"Naw. Naw. S'all right."

Hector twisted his body, fanned his fingers in front of the bulge in his pants, and then hobbled along in a semi-crouch. She was a neat girl, Angela, dainty, firm chin, bold as brass some said. But she need not have worried about her dress. At that moment Hector wouldn't have noticed whether she'd changed her frock or not. He was tall like his father when he was walking upright.

"Sump'n the matter with your back, Hector? Strained it, did you? Balin' hay, was you?"

The guys who were now mostly dead used to lie in their teeth, he was sure, about all matters to do with fornication. About the size of their genital organs and rate of expansion, the number of times they'd done it in one night. All the girls they knew were nymphomaniacs according to their stories of voracious females; begging for it the girls were, tongues hanging out.

"Any of you young fellers ever done it back'ards," big mouth Jake had asked one night over bully beef stew when the line had been fairly quiet for more than a week.

"I done it that way with this broad once," Jake said. "Her dad was a minister of God, you've got to believe. She's on her hands and knees like and we gets her ass bare and I gets on top. She loves it, you can tell the way she's squealin' and gurglin'. But when it's all over she gets mad at me and yells. 'Now don't you do that again, Jakey boy. Disgusting it were. I feels just like a dawg,' she hollers." Jake rubbed a smear of gravy off his chin and looked round, smirking. Hector did not believe a minister's daughter would do a thing like that, or talk like that. Yet the story set him thinking. He wondered if Aunt Sammy would ever...Shit no.

"What about you, Celine?" he found himself asking. "You married like?"

He raised himself and leant on his elbow and thought of the last time he had been in a barn with a woman. The layer of cynicism over Celine's face cracked a little and was replaced by an infinite sadness, but it was not harsh, more resigned, softened in the whitening moonlight. Tyler farted, long and low, and M. Trou snored, uttering a croak like a dying man's at the end of every sonorous breath.

"Where have all the husbands gone, cheri?" She paused in the night. Something rustled in the damp hay. "Where do you think?"

She drew a mittened forefinger across her fat throat.

Hector wanted to ask her how long she had been a hooker, how she had started on the game in the first place, but then he thought ask a silly fucking question, what do you expect? A silly fucking answer. He was learning.

"And Suzette. Is she married?"

"The same's happened to her. She is my cousin. There are a great many widows in France, my friend."

"Everywhere there is."

"That's true. Widows and fatherless kids."

"And Tina...where's she fit in?"

"She's Suzette's little girl."

"And so her daddy's dead?"

"Who knows?" Celine shrugged.

Hector was surprised. He had not heard Tina calling Suzette "maman". He was calming down, the facts of loss and desertion becoming both more and less acceptable. He owed this whore, that was for sure. He wondered whether he were becoming too categorical, after all who was he, especially now, to make moral judgements. How many times did a woman have to be paid for it to be labelled whore. And why only the woman to be stigmatized. There were whispered tales of his Uncle Sammy in the red light district of Calgary, but that was different they said. A man needed it. A single man was expected to break out from time to time, and his unimportant copulations were winked at. Even so, supposing his uncle had copped a dose. Suddenly a great terror to add to all the others struck at the heart of Hector and he started trembling as though he had convulsions. Supposing Sam'd passed the pox on to his wife and Aunt Sammy was infected? Christ all bloody mighty, where did that leave him, Hector?

"Come, come, my dear, calmest thou."

Celine was tutoying him, soothing him once more, caressing his cheek, patting his shoulder. After all, Aunt Sammy and all her works were an eternity ago. He was bound to have noticed something by now, pissing red hot needles, something like that. The clouds were gathering again, covering the moon in the hole in the roof, and the barn became dark.

# FOUR

### MARIE

"Excuse me, my dearest Bridget. My head is in a whirl. Did I hear you aright? You say you are…"
"Pregnant."
"And that the father is… "
"Hector."
"My son? That Hector?"
"Your son and my nephew."
"And you are not ashamed, darling?"
"What slightest good would that do?"

Aunt Sammy, as the children call her, looks at me with cold eyes and speaks in her most squashing Lady Icen voice. I know that accent only too well. I often think it is put on to protect herself from her past, but on this occasion I am too dumbfounded to conjure with any nice analysis. I realize fairly soon that she is right and that accusations of shameful behaviour will not get any of us anywhere.

I am standing by the flower bed on a late summer morning and I remember that earlier Michie had galloped off full of excitement to show Hector's letter to her aunt. Both my children are devoted to Bridget—obviously one of them too much so, I think bitterly as the horror expands. The flower garden is a deal more established than when Chuck, one of our help, the cowboy with the ghastly limp, sowed some poppies for me the year Hector was born. The red poppies are still there seeding themselves season after season, but over the years we've gotten imported seeds and cuttings and it's amazing how well some of them do in this frigid climate. Chuck is still with us and helps me with the heavy digging. He can hardly get on a horse now. To tell the truth, I don't know how he ever did. I think Nick keeps him on out of charity. I am taking the deads off the petunias, brilliant purple and white ones, and staking the antirrhinums which tend to flower rather late, just beating the frost, when I see Bridget walking round the knoll which conceals her house from ours. I holler and wave at her and go to meet her. She gives me the news of her pregnancy immediately, and I suspect there is more than a dash of bravado in her telling. Son of a gun, as Nick would say.

"And you are sure of this, darling? Absolutely?"

She looks at me scornfully.

"You needn't put on a face like that, dear Bridget. There can be false alarms. Especially at our age when the period can stop suddenly, forever."

Her scorn is mixed now with a streak of anger.

"Don't look displeased, I beg you. We are sisters-in-law, aren't we? We love each other, non? I am only trying to console, to look for some escape, anything."

We reach the flower beds. Chuck is wheeling a barrow load of manure from the stables, and the barrow gives a great lurch at every limp as though the stinking pooh and straw will spill over. A trail of it marks his path. He says he likes to keep the garden well nourished, even at this time of the summer, but perhaps he has nothing better to do. It pongs for a day or two, but in any case we live so close to the beasts it doesn't make a great deal of difference. Bridget bends down to touch the yellow petals of a snapdragon just pushing daintily out from its slender cone of buds. We wait until Chuck has deposited his spadefuls of horse turds with their weft of straw and has gone.

Bridget crouches again by the snaps. Pregnant or not she has a wonderfully good figure still.

"Isn't the colour so—God, I don't know—fresh?"

"Étonnant."

"You are not angry? By Christ, Marie, you are a saint. I am at my wits end."

The cut glass voice. I do not know whether I am angry or not. The full meaning of the message has not yet penetrated my understanding. The words are not telling me anything. My son a prospective father. The mother of the babe-to-be my sister-in-law. My grandchild growing in that womb near the petunias and red poppies and fresh manure. Dear God, he is not old enough. Where is his youth? Where was it? Swallowed by this foul war and prospective fatherhood and him only a boy. And who is this evil witch, this siren who has seduced him. The Lady Icen voice is beginning to crack, however, the aristocratic composure to crumple. She gets up and her face becomes old and ugly.

"I don't know what to focking well do, Marie."

The accent now is slum Irish. I'm used to Bridgie's cuss words—it's no use being shocked by bad language out on the edge of civilization. She bursts into tears and flings her arms around me. I make soothing noises and help her into the living room and sit her down, appropriately enough, in my old nursing chair which I still keep near the window. She likes tea, I know, not thin parson's pee as you might expect, but thick stuff in which the spoon will practically stand up on its own. I brew her some and add an ounce of rye to make it truly Irish. She gulps it greedily, scalding hot, and a spot of red appears in each of her cheeks.

"I suppose I'll have to get rid of the little bastard."

She's back to her superior voice, condescending to the world and its outrageous slings, trying to shock me. But even in my numbed state I figure this is horse feathers, as Nick would say. Camouflage. She adores children—witness the way she loves mine. Oh dear! What am I saying!

"Do you think Dot Howard would do the dirty deed? How good is she with knitting needles?"

"Dot would do nothing of the sort, Bridget. Pull yourself together, cherie."

My head is still in a whirl, but right now I am the stronger of the two. Bridge and I, the two Mesdames Plouvier, have much in common. In a perverse way, although we are both, warmly and affectionately I think, established in this isolated community, we are still in a fundamental sense foreigners. Me simply because I am French Quebecoise and Bridget because of her la-di-da ways and refusal to speak cowhand's lingo. Little do they know.

"The women were up to all the tricks in Dublin, mortal sin or not. Take hot baths, they said. What a joke! We got a luke warm bath if we were lucky once a week in a little tin tub in the back kitchen and all the family had to use the same water. Except my father who never washed. Every other woman under forty you met in Dublin was expecting. Drink a lot of gin, they said. Run up and down the stairs till you drop. Go for a hard ride on a horse, they say here."

"Who says? Who's they?"

The tea and rye are helping her back to more of her old self. So damned sure of herself. When Sam brought her home in triumph to live on the ranch I was as pleased as a dog with two tails. Her lovely clothes. She was a beauty then, still is, with her thick dark gleaming hair and shining complexion despite her having been brought up in those Dublin streets. I can't imagine them. The prairie sun had not at that time dried up her face. Even now her skin is not at all bad. No wonder that my son was enchanted. What devil words am I saying? Condoning, conspiring like some maternal bawd. I do not yet realize the horrendous fact of what has happened. Where, holy blue, did they do it? Has it been going on a long time, under our very noses?

"Are you so determined to get rid of...it, Bridget? Have you no feeling for it?"

I can't believe I am saying this, what monstrous prospect I am holding out.

"Wouldn't you like to keep it? The baby?"

At first we were wary of each other, but the barbarity of the community drew us together. Don't forget I am not very sophisticated myself. I got a taste of the finer things in Montreal and then like a bolt from Heaven, wham bam, Nick had nailed me in Winnipeg and incarceration here soon followed. The folks on the whole are good in Higgins Bend, unimaginative a lot of them, but warm-hearted, steadfast. And though he would hate my saying this, Nick's and my passion for each other has remained as strong as ever. Incredible. Modified now, naturally, but sturdy. Yet we are still isolated and the sheer feminine society that Bridget promised on her arrival was in itself thrilling, a cut above cooking, washing and cleaning for the cowboys, but you must remember we had to do that too. And even when years later she confided in me that her life as a lady's companion was a fortuitous assumption and she disclosed the tawdry facts of her Irish upbringing, I loved her all the more for it. Dear Bridge. And now look at the dilemma the reckless bitch has landed us all in.

"As you know, Marie, I've never had a child. I've always envied you your two. Oh my stars!"

She rose out of the nursing chair, the cup rattling in the saucer.

"It wasn't his fault. You must know that, Marie. None of it Hector's fault. I must take all the blame."

I look out to the garden and see that Chuck is limping along with another load of steaming hoss-shit. I move over to close the window. This confession of a noble dame is all very well. I pour another slug of rye into her teacup. What was she thinking about, though, when she pulled up the skirts of one of those lovely dresses. Maybe she didn't have to, maybe they were both naked in that wonderful bedroom of hers which I must admit I envy. I'm not squeamish—there's no way you can be on a ranch in the wilds—but the thought of my little boy doing that to his lustful, middle-aged aunt makes me want to throw up. And she egging him on. Of course she was not thinking about anything other than getting it, insatiable. Dousing the heat in her loins, filling the blank in her heart. I felt so sorry for her when Sam died in that awful way. They had everything going for them. Yet that does not excuse this incestuous conduct, fucking her nephew, putting us all in a horrendous situation. Whatever will Michelle say? She will have to know I suppose.

"There must be some other way out, Bridgie."

"Tell me."

Her skin is very white and never freckles in the fiercest sun. When she arrived this morning, she was wearing a straw hat with a broad brim and a saucy lemon coloured bow which is now on her lap as she sinks into the nursing chair. As she leans her head back to look up at me, pleading, eyes half-closed but no longer cold, I am fascinated and touched as always by the doll-like cast of her features, their smallness and daintiness which take years off her real age. The white face, the black hair, the shiny dark eyes. She's a colleen all right, of myth and dream, and no one would ever believe she was dragged up in the stews of a mean, uncaring city. She can also be a most calculating madam, selfish, hard as nails.

"I repeat. Do you want to keep it?"

"How do I know, Marie? I've only become certain in the last few days that I've got a bun in the oven. I came to you. I need time."

"I understand, cherished one. We'll think of something, never fear. But first Nick will have to know."

"Be Jaysus, no!"

Her face is made ugly with horror.

"Of course he must, darling. Whether we keep it or get rid of it, he'll have to know."

಄

"Figure as sump'n onusual's going on, Billy. Sump'n to do with young Hector."

Chuck Turner sat on his iron bedstead in the bunkhouse. He was chewing tobacco and whittling a piece of two by four which was black with old creosote.

"So."

Billy Lilley looked up from last week's Calgary newspaper, The Herald. He had been reading it slowly, his forefinger following the line of print just ahead of his eyes.

"Miz Bridget was in a rare old stew this morning. Steamin' inside she was when she come by the house."

Chuck's knife, which he kept in a sheath on the back of his belt, had been sharpened so many times that it had a concave cutting edge. He eased out his bad leg, which was inches shorter than the good one.

"Really."

Nick had excused Billy work that day because of a poisoned knee.

"Yup. They goes all quiet like a pair of field mice when I wheels the barrow along of they. Not like Miz Mary-Loo that ain't, Billy. No sir."

Billy Lilley looked up patiently, his finger keeping his place on the latest war casualties in the paper. "You get that there knee fixed," his boss had said.

"Today. Get yourself down to Dot Howard, mind." Billy had obediently been to Higgins Bend, and Dot had lanced his knee for him and bandaged it up. Wonderful what she could do, that nurse. Hardly hurt at all.

"She allus has a nice word or two to say to me. Bin working for her a long whiles, Billy. But today not a squeak outa her, not even when I spreads the hoss muck round the rose bush she's so fonder. Not even a good day. Then there was a heck of a row inside the house. She closed the winder, Miz Marie did, but I could hear them awright, hollering away at each other they was. In a posh way like."

Billy patiently laid his paper on the brown blanket folded at the head of his bed. They had to keep the bunkhouse tidy. There were ten beds in the long dark room, more of a shed, but many of the hands had gone off to the army. To the Canadian Expeditionary Force in France. "Uncle" Tom Stewart had been blinded and was in a hospital in Ontario learning Braille as the top half of his face healed, and Jonathan Cobberly had been killed early on. Young Buzz Blairmore was missing in action, as good as a goner, folks reckoned. Billy scratched his head where the grey hair was springy. He had been too old to join up but he had tried. "Thanks grandad, but it ain't worth the trip down here," the recruiting sergeant had said. Billy had told him that he could ride a hoss all day every day for a week at round-up time, but the sergeant said it was out of his hands. He would not even send him for a medical examination. So had the boss, tried to join up, but they said he was doing more for his country raising cattle. Not to mention that he too was getting old in the tooth for the army, they implied. Nick could have marched forty mile with a full pack at the head of an infantry battalion and taken them into the jaws of hell before breakfast. Or led the charge of the Light Brigade if necessary on his old hoss, Jacky.

"What's it to do with Hector? Them two having a spat, if that's what it were?"

"Cain't figure it out. Leastways, not yet."

Chuck spat a brown jet expertly in the direction of a spittoon and it landed in the dead centre of the funnel. Almost as soon as she could take breath after her arrival at the ranch Nick's new bride had told him she was not going to have the bunkhouse a cesspool of saliva, so the spittoons were installed. You can't stop a cowhand from spitting, missy, Nick had said, unless you sew his lips together, but he had to obey the rules too no matter how much his mouth filled up. A month previously she had not known what a bunkhouse was. No spitting in the yard either.

"But I seen them together often enough when they never thought I hadder. Down by the slough. Holding hands they were. In the barn.

Up at Sam's house," Chuck said, wagging his knife to support his dark inference.

"Seen who together, for Pete's sake?"

"Hector and Miz Bridge." Billy Lilley gave a dry contemptuous laugh. He looked across at his workmate. When the bunkhouse was full before the war the guys used to tease Chuck, but a lot of it was jealousy because he had such an easy time of it, spoiled and pampered by Marie, never up and away with the rest of the fellers, never on any of the long hard slogs in the saddle on the vast empty reaches of the foothills with your ass sorer than hell and your throat dry.

"Course you seen them together, you jerk. Them kids thinks the sun shines outa their auntie's rear end, allus has done. Allus up at Sam's place they was as soon as they could toddle. She's bin a second mother to them. A nice lady that one and don't you tell me she ain't."

"Sure, Billy, sure." His wad of tobacco pushed out his bristly cheek, and his chin retreated quickly into his throat, a big bobbing Adam's apple. "But she don't have no time for the likes of us."

"True."

"I don't think you is getting my meaning Billy."

Billy pulled his pipe and a tin of twist tobacco from his pocket. His shock of wiry hair gleamed silver in the shaft of light coming through the doorway. His shirt had once been gaily checked but the colours had run together into a sludgy brown. Round his neck was a faded green kerchief twisted round the wrong way. His face was in feature the opposite of Chuck's, compact, firm, a square chin, bristly also, eyes distantly humane. Before he filled his pipe he cleared his throat heartily and spat a gobbet of phlegm carefully into the spittoon, holding his head over the funnel till the last dribble had dropped off.

"I sure as hell ain't getting your meaning, old son."

Chuck Turner looked uncomfortable. Wrenching his body into painful angles he stood up and his big hands at the end of his dangling arms started to brush the shavings off his pants.

"You're not going to leave that crud down there?"

"Do I ever leave a goddam mess anywheres, Billy Lilley? I'll clean 'er up in a minute. Like I allus clean up after you hunks."

"You know what, Chuck. You got a dirty mind, I tell ya. You get sitting around here on your ass all day and you start thinking dirty things about other people cos you got nothing better to do."

"I ain't said nothing about nobody."

"No?"

Billy scratched a match on his boot and lit his pipe, waving the smoke about with the hand that held the match box. He looked worried and sad and old. The casualty lists depressed him. None of the hands disliked Chuck Turner, but he was a real old woman, gossiping at random about his employer's family. He'd go too far one of these days and the boss would give him the bum's rush, except that he was so well in with the boss's wife. What in the blazes was he getting at today for Christ's sake? Did he mean that young Hector, whom Billy had taught to ride when he were a kid, were doing things he shouldn't with Miz Bridge? Shit, no. Impossible. Only a crazy loon like Chuck could imagine that sort of garbage. Heck, she were respectable and old enough to be his mother, and she loved those two as though she was their mother. Billy was a firm believer in the ordained order of the universe. The stars was up above and so were the sun. It was cold in winter, goddam cold it could get in the mountains, and cowhands was cowhands and ranchers was ranchers.

"You want to watch that fucking mouth of yourn, Chuck Turner. It'll get you into trouble if you ain't careful. What would the boss say if he heard you spreading stories like that?"

"I ain't said nothing about nobody," Chuck repeated, his face blank, offended.

He was making atrocious jerks and heaves between the two beds, sweeping up his wood shavings with a broom which was worn down to the handle.

"But you ain't seen what I seen, Billy Lilley," he mumbled. "And if you had of you'd play a different tune on your old fiddle. And I ain't no hoss's ass, Billy, I can tell you. And put that in your stinking pipe and smoke it."

෪ ۞ ๛

Nicholas Plouvier galloped towards the western boundary of his spread, stopping only with ragged impatience to open and close a gate, and then racing off due west across an open valley where a tongue of the prairie had penetrated the foothills. His mouth a grim horizontal slash, his teeth clamped hard together, a plug of tobacco forming the shape of a gumboil in his cheek. To his south the Canadian Pacific Railroad snaked its way to Banff and Field, cutting through the mountains on miracles of engineering. A Sunday afternoon when things were fairly quiet on the farm and his sister-in-law had come to the midday dinner. She generally came every other week, formally, as it were, not counting the many droppings by, and he looked forward to that. She was always pleasant company and cheered him up. But this Sunday, good Christ, the roof had fallen in. He was a natural rider and his horse would not stumble in gopher burrows, but though his body and reflexes were guiding the horse his mind was not there. Fate, he thought, could be a vengeful critter. Delayed vengeance at that.

"It's more than a feller can take, Missy," he'd said as he stumped away from the table. "I gotta to get to hell out of here and cool my head before it bursts with all this rat shit"

After half an hour's hard gallop he turned north through a cleft in the hills into a green landscape, dusted with the summer, rolling acres mounting into knolls, sliding through gulleys, dotted with stands of trees, small woods. He could no longer let his horse run like crazy but had to walk it along a broken trail through shrub and brush. The horse Jacky, a roan, great barrel chest heaving, shook his head and flecks of saliva flew onto the wild rose bushes. The homesteads were widely scattered and only poorly maintained gravel roads ran in the vicinity, and often not up to the homesteads so that wagons and carts had to be left at a distance.

He'd tried all the self-deceiving tricks that an outdoors man, used to the lonely boondocks, could employ to clear his mind of nauseating thoughts, letting his consciousness slip away whilst only the fact of physical presence remained with him in the saddle. The human stripped of all but animal instincts alone among the grasses and the trees and the late wild flowers, the small creatures, the impossibly graceful deer, the birds unheard in their afternoon silence.

"Just say that again, Bridge."

The gravied piece of beef had remained on his fork. He never did eat it.

"You and Hector, my little guy, you was...Shit!"

Nick never swore in front of the women. He'd jumped up from his chair, gravy smearing the white Sunday tablecloth, and thumped the table.

"Like a dawg and a bitch in heat," he shouted.

"Nick." Marie Louise's pale face was pleading. "We've come to you for advice, dear Nick. And help."

"There ain't no help on this here earth that I can see. Nowhere. Gawd help us is all I can say. And I don't think even He can."

At this time of the year the flies were a nuisance under the trees, and they buzzed around Jacky's nose. Whenever any suggestion of peace came dropping anywhere near it was destroyed by the raw images of his son on top of his sister-in-law, rutting away like any farm beast, the pair of them laughing at him in derision. He'd spent a lot of time with Hector before he'd taken off for the wars. Oh my, the brazen audacity of the boy. That dutiful, filial face. That's right, dad. No, dad. O.K., dad. Was that why he joined the army. 'Course he wouldn't have known at that time about nobody being put in the family way. As Hector had grown towards manhood, so quickly, as he'd ridden by Nick's side on the ranch, both silent for long periods in happy communion, not needing any chat, Nick had sometimes vaguely thought of his son's marrying, of grandchildren, his genetic line, his blood. It was only natural that men thought of such things. Well there was a grandchild all right on the way now. Christ almighty. As a rule Nick did not allow profanity in his hearing.

He arrived at a broader gravel road which ran due north. To the right of it homesteaders had already begun to establish fields for grain, dairy cattle, and to its left was the beginning of a comparatively small reserve, part of Queen Victoria's atonement to a small Indian band of Stoneys. Like Billy Lilley, Nick believed in the universal order into which he had been born, where everything and everybody kept to their proper place. He prided himself he was not sanctimonious, no bible belter, he was tolerant of small sins, and of bigger offences committed by men and women driven by harsh circumstance. But he was a believer in law and order and swift punishment where necessary. And decency. And marriage and the family. Of course men did stray from time to time, in drink or out of it. This was not a perfect world, especially out here, but probably just as bad in the cities. Take himself and Missy for instance when they first met in Winnipeg. A flicker of a smile played for a second at the hard ends of his grim mouth. He did not go to church much but he supported in a general way what Christianity stood for. He nudged Jacky onto a faint trail which led into the Indian reserve. Thicker woods, larch and spruce which made a glorious gold and green in the fall. He had to be careful guiding Jacky round old tree trunks lying across his path and at times had to dismount and lead his horse.

ᛯ☙

"You got yourself inna heapa trouble again, Big Nick?"

The Indian, beat up face, shoulders sceptically hunched, was waiting for him in a clearing of thin trunked aspen, leaves shivering in the slightest breath, a romantic spot, idyllic, except for a smell of human shit hardly smothered by a pervasive odour of acrid wood smoke which always made Nick's eyes water. He was sitting cross-legged in the centre of a pool of sunlight wearing the same kind of floppy domed hat as Nick, stained work shirt, pants, boots with their soles coming away from the uppers.

"Hi there, Clarence Manythumbs. Talking drums, eh, you old rascal. Or just a blind goddamn guess. How'd you know I was coming?"

"By them smoke signals, big white boss. Your Missy send 'em."

"Stop talking shit, Clarence."

He handed the Indian a package of tobacco.

"No firewater, boss? A fine fucking peace offering this is."

Clarence Manythumbs, Nick thought, could not be all that old despite his seamed, ruined face, the noble nose pitted with enlarged pores, eyes half closed but bright with ironic welcome. The other ranchers would not approve of Nick cosying up with an Indian.

"If I would of brung you a bottle of whiskey you would of been zonked out of your mind before the end of the day."

Clarence laughed, showing his black teeth. He brushed at the flies buzzing about his nostrils and mouth.

"Sit down, big fella. Tell me what it is. You ain't come to see about old Clarence's health, that's for sure. Nor 'bout Rachel's."

The rancher dropped Jacky's reins and hunkered down. The joy in his face at meeting the Indian had passed.

"How's Rachel doing?"

"Gettin' along real fine."

"And the boy?"

"He's okay, but he ain't a boy no more, mister."

"I guess that's true too."

Nick took his hat off and spat a stream of juice in the direction of Jacky's hooves. His thick black hair flattened. Darn strange that Hector should have been born fair and both his parents dark.

"You'd better believe it. And there's sump'n else you oughta know. He's goin' to get 'issel wed."

The rancher's concrete face seemed to set even harder. Every so often the clamped jaws would move as he shifted the wad of tobacco from one cheek to another. Right from the start Missy had not let him chew in the house. "Disgusting habit, cheri, you can do as you please out on your old horse, but not here, please, darling." He glanced up at the leaves trembling in a shaft of sunlight. He had ridden out to seek from this ruined aboriginal, not for the first time since that humiliating business of long years ago, God knows what? Comfort, advice, teepee wisdom. Bearshit philosophy? The other ranchers would think him a stark staring case for the bin if they had the slightest inkling that he came to consult an illiterate native, and Nick sometimes wondered whether he were in his right mind himself. Yet it had seemed an inevitable progression after the Rachel affair, when for some inscrutable reason Clarence had come out of the woods to help sort things out, mediate, patch up a nasty little betrayal. This had been before he met Missy. Of course, he could have told them all to go hang. Most white men he knew would've.

"Getting wed, eh? Is he? I'll be darned."

Long pauses between the three phrases.

Even so, his coming to Clarence was highly improbable whichever way you cut it. He'd never breathed a word of it to his wife, still less a murmur about the Rachel business. No doubt there were secrets in her own past that he never wished to pry into. But the main reason he didn't tell Missy about Clarence was that she would think him plumb crazy, fou...and why not? That this tall hard rancher carving a place in the west, unflinching against all the hostilities, assured, confident, reliable, giving counsel and succour to the weaker brethren of the community, emotions under a tight rein—all that and more—should seek out a chronically drunken bum to commune with, hell no. But hell yes.

Clarence, Nick would like to tell the scoffers but never did, was no dumb Injun. Under that slurred and broken drawl, if you were prepared to listen, he could go direct to the simplicities which lay at the heart of consolation. It was both as simple and complicated as water divining. A stripping of pretension from the mouths of babes and Indians. Ages ago he'd told Nick he was a Stoney, had been a young brave once who had gone big game hunting in the mountains. The Assiniboine word, Assinipwat, means Stone People, descendants of the Sioux. Nick would have liked to know him then when he faced the sow grizzlies protecting their cubs, but by the time they met middle age, indolence and alcohol had begun to corrode Clarence.

"And Rachel. What's she think about the wedding?"

Clarence cackled. He'd filled an encrusted pipe with Nick's tobacco and his face was hidden in a veil of smoke.

"It don't matter one lil' ol' chicken fart what she think, do it, big Nick? Weddins is for a man to decide, ain't they?"

The rancher began to tell him about Hector.

# FIVE

The rains eased, but November fogs and rimes settled over the countryside. Having slept in reasonable comfort in the dry, the Trou family and the two deserters moved from barn to barn. Each night Celine contrived to lie beside Hector and hold his hand in her mittened one.

"What you doing old buddy? Getting into that bag of lard? Nightly ration, eh?" Tyler asked one morning after he'd had to get up in the night for a pee. "I reckon she's not a bad old rattle, eh?"

Celine knew enough English to catch the gist of Tyler's remark and for some reason felt ashamed. She was pleased though when she saw that Hector turned away embarrassed also.

"Go fuck yourself, Tyle," he said out of the side of his mouth.

"Keep you hair on, pal."

As the rains stopped so the temperature went down and the muddy roads began to harden into frozen ruts. The little group of fugitives was beginning to move out of the warscapes where all the trees and fields were violated and the land one shitty brown. The countryside now, though unshelled, unpocked, not soured by poison gas, wore nevertheless its gaunt winter dress which could make the land they marched over depressing enough. Celine's spirits, nevertheless, had risen minimally, against all the odds. At night when the others had flopped off immediately to sleep (Tyler had made more forays and scrounged a good supply of rum, but it was getting less easy to steal the further they moved from the front) she and Hector would talk in hushed voices like lovers. His French was strange to her but understandable and fluent.

She told him about the farm and the apple harvest and the cider making. They made a liqueur too from the cider. "My faith, how that was strong." Her father had inherited a little farm and orchard which had been in his family for ages as well as the estaminet. "How Uncle Joseph loved that apple liqueur, Calvados was the Norman name for it but they made it in our valley as well. He said it would blow off the top of your head. Pouf!" Celine laughed when she said that, the first time for long enough.

"When did your uncle get that sore on his neck?"

"A long time ago. It has got worse this last two years. Poor Uncle Joseph."

"He needs to get it lanced. Why does he not get it treated?"

Celine laughed again, but this time with her old bitterness.

"You seen any doctors for civilians round these parts? You show me and I'll tell Uncle Joe and he'll be off to him like a chicken from the fox."

They loved Joseph, a favourite uncle in the days when he hadn't got that horrible growth and before his mind wandered. She pressed Hector's hand to show that she was not displeased with him. She remembered the glorious days before she was married and how the family would gather on Sundays and Feast Days at the farmhouse which was scarcely half a kilometre from the estaminet. Uncle Joe would come from the next village where he was a wheelwright and also Suzette who was one of five daughters of Celine's mother's sister, Aunt Claude. How slim her cousin was in those days. Whenever it was warm in the spring or summer they would eat out of doors on a patch of grass by the orchard and Uncle Joe in his Sunday best, newly shaved for the Sabbath or a holy day, a straw hat with a red and green ribbon round the crown and a striped shirt and a floppy tie would play the accordion, dancing to his own music. There was not even a pimple on his neck at that time, and he was quite a one for flirting with the ladies.

"Thou just keep thy snoopy eyes to th'sen, my man," Aunt Bernardette would say to him only half kidding.

As the evenings drew on, M. Trou would take the grandfathers to wet their whistles in the cool of the estaminet which was being looked after by one of the village lads he hired from time to time, but Uncle Joe would stay with the younger ones who played around and skipped to his melodies, merry and sprightly and sad and sentimental. When it was hot the grandmothers and aunts would sit knitting or crocheting in the shade of the apple trees on kitchen chairs fetched from the farmhouse. One of the old ladies, grandmaman Flautier, if Celine remembered correctly, smoked a little clay pipe much to the exasperation of the village curate. She had no teeth and a sharp thin nose, but her chin instead of balancing it receded disappointingly leaving her pipe and nose to jut out in lonely profile. Rain or shine she always wore a black bonnet.

"My mam used to say she must have had very hard gums. And you know what? However tight she tied them ribbons grandma Flautier's bonnet would never stay fastened. They slipped over her little chin, well no chin at all really, and got caught on her nose," Celine said to Hector in one of their barns and she could see that he smiled in the half dark.

"How I loved all the out-of-door seasons, Hector chou. The trees covered in white blossom seemed to stretch for miles. The smell of the hay with the dried thistles in it. My daddy had horse and a plough, and I would watch the share cutting the soil and the birds, gulls, wheeling and screeching behind him. I had brought out his food and bottle of wine but had to rush back to do my chores."

Celine, the fat whore, sighed. She was on her back, her plump knees drawn up, gazing at the roof of some alien barn, no shell holes in this one, and Hector was leaning on his elbow listening and looking at the blotch of her face. She insisted on holding his hand. The usual night noises, farts, belches, snores came from Tyler and the others. Joseph was windy and raucous that night.

"But, my God, times were not always good. Though looking back one always forgets the bad ones. When some blight got on the apples and they went brown and mushy. Every blessed little apple. And sometimes the hay would be soaked and rot in the fields and a horrible disease would happen to the cows' feet and the fowl would stop laying..."

"Same as happen to us," Hector said. "My dad said you cain't piss against the wind."

"There was one wicked summer..."

She took her hand away from Hector and rubbed it across her face as though trying to erase a memory.

"The summer when Suzette's two sisters were drowned."

"Really?"

"Them two girls was too young to die."

She shuddered at her memory of the bodies when they had been recovered from the deep pool by the weir, how utterly dead they seemed, like gaffed fish. It was a mystery how the girls managed to fall in. Her father and Uncle Joe used to fish that same pool but not for a year or two after the drownings. Celine snuffled a while and then recovered.

"Mind..." She smiled grimly in the dark. "When you think of what's happened to those who are left, maybe the good God was merciful."

She thought of the men who had mounted her. It was enough to make a cat sick, though that kind of sensitivity, remorse, whatever, had only partially and recently returned. Much of her grief was the fault of the Boches starting the war, not all of it, but they exacerbated it. One of the grandfathers or great-uncles, she could not remember which one, was forever warning them. "It won't be long before the Hun comes again. Mark my words. And then watch out. Then you girls will have to take care." He got to be quite an old pest he was so obsessed, and they only half-listened and mocked his squeaky voice behind his back. Suzette described how he tried to feel her up once behind the blackcurrant bushes and had given her some money not to tell her parents. He must have been a great-uncle. Celine held Hector's hand tighter. She herself had discovered to her personal cost early and late that it was not only the Boche they had to be careful about.

One summer when Celine was in her late teens and the sunny days seemed as if they would never cease, formations of the French army had been camped near the Trou farm. They had assembled in all their pomp and blowing of trumpets and bugles at the orders of some remote ministers and generals in Paris for military training in the field. Celine, Suzette and the others had been thrilled to see the soldiers in their blue uniforms, the sun gleaming on their equipment, marching and counter-marching, and the cavalry prancing in as though they were the lords of creation. On a holy day, the Feast of the Assumption, Celine had been raped by one of them, a brigadier, who had lured her down to the river to show her his magnificent horse.

"Come, my pretty one, come and see my horse," the corporal with the splendid plume in his hat had said. "It is not far. My mare has such a magnificent tail you'd never believe. A green one."

His spurs were shining at the back of his riding boots. Celine had giggled and looked around for Suzette, who had disappeared. The two cousins had strolled to the far edge of the orchard and could hear the music of Uncle Joseph's accordion in the distance. Suzette was older than Celine by a few years.

"A green tail! I don't believe you."

"Well just come and see."

She flapped her bonnet against her long Sunday skirt and looked shyly at his arrogant, flirtatious eyes.

"I shouldn't. Maman says I mustn't go with the soldiers."

He took off his gauntlet and led her by the hand while she looked back vainly for her cousin or anyone. The green apples had not yet begun to turn colour. Later she hadn't dared to tell her mother, who died shortly afterwards, or M. Trou, who would have boxed her ears for being such a simpleton. Where had they been when she needed them? She could smell the apple brandy on his breath as she struggled with him and his spur had torn her dress. When he finished he got up, buttoned up his breeches, mounted his horse, saluted and cantered off. The mare's tail was black.

Celine sighed in the barn.

"What's the matter?" Hector asked.

"Nothing at all. I was just dreaming backward, to when we were children. Younger at any rate. I was married when I was nineteen. A girl was on the shelf if she was not married before she was twenty. Uncle Joe played his accordion at the wedding feast."

At least the cavalry corporal had not made her pregnant or infected her with the pox. He had told her to pull down her dress as from high on his horse he'd looked down on her sobbing in disarray. Celine did not question why she was reminiscing so much, why her apathy was not such a dead weight as two weeks ago. She did not consider what she could expect from this young foreign soldier, now deserter, who spoke French with a Canadian accent, never for one moment contemplated the hopelessness of the case. There was a dream world of youth, ages before the war, which had been kept screened and suppressed in the misery of the present lest thinking about it would drive her mad.

Until now, the final surrender, her father would not give up his patrimoine, unluckily situated on the edge of a massive conflict, no matter how much the war destroyed his land and family. Their desperation drove them to shameful indignities. At first it had not been easy, but for the past eighteen months, two years, Celine would lie on the bed by the bar for any soldier who came along and wanted her, lift her skirts and take the money. M. Trou scarcely bothered to turn his head as the riff-raff of different armies fucked his daughter. A passive indifference had settled on her and her father and cousin, a cauterizing of the emotions. The monstrous swelling on Uncle Joe's neck seemed to drain power from his mind and speech so she might as well have been washing dishes for all the notice he took as she earned a few francs for the harassed family. And Suzette was on the game as well. She had to be.

In the barn she could tell Hector was getting drowsy. He'd had a swig of rum tonight to settle his nerves after the fright they'd all had earlier that day with the General and the police. Celine was determined she would never tell Hector how she was raped by the river, even though in retrospect one penetration of her body more or less could scarcely matter.

♦

They had been lucky that afternoon. The hedgerows hereabouts had not been flattened by Fritz's artillery, but they'd been splashed with mud and were depressing in their leaflessness. Three men had suddenly leaped out from a ditch bordering a row of hawthorns and run over to the Trou cart. Celine at first thought they were brigands. Despite all the armies and police, civil and military, that crowded the French countryside, marauding bands of desperate men, deserters of all nationalities, terrorized farms and villages for money and food. They formed an ironic underclass in the war to end all wars and yet held for each other a comradeship of outlawry. Nothing was sacred to them. One group had audaciously raided the stores of a crack infantry division, knocked senseless the cooks and the odds and sods and went triumphantly away with some of the choice rations intended for the senior officers. Since it had been agreed among the members of the Trou group that once out of the range of shells the two women would walk by the cart and only little Tina ride, Celine was waddling heavy hipped beside Hector, occasionally bending to help push, when she saw the men burst from the hedge. She screamed. One was carrying a small scythe.

"Stop. Stop right there."

The villainous looking one with the scythe waved it frantically. Tyler and M. Trou, who had been pushing, lowered the shaft to the ground. There were no other refugees on this stretch of road, no troops, no horses, no trucks nor carts. Just the grey sky, the puddles on the road with a thin film of ice. Across a field was a cottage with a smokeless chimney. "You fellas got discharge papers?" The question from the oldest of the three. He'd grown a beard which had streaks of grey. He stood with the erect posture and grim neutral face of a regular soldier and wore a khaki Balaklava helmet, knitted by some patriot in France or Britain or maybe even Canada.

"What's he talking about?" Tyler asked.

"For Chrissake, Tyle, don't speak English," Hector whispered.

The man with the beard laughed. He was in a shocking condition, peasant disguise like the two Canadians but pants filthy and torn, an open gash on his cheek above the beard, eyes swivelling, looking at them all in turn.

"Keep your hair on mates. No one's going to 'urtcha. But answer a bleeding question, cantcha? For your own fucking sakes. You got your papers?"

A hairy leg showed through a rent in his trousers. A pity someone hadn't sent him long warm underpants and loyally knitted socks.

"O my gentle Jesus," Celine said to herself. "This is all we need, just all we fucking well need now."

The third man, smaller than the others, almost a dwarf, started to cough violently. He bent down, spewing a brown bile on the road. Uncle Joe patted his back and held his forehead.

"Why?" asked Hector in French. "Why do you want to know?"

Celine felt proud of him, talking bravely to the brigands, as though she had a special interest, as though his fluency took her out of her apathy. The man with the cut face pushed his Balaklava back on his forehead.

"Never heard anybody speak like you, young fellow. Which part of this infernal country do you come from?"

Hector eyed the man with the scythe.

"What's it with you guys anyway? Who are you?"

"I got this feeling you ain't very different from us, sonny, if you want to know. We're just trying to warn you. You and the women and the old fellers."

At that moment a fourth man came from the hedge and waved at the others.

"Get out of here, Emile," he shouted. "A whole mob of bloody soldiers is coming. Skedaddle!"

"We was just trying to save your hides, mister," the beard said as he started off. "There's a check point down the road. Lousy with police hiding behind a big four wheel waggon. Just waiting for the likes of you, sonny boy. And him." He pointed at Tyler. "Thought you might like to know. Just watch it."

With that they simply disappeared, like hedge sprites, no sign of them on the plough on either side of the road, not anywhere. Despite the raw day M. Trou took off his beret and mopped his brow. He was taking out his pipe when they all heard the sound of horses and round a bend in the road came an awesome group of military splendour.

"Get that ruddy heap of stinking rubbish out of the way," an officer screamed in English, pointing accusingly with a gauntleted hand at the Trou cart. "Get it to hell out of here. Make way you bloody scum for General H***."

M. Trou and Uncle Joe, Hector and Tyler heaved desperately to move the cart and stood by the hedge as the great man rode gloriously by. Celine had never seen anything like him. God knows how many hands high his horse stood, but it seemed as though the mighty leader of men were half in heaven, towering above them from the grey sky, just as the corporal had been who raped her. How blood red the band on his peaked cap was, how all his brass buttons shone and so did the trappings on his horse. His face was pink, a shade or two lighter than his cap band, well fed and wined, an impressive iron grey moustache under a firm Roman nose, wide shoulders, upright carriage, breeches a very light brown, almost white, the leather on his boots smooth and brown like a chestnut. He was flanked and followed by other important looking officers who answered the General in a fruity god-like English which reminded Hector of Aunt Sammy. They rode past the wretched Trou group as though it were a pile of horseshit.

"It's too near the front line for the likes of them bastards," Tyler said.

"They didn't take no notice of us anyways," said Hector.

He turned to M. Trou. "What we going to do about the police, boss?"

"What police?"
"The cops them fellers were talking about."
"You and Teelair will have to go in the cart."
"And suppose they search it?"
The old man shrugged.
"There's no other road. And the country's as flat as a pancake round here."

ଓଷ୍ଠ୍ୟୋ

The year after she had been raped, Celine's husband-to-be came courting her from a neighbouring village. As she lay by the side of Hector in the barn she wondered whether she would ever tell him about Jean, big, handsome, strong, with wiry red hair and a fierce ginger moustache. And his sudden brutal temper. Life before the war had not been all roses. The police at the check point on the look out for deserters had not searched the cart. Hector and Tyler had hidden under the tarpaulin with Tina very visible and propped up between them.

"What the blazes have we here, Jack?" one of the police asked as the estaminet group approached, Celine and her father pushing, Suzette holding on to the flapping cover and Joseph, head askew, trotting by the side like an uncoordinated puppet. "You sure see some god-awful sights in this asshole of a job."

There had been a moment of anguish when one of the policemen had leaned across and patted Tina on the cheek. She had cowered away from his touch. He looked pained, held out his palms on either side of his body as though testing for rain, but then waved them through.

"You'd better get that neck seen to, you filthy old man, you. It's enough to turn me stummick," the policeman shouted at Joseph.

He turned to his comrade. "Innit, Jack?"

M. Trou had taken an immediate liking to Big Red. The local proprieties had all been observed. Jean and Celine had been properly introduced at a wedding reception appropriately enough, no back lane pick up theirs. In any case M. Trou with his social pretensions would never have countenanced such a thing. The young giant asked Trou, who by this time had lost his wife, if he may visit his daughter and Celine's father had been delighted.

"You've got quite a catch there, sweetheart. Look at the size and power of him. His shoulders. As strong as a horse. Think of what he'll be able to do on the farm."

"But, dad, I hardly know him yet."

"You will do, my girl, you will do."

Madame Trou had been a chronically sick woman and it was only after a number of miscarriages that Celine was brought safely to term. As things turned out she was to be the one and only child and there was therefore no male heir for M. Trou. He faced his bitter disappointment stoically and worked reasonably hard on the little farm where he was helped by two village men he hired and by a moderate but steady intake from the various liqueurs in his estaminet. He never married again, though there were a number of women in the neighbourhood who would willingly have come to him had he so much as lifted his little finger. When Big Red happened along, M. Trou was delighted and hoped here was someone to share the family responsibility. His own father, who legally still owned the land, had for years been crippled with rheumatism, living on apple brandy and was now more dead than alive.

"You'll please your father, miss, if you give Jean the glad eye."

Celine grinned shyly, conspiratorially. "It's not up to me, dad."

She had not minded his sort of persuasion. She and her father were very close and fond of each other if not very demonstrative about it. And besides, the attentions of Big Red were flattering. As a girl Celine had not been slim like her cousin, Suzette. She was not grossly fat either when Jean was courting her but substantial, sturdy arms and legs, and yet she moved with a kind of powerful grace, if not exactly daintily. Suzette was always the dainty one, the grandmothers and great-aunts used to say.

Her mind had never been so full of the past as when she lay by Hector in the barns. She let the memories unfold without analysis or even shame. She never tried to understand fully why she had not gone weeping to her father when she was raped by the river. She had bottled it up and sneaked in the back door and washed herself and put ointment of her mother's on the bruises and scratches. But she was timid and suspicious from then on whenever males were around and at first would not let herself be out of sight alone with Jean.

"What are you frightened of, my little one?" he would ask. "I shall not harm a hair of your pretty head."

"Off you go with Jean," her father said. "He will take good care of you."

During the whole of the courtship period he was indeed a gentle and caring giant. Since her mother had died she was busy almost every minute of her waking day with the "woman's work" in the house and on the farm, and Jean was not too proud to help her occasionally with her many tasks. Her father did not require much looking after, but besides washing and cooking and mending clothes there were the constant needs of the chicken, geese, the milch cow, the few pigs they always kept, the vegetable garden. Though never in love with him, Celine grew fond of Red and dependent on him.

"I like to see you smile," he said. "That dear white face. You know what, my darling? I never know what you are thinking."

Celine was not sure whether it was a compliment, but she hoped she knew what he meant. Other people had said it. One horrible cousin said she had a face like a square mask, with slit eyes like a Chinese, and a gash for a mouth. Bad cess to her, the silly bitch.

M. Trou spared no expense on the wedding, and all the family—grandparents, in-laws and scroungers from along the valley—came and the apple orchard rang with music and laughter, with Uncle Joe playing and Big Red a dominant and entertaining bridegroom. The girl cousins told Celine how lucky she was. Though a notch above the labouring peasant class, the Trous were not the sort of people who could afford to go on a wedding holiday, so after all the traditions and customs had been followed, including some crude and suggestive antics in the back lane by a few drunken rowdies, Celine and Jean retired to the main bedroom in the farmhouse. Since his wife died M. Trou had moved out of it anyway.

The physical submission of the wedding night had been something of a shock but the new husband was nothing like so rough as the cavalry brigadier had been by the river. Nevertheless she had cried out. Big Red was so enormous and had ginger hairs all over. But when he was finished he did not turn away from her and go to sleep but petted her gently and cradled her head in his enormous arms.

"There, there, little one. That didn't hurt too much, did it?" No doubt he thought she was a virgin.

The first year was generally happy, seasons coming and going, normal marital ups and downs. Her grandfather died and M. Trou became legal owner of land and property. Celine showed no sign of becoming pregnant. As she lay beside Hector in the last barn they were to share as a fleeing group of refugees, she wondered whether she could ever bring herself to tell him how her husband first attacked her, seemingly without any prevarication.

"I couldn't believe it, chou," she might say. "We were about to go to bed and I had just finished preparing the pig food with some of the leftovers of our supper when he suddenly gave me the most almighty clout on the head with his fist. I staggered, more shocked than anything, as he came at me, red eyes blazing, moustache bristling, his thick lips drawn back in a maniacal snarl and then another smack on the other side of the head with his other fist. I was dazed, Hector, and it was hard to breathe or to speak.

"'Jean' I began with great effort, my head spinning like a top, 'what are you...'

"'Bitch! Whore! Damn you!'"

"This time I got a smack full in the mouth. My lip was cut badly and a tooth came loose.

"'What the fuck is this shit?'

"He had never cursed in front of me before. He took the pig bucket and flung the contents over the kitchen floor. He picked up a chair and threw it at me, and as I tried to dodge it I slipped and fell into the pig swill, my face sliding among old potato peelings, fish heads and chunks of turnip skin. I started to cry, chou, more out of misery than because of the sting of his fists, though that was bad enough. It seemed as though my little world had come to an end."

Of course she would never be able to tell Hector of this the first of her indignities, still less of the many more to follow. She must have passed out for a time among the swill and when she woke she could hear Jean rampaging about the house. Her father was at the estaminet. It was a curious fact, she began to think after a while, that Big Red never attacked her when M. Trou was at home, as though the assaults were calculated rather than ungovernable outbursts. And another perhaps more alarming fact was that whenever Big Red hit her he was stone cold sober. As she got up shakily and started to clean up the mess, she heard the front door slam. At first Celine wondered whether her husband had heard anything about her disgrace with the corporal, whether her ravisher had been boasting in some bar or other about how he had laid a broad by the River T*** by telling her a fairy story about his horse's tail, whether Jean had put two and two together. That was unlikely and it was soon obvious it was not the case.

Celine made the kitchen as tidy as possible and daubed witch hazel on her cuts and bruises. She fed the cats and went miserably to bed. She heard her father come lurching up the stairs to the back bedroom, she knew his tread so well, and then hours later Red returned, tore off his clothes and fell sobbing into bed beside her without bothering to put on his nightshirt.

"Oh, my poor one. What have I done to you?"

He embraced her and kissed her swollen cheeks and then penetrated her gently and considerately.

"I never discovered what set him off," she imagined herself confessing to Hector. "I mean it was not the full moon or anything like that or regular like. He could bash me three times in a fortnight and then not again for months."

"The attacks always came out of a clear blue sky and I became a nervous wreck. I started to eat and eat and get fat as though that would make me forget his savagery. There's always plenty of food on a farm. He was like a mad beast when the fit was on and then always afterwards he would come weeping begging for forgiveness. It went on for two or three years till my father had had enough of it and half killed him one night with an axe. Red made no attempt to defend himself and he disappeared from the valley. He brought no charges against my father."

"I think maybe my not being able to have a baby had something to do with it, but then that could have been Red's fault just as much as mine, couldn't it? There was generally but not always some particular thing like the pig swill seemed to madden him, some paltry article or event which made him lose his marbles. Oh dear, oh dear, oh dear. Hector, I think it was about this time I started turning to other men. For comfort like, and sympathy. You see, dear friend, I became the local whore, sneaky like, long before the war began. It weren't the war what started me on the game. I don't think my dad knew, not for a long time after my husband left anyways. It was all very hush hush, a whisper, like, behind the back of the hand. I was not publicly branded and shunned, you see, and the village kids didn't shout at me in the streets and no one shaved my hair off. But if any feller along the valley wanted it, they knew where to come for it. The money was always useful, especially after Big Red was sent packing with his head split open and things started to go wrong."

Celine would never be able to confess this shame to Hector. Never in a month of Sundays.

CB❀SO

It had all started by chance on the morning after a night of brutal pummelling. She'd got up in the dark to use le vase de nuit. That homely receptacle must have been the trigger this time—hard to believe. The sound of her water splashing in the chamber pot must have woken Jean. He had bounded out of bed and thumped her with such force on the shoulder whilst she was still pissing that the pot had cracked under her and made a gash in her buttock. She still had the scar to this day. Because of her recent gorging herself she was also becoming plumper and that had not helped. He had gone on battering her in his frenzy among the wet shards of the broken pisspot till she had passed out. On this occasion he did not help her back to bed in an agony of remorse and make penitent love to her. When she woke up, all wet and sticky on their bedroom floor, haunch bleeding, there was no sign of him. Her father was away for a few days visiting an aging cousin who had left the district and was now gravely ill with St. Vitus's dance. It's usually a kid's disease, M. Trou had told her as he left.

"Oh, dear Hector, if I could only tell you…explain how it all happened. It sounds a poor excuse, I know. I've noticed you looking at me quizzically as though you're wondering why I am a fat pig of a harlot, up for sale to anyone. I only wish I hadn't done it that night with Tyler. You was there a few weeks ago, you remember. He had no money anyways.

"That morning I once again bathed my wounds. I couldn't stop the blood oozing out of my behind. I noticed my thighs were getting too fat. I brushed my hair. I managed to get some breakfast down, eggs, bread, butter, cold ham. I could always eat after a bashing. I then wandered out to the orchard, my head still woozy and my eyes blinking in the bright autumn sunshine. The apples were red and golden and I picked one and chewed at it though my jaw was sorer than hell.

"'Someone as I know ain't looking best pleased this morn.'

"He came towards me from the barn with bits of straw in his hair as though he had slept there all night. He brushed his pants and shirt with his hands. He was a lanky feller with dark hair who come from two villages down the river and claimed he was a friend of Uncle Joseph. Joe said he was decent enough when he was not on one of his binges.

"'What you been doing in our barn, Ferdi?'

"'Had a drop too much, didn't I, missus? Last night.' He turned to one side, held his nose between thumb and forefinger and blew snot on the ground. 'Sorry about that, ma'am.'

"I didn't want his ma'aming me, Hector. I knew him all right. He were a very good dancer and I'd danced with him once or twice. Handsome too. Joe said he could make his way in the world if only he bothered. He certainly were no bum if you get my meaning. Everyone called him Ferdi, not mister anything 'cause no one seemed to bother with his last name.

"'Have you had any breakfast?'

"'No, ma'am.'

"'Well you'd best come in…'

"Whilst he was eating, he had nice table manners, not like a lot of the men round us who eat like pigs, he looks up at me and touches me on the elbow, gently enough.

"'You all right? Last night I thought I heard…'

"'Sure I'm all right,' I answered, drawing away from him. There must have been gossip in the village about Big Red and me. 'And you never heard nothing last night. Understand, Ferdi.'

"I can't begin to tell you, Hector, the effect that man had on me. Just watching him eating his breakfast, his dark hair falling over his forehead.

His eyes were glazed over with the booze of the night before, but even so he could look at me as though he was daring me to...My heart started to thump and I began to feel hornier than a fiddler's bitch."

As she lay in the barn, Celine was too embarrassed even to imagine telling Hector how she started on the rosy and thorny path of sexual promiscuity that morning, the morning when her bum would not stop bleeding. She'd gone over that day many times, the day when the backsliding had started, a moral and erotic watershed. She'd looked back on it at first with agonizing remorse, but later, as custom and repetition dulled her sensitivity, with increasingly cynical detachment as though she were analysing someone else's obsessions and bravado. Until she met Hector she had entirely got past the stage of worrying about it. It was done, non? And part of her blasted existence. No use picking at it.

Ferdi had obviously guessed she was having a grievous time with her husband but she doubted he would have tried anything on for fear of Big Red, who had a formidable reputation along the valley. Ferdi would never have made a pass at her of his own volition. What was too shaming to admit to Hector, even in imagination, was the way she had become sexually excited as she watched Ferdi wolf the bread and hard-cooked eggs, just as after being savagely beaten by Jean she would respond passionately to his lovemaking while all her being cried out in hatred and pain against this beast.

"Have you made a mess in our barn?"

He wiped his mouth with the back of his hand.

"'No, mum! S'elp me that's the truth."

He was of course unshaven that morning with dense black bristles on his chin and cheek. His breath and his body and his clothes smelled. His male grossness served only to make her more excited, almost uncontrollably so.

"Well maybe you have—and maybe you haven't. We'd best make sure."

She took him by the hand and led him out as the cavalry corporal had guided her to the river. As they approached the barn, Ferdi bent over holding his groin.

"Mum," he said, "I'm busting for a pee."

"Very well. You can do it here. Up against the wall. Here let me...."

She so wanted to say to Hector that she couldn't think what came over her. What made her do it. She pulled out his long thing like a snake from his trousers, of course it was getting bigger all the time. Then there was this enormous scalding jet and he just about pissed a hole in the barn wall.

They hurried into the Trou barn, half of which was filled with pieces of farm impedimenta, wagon wheels with spokes missing, buckets, barrels, a feeding trough with a side torn off. The other half, earth floor, was fairly clear apart from a scattering of corn, patches of dried chicken shit and a heap of straw along the south wall where Ferdi had obviously spent the night. Celine pulled him to it, dragged him down, tugged at his clothes.

"Are you sure this is all right, missus? I mean suppose...."

"Don't worry. He won't be back for ages yet."

And so that's the way it was. Understandably no money changed hands that day. Ferdi hadn't a sou in any case, but the idea of being paid for it never entered Celine's head for years.

There was no need. She would have told Hector that this was one way of getting her own back, of thumbing her nose at Jean. He came back of course, late that day but before her father got back from the cousin who had died in the middle of a grotesque fit. Red's sorrow and remorse were seeming to be forced, Celine thought, and his after battering copulation was losing something of its passionate edge. Ferdi was a gentle lover, and she met him a few weeks later and seduced him again though he was scared out of his pants. And then more frequently. After a time one of his friends was introduced and had a go, and then another, always in great secrecy—no one wanted Big Red to find out—until there was a satisfied conspiracy of Celine's lovers along the valley to which young men were absurdly proud to belong.

This indiscriminate coupling with men from up and down the valley went on after Jean was chased out by M. Trou, and Celine never knew whether her father was suspicious about her goings on or not. She did not start charging for her favours till things started to go badly wrong on the farm. By that time she was becoming plumper and coarser and her cynical mask was beginning to form.

Celine dreamed more and more of her early life as she lay by Hector's side in the barns. They never embraced. They held hands often but no more. Then came this last barn the refugees were to sleep in as a group. After that they reached towns and villages where many of the population had remained—had even increased by the arrival of refugees like themselves. Life in the sad, bereaved places they came to now, though harsh and bitter, was less nerve-racking and their buildings were removed from immediate danger of destruction. Some form of civil administration was in effect which, though beneficial on the whole, was two edged. They were assisted in food and lodging but also they had to be careful that Hector and Tyler were not seized by the police and handed ignominiously over to the military.

"This is more like it, Hec," Tyler said. "I'm all for the quiet life. But where do we go from here?"

"We gotta watch out, old buddy. Maybe we oughta just piss off. We're only putting these guys in danger."

But M. Trou said tersely he'd be happy if they all stayed together, and Celine looked woebegone at the thought of their leaving.

## SIX

"Good Christ," Nick said to his horse. "Looks like we got us a fire over there, Jacky. Some poor blighter's barn, maybe. Maybe even his ranch house."

He kicked the horse's side and started to gallop, even though it was getting dark and galloping was not the safest way to ride. He'd spent a long time talking to the Indian in the woodland glade. As usual he'd drawn some comfort from the old man, but this situation with Bridget was a real bitch and required a lot of thought and working through. He had not mentioned her by name but he was positive that Clarence Manythumbs knew who the woman in the case was.

He could see flames now in the pall of smoke. It was getting to the time of the year when both the well-to-do ranchers and the poor families with small acreages, scrabbling away at the thin soil for a living, would deliberately set fire to a parcel of land to clear it of rubbish growth. Usually they would start in the morning and watch over the burn—especially if it were in the vicinity of Higgins Bend or anyone's home or barn. Perhaps some dummy had got lazy or drunk and let the blaze get away from him. Nick knew of a few shiftless jerks who just didn't give a damn. Somehow, though, this did not look like an ordinary scrub fire.

Nick's mind, his reflections and thoughts, were, on a routine day, clear and uncomplicated and sent out decisive signals. Basic assumptions held, two hosses and two steer made four critters, and so he acted and reacted accordingly. On a routine day he was satisfied and happy with his work, his wife and his kids. Peripheral disturbances, accidents and hard luck cases could affect him but not seriously injure his central certainty nor break the severity of his hard face. He was dimly aware of the basic selfishness of this but what the heck, why sweat unnecessarily, why not without surrendering too much principle simply accept the punches that other folk were taking. He could roll with those that came his way. The irritants were at varying emotional pitches. Why worry, for example, about his chronic itch for his brother's wife, the one who was at the root of all this latest crap, the one who was the cause of his being out of doors right now. He'd always had a secret desire for Bridget from the day that Sam had first brought her to the family home, but he'd never done a thing untoward, never placed a finger where he shouldn't, had he? Perhaps once. And don't forget she could be something of a temptress, could she ever, but he handled that mostly okay in the past and was handling it now, no great problem, nothing at least that Nick couldn't tough out, with Bridget that is. But when it came to her and his son that was a different kettle of fish. It was darned bad luck when some breadwinner broke his leg, or his daughter was stricken with meningitis, or his business went belly up. He was sorry and he would give help in deserving cases, but these little outrages did not keep him awake at nights. No sir. But now with this business of Hector's up his nose he figured he would never sleep again.

"That ain't no barn, Jacky. That's the whole fucking town going up."

An angry red glowed on the black clouds of smoke on the darkening horizon. Nick rode his horse hard in the direction of the fire.

Though he was not afflicted with too much introspection, Nick guessed he was lucky in that pressures of any sort rarely seemed to get to him as they did to most other people, though judging by the customary set of his face, as Marie Louise often teased, you would think he was defying the outrageous arrows of the world most of his waking hours, staring down some demon archer. Yet occasionally he was thrown for a loop. That Indian thing which Clarence Manythumbs had helped straighten out for him ages ago, for instance, gnawed at him for months, years, in a muted way it still scratched the edge of his conscience. His later meeting and marrying Marie turned him upside down, ripped apart his stony placidity, but that was a disturbance of sheer joy and still was, soothing to a small degree the Indian betrayal. Through strength of character, a little bullying, good luck and good management he had survived successfully all other hazards...until now. Until his dumb son Hector and that fucking sister-in-law had really messed things up.

He kicked Jacky's sides. He rarely wore spurs.

ଓଃଃ ଚ

The fire that wiped out the poorer half of Higgins Bend in the Great War (it was a miracle that every darn building did not go up in smoke) caused a deal of grief, naturally, to people who could least cope, but years later it was agreed that it was a blessing in disguise. The place needed cleaning up, straightening out. As in most of the developing west, town planning was zilch. Folks were concerned with surviving and to heck with the landscape and aesthetics. It was a hostile land anyways and all they wanted in the winter was protection and warmth and not one cared a cow's ass about wide boulevards or siting the wooden huts on the contours of the land. The part of Higgins Bend that was destroyed in the flames consisted of shacks built higgledy-piggledy between the brickworks and the sawmill. The race track and the polo field lay between the mill and the Bow River, and it was in this open space that a couple of police and a group of volunteer firemen were trying to organize a chain of water buckets more in desperation than order when Nick came galloping in. It was pathetic. It made a man want to weep.

"What's happened to the fire wagon?" Nick shouted to a farmer, moon-faced, sweating, passing the dripping buckets. They were more than half empty by the time the got anywhere near a burning shack.

"The hosses got spooked by the smoke. The shaft's broke."

"Them buckets won't do no good. You might as well piss on the fire."

"Suit yourself, big feller."

Nick went to the town end of the chain and watched as sweating men, mainly older guys, threw water into the inferno. There was no stopping it, a wall of flame, twisting in different colours, roaring, seemingly impenetrable, evil-smelling smoke swooping down, choking, blinding. The goddamn archer with his flaming arrows. Nick was right, urinating would be just as effective as the pathetic buckets, but something had to be done even if it was as futile as a thimbleful of piss. The only hope was that what wind there was was blowing away from the rest of the town.

"There's some poor bugger still in there, Mr. Plouvier."

Nick recognized Billy Lilley, black-faced, leather jerkin scorched, up near the flames. Even the buckets were getting hot.

"I can hear him hollering."

It was hard to make out any voice above the roar of the fire, even Billy's who was right there beside him. Nick grabbed a bucket from a guy at the head of the line and flung in his two bits of water. He listened to it hiss like a blob of spit on a hot stove and then stood staring at the fire. Suddenly he took a pace forward, his arm shielding his face.

"Christ, who's this, Billy?"

Unbelievably in a fractional break in the wall of flame a woman came rushing through from the burning shacks, parts of her dress smouldering, sparks on her head, the smell of burning hair.

"Throw that bucket of water over her, Billy. Now, for heaven sakes!"

The water drenched the woman, half knocking her over, and she crouched, catching her breath. Nick bent over her.

"Sorry, lady. We had to..."

She was sobbing, putting out an arm to Nick. At least she was no longer on fire.

"It's young Angie Leech," Billy said.

Nick helped her up and put an arm round her shoulder. He could feel her taut, trembling body through her soaked dress. Memories raced through his mind as he tended her. Angela Parkes that was, the one that Hector had gone out with a couple of times and Nick had not been best pleased. She'd only been married a month or so to Dick Leech. Local gossip said they'd had to get wed. If Nick had not sneered at Hector's young love, put her down, then perhaps this god-awful mess with Bridget might never have happened. Angela twisted suddenly and reached up to clutch Nick's shirt collar.

"Mister. My Dicky's in there. He's trapped under a beam. His leg's busted. I can't get him loose. You gotta come in with me and..."

Her words came tumbling out, agonizingly importunate, rising to hysteria. Yeah, if only he had not interfered, but then would he have wanted Hector to be living down here in a shack in these slums? He could have fixed them up with something better on the ranch. But meantime here was the girl pleading with him to risk his life to save the boy she did marry. He'd best stop being such a jerk and get a hold of himself. The events of the day were making him soft in the head, him, Nick Plouvier. He held Angie by the wrists.

"Listen up, lady. Listen."

She writhed and shouted and begged. He shook her wet arms.

"There's not one man jack of us can get in there, Angela. Mrs. Leech. Just you take a look at it. You oughta know. I don't know how the heck you managed…"

"Mister. While we is arguing my husband's darn well roasting to bits. Like a hog on a lousy spit."

She wrenched herself away from him and made a mad dash for the furnace.

"Catch her, Billy. Damn fool girl'll kill herself."

But even Angela was driven back by the heat and collapsed at the edge of the fire on the dirt street, this time completely unconscious. Nick pulled her by the feet along the ground, the skirt of her woollen dress riding above her knees. He knelt beside her and lifted her head.

"Is Dot Howard anywheres about, Billy?"

"No one's seed her, boss. But your missus and Mrs. Sam and some of the other wives is helping folk what got burned or hurt like. Or ain't got no houses left. They's with the doc in the church."

"Is that right? The doc, eh? He's sober enough, is he?"

"Yessir."

The wind was strengthening, making the flames more furious, intensifying Dick Leech's pyre, but blowing them away from the river and the rest of Higgin's Bend.

"I'll take her, Billy."

Nick lifted up the woman easily—she was too much like a child still—and headed for the church. What else could come up and smack him right in the heroic chops? Life would go along tolerably well when suddenly a double whammy like this one took the wind out of a feller's sails. The fire was a disaster, okay, but it was the sneaky hits that wounded the most. In a different set of circumstances this girl could be his daughter-in-law. Under the black smudges and the scorched hair her face was pale.

As he trudged along he wondered how much of the township had been destroyed. And God knows how many had been fried to death beside Dick Leech, who was a goner for sure. He'd seen Dick around, two years older than Hector, a thin inoffensive lad, not much good on a horse, lived in the shanties, likeable enough. He had a job in the brickworks. He'd tried to enlist but had been rejected because of fallen arches. Nick did not know whether his marriage to the girl he was carrying was a shot-gun affair or not and it was none of his business. But he remembered he'd shaken his head in sadness when he'd heard of it. They were too young and too poor. They did not know what trouble they were storing up for themselves. But then if there were a young 'un on the way what else could the blessed pair do? For that matter, what was he going to do about Hector's young 'un on the way?

The door of the wooden church was open as he staggered in, and he saw a crazy scene inside. People were lying stretched out on the wooden pews, wild-eyed, blackened, burnt, half undressed some of them. The doctor had pulled himself together and, though bleary and his breath smelling of liquor, he was moving from one to another, doing what he could.

"Has anyone seen Dot Howard?" the doc shouted.

Nick carried his damp burden, smelling of smoke and burnt hair and cloth, up to the front of the church and found a space near the altar and laid her down. Marie came up, efficient, sleeves of her gown rolled up.

"Who is it, Nick?"

He looked wearily at his wife. He was glad to see her. Their own disaster and acrimony were forgotten for the time being.

⊗❀⊗

Three women boarded the train for Winnipeg—Marie Louise, Bridget and Angela Leech, who had recovered enough to make the long journey.

Nick Plouvier and his daughter, Michelle, saw them off. Angela had taken a lot of persuading.

"I don't like it, Mrs. Plouvier. Not one little bit. It ain't right."

"We know that, Angela. None of us likes deceiving people. But what else can we do?"

"Mebbe you shoulda let the truth come out."

"Angela!"

"Mebbe your Hector should do what's proper. Be a man. Like my poor Dick did."

Angela began to sob, but gripped her little fists into hard bunches and stopped. She was wearing a stylish tweed coat with fur trim at the collar, very smart, a gift from Bridget.

"But, my dear Angie, he can't marry his aunt."

"Then he oughta thought about that, shouldn't he? Afore like."

## BRIDGET

I've thought and thought and thought again about having an abortion and then everyone's peace of mind would be restored and honour satisfied all round. Except perhaps for Marie's. She's sitting opposite me in this train racketing its way to Winnipeg. It's her devious idea that we should go to stay with this French family and attempt the most impudent deception. French Canadian that is. I'm going to lose my child anyway, so why go to all the trouble of this lying charade. I can see why Angela Leech is jibbing at it. She's about had enough, losing her own baby just two days after her husband died that horrible death. His body was so charred it was unrecognizable, Nick said. She was not very far gone—you wouldn't know she was pregnant—but it must be a ghastly wrench. I can sympathize with her.

It was Marie's idea, and I expected Nick to explode when she first comes out with it. The whole situation is so grotesque anyway. This child I'm carrying is their grandchild, haven't I been over that ground enough times in the agony of the sleepless nights. And they think I'm hard as nails. Angela came to live with me after the fire and Marie worked on her remorselessly. I didn't believe she could dream up such a crackpot plan. When I look in the mirror I can see my tummy beginning to swell, finally. Soon I should not be able to get into that nice coat I've given to Angie so she might as well have it.

"It's for her benefit as well as everyone else's, Bridge, can't you see? Angela's good, too," Marie argued as she worked on me. She wears her clothes with French chic as though they were part of her. Lady Icen approved very much of her and said she was wasted in our backwoods. A fetching pale lemon overcoat today, not too warm for the time of the year.

"The three of us go to Winnipeg as I've said. We haven't got much time to make up our minds, you understand that, Bridgie, darling. We can stay with my friends. I can come back with some cock and bull story about..."

"Cock and bull!" Nick had snorted. "That's about the size of it."

He was grim faced as he waited for my decision. I've never known him at a loss like this. He goes about the house and the ranch as though he's in a dream, or a bad nightmare more like. Poor man. He no longer sidles up to me all bland and innocent like, no longer gives me little nudges and squeezes.

Angie's a sweet kid but not as soft or naive as she looks. She reminds me of my own growing up in Dublin. The worst burns are on her arm, and though they are not fully healed yet they are mostly covered by her gown. There is one livid streak along her jaw line, about an inch and a half long and narrow, which looks very angry but you can't say disfigures her and in any case it has almost dried up. Her eyebrows are growing back. She's got a bit of a hard face anyway, not bitchy, not insolent. It's difficult to describe other than knowing she's not had an easy life and it shows. And, let's be honest about it, she's going to do well out of this crazy scheme. Sheer bribery on Marie's part. Get her lost motherhood back, a baby to nurse and love, and live comfortably for the rest of her life.

No one's going to believe us for one minute, so who are we trying to kid? There are too many holes. It's all so crass, so obvious. Sometimes, in the hour just before dawn I think, to my great shame no doubt, that I'd rather abort it than hand the baby over to Angie. Okay. Such a monstrous thought may come unbidden but there's a problem, a big one. The trouble lies in where to go to get rid of it. Some furtive back street in Calgary presumably, but exactly where? There have been abortionists from time immemorial, indispensable, lurking in the shadows of respectable society. There are plenty of them in Dublin, that's for sure. They stick a long sharp instrument up you.

"But what will its name be?"

"Leech, I suppose. It will have to be, won't it? But let's cross that bridge when we get to it."

Angie had brightened up at this. She was present during all the discussions, she had to be as the prospective "mother," and Michelle and Nick were there for many of them. Marie had seized on this solution like a terrier on a rat. That was a great sport in Dublin, ratting. The little dogs would toss those beady-eyed evil creatures in the air and we'd all clap and shout. Outside the train window the prairies sweep by us in full majestic growth, miles and miles of ripening grain, cornfields we'd call them on Lady Icen's estates, and as long as I've lived here I find it hard not to think of them so. Apart from Angela, no one had breathed a word about Hector in our discussions. Not even Michelle. I believe she's very hurt, let down by both Hector and myself, the two people most dear to her, even if I say so myself, justifiably to some extent because there is often friction between her and her mother. I can hardly bear to look her in the eyes, but she is not reproachful by word or look, just quiet and sad. She is normally so full of spirits and cheers me up. God blind me, O'Riley, how wretched can you get?

Naturally I'm in a vulnerable position, in fact I'm the villain, that is understood and I accept that. They say it takes two to dance the polka but I know only too miserably who started things, who did all the enticing, and I am certain that Nick and Marie think that I was the fucking prime mover and shaker, and considering that, they believe that they are treating me wonderfully. But then they never saw their darling Hector in a frenzy of lust in the sick barn, eyes popping, thrusting at me like a lunatic, coming too soon. Just as no one is mentioning Hector, no one is telling him about his prospective fatherhood either.

"What good would it do?" Nick asked. "The boy may be sent off to France any minute now."

"I thought you said he'd get embarkation leave," Marie Louise said plaintively.

"They don't always give it these days. The papers say they're desperate for more men. Over there. In France."

Nick shut up after this and Marie sobbed.

"I think he should be told," Angie said.

I shan't make the excuse of not knowing what came over me, of being carried away by a fit of passion and madness, simply because it was not like that. When I'm being less hard on myself I can whitewash past events and moods. I can present in mitigation the empty years since Sam died and I was shut away in the bloody backwoods like some frigid and deprived hermit. I can bring to my defence the sneaky tantalizing visits of Nick, breathing down my neck from his hard thin-lipped mouth, his tumescence brushing my hip. I had only to lift a finger or a skirt and we'd have been off to the races. What would Marie think of me having a little bastard by her darling Nicholas, eh, I ask you. Would she ask Angela to mother it as though it were her own. Fortunately for Nick, the kids, his own children, were most often close by.

Eventually Angie gave in to Marie's persuasion and bribes and then I began to have doubts about this damn mad plan myself.

"How do we know this family in Winnipeg, what's their name again?"

"Chansonnier," Marie said.

"How do we know they will agree to this?"

"They will," Marie said.

"And who's going to forge the names on the birth certificate?"

"Courage, darling. The priest will arrange all that."

"The priest!"

"Anything to save a soul. You ought to know, dear Bridget, since you come from Ireland."

Of course I ought to have known, but in the slums of Dublin the finer hypocrisies of religion mostly passed us by. I'm sure as hell they were in the air like incense and prayers or the smell from the lav in the cobbled backyard. There was the church and there was the street. And there was a drunken father coming into your bedroom and trying to feel you up. The stinking rotten turd, how I hated Michael Donnelly. Yet how can any daughter say she hates her own father—that's worse than a mortal sin. He thought he was selling me to an English lord but my pissy old da didn't know a lord from a sow's arse, did he now?

"She's a foin lass indeed, your worship," my da said, plucking at my shoulders and bottom as though I were a prize pig. I suppose that the only faint justification you can make for him is that he was drunk out of his mind, as he was most of the time I lived at home.

I don't know exactly how many sovereigns that bastard Michael Donnelly got from Sir Reggie Slatters, an English lord my foot, not many according to Reg, but I do know I went willingly out of the pub with the buck-teethed, jawless git. Two nights before this "sale" my dad had come on and on at me, trousers half down, pulling the blanket off my bed and my sister crouched against the damp and peeling wall and me screaming blue murder. Then my mother came in and beat him with the poker until he fell down with a drunken stare of incomprehension on his face. We left him on the floor and my sister and I went and slept with our mam. Oh the shame of it all, she moaned. She was a physical ruin, my mother. Figure shapeless, hair ratty and greying, hands red and raw, nails bitten down to the quick, calves bulging with varicose veins, ankles thick. An old piece of sacking for an apron, her "pinny" she called it. There was a picture of her in the front room on her wedding day, a lovely young raven-haired girl, which didn't bear looking at.

Sir fucking Reggie, smarmy, whey-faced, a suspect baronet, an indigent cousin of Lady Icen who had followed her to Dublin, I learned later, took me in a cab to one of the posh hotels. The horse farted continually. It was raining, a Dublin drizzle, and since I had no bonnet on I could feel the damp on my hair. I noticed the man at the reception desk give him a funny look but didn't dare say a word, and I was hurried up to the knight's room.

"Well, my beauty," he began as he unlocked the door.

"Well, my beauty, what?"

If Reg had had a jaw it would have dropped. It was the first time naturally that I had set eyes on the Lady Icen. She sat upright in a chair by the fire with eyes and voice as chill as her name, enough to put the fear of God into any poor relation. I rushed across the room and knelt on the floor and clasped her knees. It was like a scene from one of those melodramas she and I used to go to later in the Strand.

"Get up child," she said. "Don't grovel. Get up at once." But there was a kind edge to her sharpness.

"I suppose he's paying you for this."

"No," I said, standing up, indignant, smoothing down my grey dress which had stains on the skirt. "He is not indeed. My da got the money. This gentleman bought me."

"He what?"

"From my da."

Lady Icen also stood up. She was young and slender and I thought beautiful in those days. At first I believed she was Reggie's wife. You must remember I had never been in anything resembling this hotel room in my life before or among such people. No, that's a fat lie I'm telling. I'd been to the parish priest's house on some errand, and there the floor was not made of stone like ours and our neighbours' with the occasional rag mat over the damp bits and the cramped rooms and the rickety stairs and the one cold tap in the scullery. The priest's house was wonderful compared with ours but nothing like this splendour, thick rugs, comfy armchairs, roaring fire.

"I say, dash it, Kate. Why are you in my room anyway?" Reg put on a brave face, pushing his luck.

Don't misunderstand me. I'm not claiming I seduced Hector because I was born in a harsh and evil Dublin slum. Yet when I look across at Angie's pouty face, quite pretty in its way, her sharpish eyes closed as she dozes despite the swaying of the train and the clacking of the wheels, I wonder if she's really had it as tough as I did. She wouldn't believe I had anyway. She thinks I'm a lady and that I look down on the likes of her who live near the brickworks. I got to know Lady Icen intimately of course, and time and familiarity dulled some of her early glory, but that first night I adored her. I thought her the most magnificent lady in the land. She shrivelled Reg with her contempt, her disapproval.

"Your room! You indescribable, disgusting fellow! And who, may I ask, is paying for your room? And who asked you to follow me here in the first place?"

"Have a heart, Kate, old bean."

"Have a heart! I've never heard such impertinence. Where's your heart so far as this wretched girl is concerned? How much did you pay the father for her?"

"A couple of quid. Three."

"You mean you bought her for the night?"

"No. Me da sold me to him body and soul. For ever. He said he'd had about enough of my whining ways."

"I must be dreaming. I can't believe this." Lady Icen said. She drew a little white hand across her forehead.

I was not really taking in how little I cost, though two pound meant a lot to us, as I was buggered and bewildered by the pair of them. I was amazed that I had the temerity to breathe the same air. As I learned my way through the intricacies of the English social classes and their incredible pretences and mimicked the different cadences of their language, I realized that Reg's family was on its way down through debts, bad luck and sheer ineptness and that he was at that time about the bottom of the aristocratic heap, and impecunious with it.

"If you have money to waste on your beastly lust you can spend some of it on another hotel. You will pack your bags and get out this room. And out of my life. The sooner the better. And you will leave the girl here."

Reg looked the picture of misery, his recessive chin quivering in the region of his Adam's apple.

"I say! Don't be so hard on a fellow, Kate."

"I will give you thirty minutes."

Reggie was so utterly taken by surprise at Lady Icen being in his room at that time of night that he had not even put down his silver mounted walking stick or taken off his velvet collared coat or his brown hat which was still at a rakish angle on his head. I'd noticed the silver and the velvet in the cab when I was beginning to wonder vaguely where we were headed and what would happen to me. Sir Reginald gave me furtive glances and made burping noises in his throat. I mean, a girl living in the Dublin slums had no illusions about what men or boys or fathers wanted girls for or what they did with their pricks apart from peeing through them, but, by some miracle, I was still a virgin. There'd been some close brushes with a fate worse than death but no dishonour so far. The nearest shave had been with a boy called Brian Murphy who had been sitting on the lav seat with his little dick standing up like a soldier and me just about to squat down on it when me mam started hammering on the door. Later when I told Lady Icen about being a virgin she would not believe me. She thought all poor girls were whores and I didn't argue too much because I soon sensed it was part of her charity to "save" me.

"You come with me, girl. And mind you look sharp, Reginald. Thirty minutes."

I followed her out of the room, still dazed at her personality, at her confident authority over the Sir my father had bowed and scraped to, at her maroon dress which fitted so smoothly over her dainty body. The silk frilly front made the top of her gown so charming and modest, her dainty slippers were in startling and pathetic contrast to my clumping boots and black stockings with holes in them under my crappy trailing skirt.

"What is your name?"

I suppose at that time I was not much older than my niece, Michelle, is now. Oh what I wouldn't give to assuage some of her hurt. Before the nonsense started with Hector I used to think of myself as a patroness, in the best sense of the word, to Michie, sort of roles reversed. What a crock I've made of that. She really believed I was a creature from a kind of girlish dreamland as I told her of grand London balls and receptions, stories of my time with the Lady Icen. Michie looked up to me then. I'm not so sure about now.

"You know you are rather pretty," Lady Icen said. "Or you will be when we get some of that dirt off. My maid will get you some hot water."

"It's ever so good of you, missus."

She smiled briefly. Her hotel suite was bigger than all the rooms of our house put together, with an enormous dressing table and large mirror. I could see the pair of us reflected in it behind all the pots of creams and rouges and silver backed hair brushes and tortoise-shell combs.

"You may call me Lady Icen."

What age was she when I first met her—ten years older than me? But that night and for a long time I was prepared to call her your holiness and grovel in front of her and kiss her ring.

"Have you been many times...with men?"

She had a prurient side to her, a kind of vicarious indulgence in dirty sex.

"Never, missus. Never, I promise."

Brian Murphy didn't count.

"Lady Icen, child, not missus. You will get used to it."

She was standing by the fireplace, sizing me up. A picture in an ornate gilt frame of an Irish mountain and lake hung behind her. Some dogs with their tails sticking up and a man with a red coat in the foreground.

"Then why did you agree to go tonight with Sir Reginald? You must have known what my cousin...what he wanted?"

The heat of the room, the excitement of the evening, and the thought which just came to me of my sisters and mother were getting to me and I merely nodded at this fabulous woman. I felt myself ready to crumble, but if you're brought up in the slums you've got to be tough to survive. We had to protect our sentimentality, shield it in a hard carapace.

☙❀❧

The likes of Lady Icen believe they have a God given right to inquire into the "morals" of the likes of what I was then, a poor teenager in the slums, poor in the sense of hard cash and education, and probably in her eyes in the sense of worthiness, though to give her her due she did not think me worthless for long. What I suppose I am trying to put together here as we three women, connected in our design by the foetus inside me, chuff-chuff our way across the prairies to Manitoba are some of the chances and reasons which have led to this embarrassing quandary. And because I know where the greater share of it lies I am not trying to shift the blame.

In the years of widowhood I've read and thought a lot, even though many of the good natured oafs around Higgins Bend believe me indolent as well as hoity-toity. Mine has been haphazard, uncoordinated reading and thinking and I don't pretend to be a philosopher or the wise witch in the Alberta woods, but it eases the embarrassment to try to figure out in a rough and ready way how I got to where I am. I've already said it's not a simple sequence. I did not fuck Hector because my father tried to fuck me. Nor because he sold me to Reggie—later I became convinced that that chinless wonder would never have been able to get it up, but he might well have had some horrible perversion in mind for that and future evenings. Lady Icen decided to "adopt" me as part lady's maid, part companion—after all her cousin had bought me—but she insisted first that I went back to my mother to get her written permission to leave home and live with my patroness.

"Our mam can't write, my lady. Hardly"

"Very well, then. I shall write out something myself and I trust you to read it to her and get her to sign it. Or put her mark on it. Do you understand, Bridget?"

The Lady Icen would not dream of going anywhere near the slums herself. For me it was a disturbing experience going back. My mother had already lost children to sickness and her grim face was a stern mask, hiding all she felt, not necessarily indicative of hostility to me, I was certain of that. She'd been out of her mind with worry since some kind feller from the pub had told her what my da had done. She'd hammered him when he got home and this time damaged his eye so badly with the poker that he'd had to go to the infirmary. We had a cup of tea in the back kitchen.

"Well, you knows best what you're up to and I'm not going to make you stay in this house, as sure as eggs is eggs."

She wiped her hands on her pinny and signed Mary Josephine Donnelly in a spidery hand. She had the rheumatics in her fingers.

"And now you're on your own," she said

"I'm not doing onyting dirty, our mam."

There were other twists and turns in my life which I haven't yet mentioned, but I don't think they had a direct connection with my seduction of Hector. In retrospect, the physical loving of Hector is now the hardest thing to come to terms with but then, whilst it was happening, it was so easy. Many's the time I'd romp around with both of the children, giving them piggybacks when they were little, hugs and kisses, acting like a loving aunt until one day alone with Hector the pinches and the squeezes became more lingering, fiercer. He laughed in an artificial way and he suddenly gripped my breast and then blushed.

"I'm sorry, Aunt Sammy."

He turned and ran out of the house and I ran after him.

"Wait, Hector. Don't go away. It's all right. I'm not cross."

The sudden manifestation of a boy man made me lose all sense of responsibility and broke through all the protective shibboleths. Thou shalt not fuck thy brother's son.

I caught up with him and held him by the arm.

"Come back, Hector."

I should have let him go and it would have blown over most likely, but the moral restraints had burst and the usual daily decorum splintered. Aw shit, as the hands would say, it were just plain horniness. I wanted my oats but, my God, that devil's relationship with Hector was wonderful, something miraculously out of this world.

We've passed through Calgary, where more people boarded the train, and are on our way to Medicine Hat.

After a brief Indian summer of glorious days with the light on the surrounding prairie so bright it made Bridget screw up her eyes and the sun mellow and warm on her swelling belly, the winter hit Winnipeg hard and early in the middle of October. A ton of snow fell and it stayed. Marie Louise revelled in it and forced Bridget out for walks in near blizzard conditions. "You must keep healthy, cherie. I remember when I was enceinte with Michie...." As she dragged her feet through the dirty snow, Bridget thought she would scream if she heard any more about her sister-in-law's pregnancies.

Angela was sulky half the time, constantly bored until one day she found herself a boy friend and had the effrontery to bring him back home. "It's no use looking at me like that," she said to Marie. "I can't be in mourning for ever, can I? It ain't natural. And you brought me to this stinking place where I didn't know nobody."

To Bridget's surprise the French family had welcomed them with warmth and hospitality and appeared to fall in immediately with Marie's scheme for her unborn grandchild. They had quite a brood of their own but a large house, and M. Chansonnier was evidently prosperous. The sisters-in-law shared a bedroom, and Angie was tucked away in the attic.

# SEVEN

A few years after Bridget's winter in Winnipeg, the rains and drizzles and frosts of November on the Western Front continued through Christmas and into January. The Trou group of refugees and deserters pushed their cart wearily along the streets of Chaubet, a small town not far from T****s, where the guns could no longer be heard.

Throughout the dismal journey they had little chance for washing — themselves or their clothes — and they stank accordingly. The two moustaches, however, M. Trou's bushy, arching in angry spikes, and Tyler Brown's, black, cropped, dapper, had both been jealously groomed despite the atrocious conditions. The deserters had no personal property, not even a toothbrush; they had cast away everything with their military identity, but Trou had brought with him from the estaminet a fearsome open razor, a pair of blunt scissors, and a little hand mirror, all of which he lent to Tyler. Whatever the weather they conscientiously performed their morning toilet.

"Your father is proud of his moustache, no?" Hector said to Celine one of the mornings on the way.

"I think he's looking for a new wife. Silly old sausage."

Celine's eyes were beginning to sparkle just perceptibly through their customary glaze.

Hector had tried shaving with M. Trou's lethal razor (Trou carried with him an old leather strap to sharpen its terrifying edge) but could not get the hang of it. After cutting himself badly he gave up. The consequence was that when Hector pushed into Chaubet he looked like a gaunt prairie Jesus with a blond beard.

"How much further to this friend of yours, uncle?"

Both Suzette and Celine had lost a lot of weight on the journey and their clothes hung loosely on them. Oddly, the weeks of slogging along and endurance had not only reduced the unsightly flab about their face and figures but had given a brightness to their skin. The journey had done nothing for Suzette's daughter, Tina, who looked pale and ill. Trou claimed to know a man in Chaubet who owned a grocery business.

"I helped him when he was down on his luck. He married a pretty girl whose father owned a shop here and they had five children. Four boys, I believe, and a girl."

They soon found the place. It was not a large town.

"Is that the shop, uncle? Over the street there. GABEREAU ET FILS. EPICERIE." Suzette read out the name above the window. "What a big house it looks."

"He's changed the name," said M. Trou. "Cunning old fox, Marcel. He always was, my dears. He has changed the name of his father-in-law's business. I wonder what his wife thinks of that? I can't remember what her name used to be."

Hector had never heard old man Trou talk more than a few words before. Perhaps his escape from the killing zone had loosened his tongue. As housewives came out of the shop, their faces worn with the care of war, they barely glanced at the muddied cart, its shaft lowered to the cobbled street, or its pathetic load or its attendant ragamuffins. One woman, however, patted Tina on the head and searched in her shopping bag for a cookie.

"There you are my little one. You look as though you could do with it. All skin and bones you is."

She looked accusingly at Hector. The air was damp and it felt as though it could drizzle with rain at any time. They took the cart round the back to the tradesmen's entrance and Trou went in to seek out his old friend, Marcel.

ଓଞ୍ଚ଼ଓ

Hector had become inured to the sights of war, to the ravages it had worked on the faces of troops and civilians, the old and the young, the ally and the enemy, but, for all his hardness, he was shocked at the appearance of Madame Gabereau. They had waited in the grocer's yard, Tyler smoking a pipe, Suzette lifting Tina off the cart and pulling the child's coat tighter around her thin shoulders. Uncle Joe, mouth partly open and his head pushed to one side by his carbuncle, placed his foot on the shaft. It had been a long time since he had played his accordion. Celine stood proudly by the side of her Christ-like deserter, tall, face prematurely grooved, but appropriately humble in peasant clothing. A good looking girl opened the back door. She paused and looked at them shyly.

"Papa says will you please come in."

She spoke quietly and addressed Hector. Unexpectedly, she reminded him of Higgins Bend, of Angela Parkes perhaps, but Angie was cheekier, robuster than this one and nothing like so pale.

"Merci, mademoiselle." He wanted to be attentive to her, kind.

"What is your name if you please?" He paused and looked round the group of refugees. "This is Celine...Suzette and Tina. Uncle Joseph. And I am Hector."

The girl gave a little bob at each introduction.

"And this is my friend, Tyler."

The former Private Brown took his pipe out of his mouth, saluted, grinned and brushed down his moustache with his forefinger. The girl smiled faintly, courteously.

"I am Madeleine Gabereau."

She has a forlorn smile, Hector thought as they followed her through the door, as though she is carrying more than her share of grief. She was about the same build as Angie, better groomed but dress more modest, becoming. A longer nose, but dignified both by feature and whatever her secret sorrow was. Hector was peripherally aware of a faint smudge of black hairs on her upper lip which he found vaguely exciting. He had not seen let alone been in the company of a girl of his own age for Christ knows how long. He did not wish to dwell on reminders of Angie and Higgins Bend for he had written them off, excised them from his life. On the tedious slog from the front line such thought and memory had been banished. Just before he'd boarded the troop ship in Halifax all those years ago (his embarkation leave had been cancelled because of what the military authorities called a "flap"—the Boche had made a big "push" at a place called Mons which later became familiar to Hector) a guy from Alberta who said he had a cousin in Higgins Bend had told him that Angie had married a kid called Dick Leech. Hector knew him because everyone knew everyone else as a matter of course in Higgins Bend. Later his mother had made a brief mention of it in a letter.

They straggled apologetically into a large kitchen which opened immediately onto the back yard. Half of the stone floor was covered with linoleum. An open fireplace was built into the wall on the left as you entered and held a smoky coal fire which gave off so little heat that their breaths still showed. A cat was curled in front of it, almost in it. M. Trou sat at the end of a wooden table with his friend and between them was a bottle of apple brandy. At Hector's home, even when it was minus forty outside, the kitchen would be full of bustle and warmth and the smell of horses and cows and people's bits and pieces everywhere and a calendar advertising a cattle drench on a cupboard door. Not every house in Higgins Bend would be snug and warm, his memory conceded. The sort of shack Angie was brought up in could be cold enough in January to freeze the balls off a brass monkey.

At the grocer's, more introductions. Little glasses of brandy were handed round, even Tina got one and burst into a coughing fit at the first sip. Suzette patted her back. Hector heard M. Trou explaining in a low voice the presence of himself and Tyler. He was attempting to put an exculpatory gloss on their desertion. The grocer turned to Hector.

"My four sons have all been killed."

"I am sorry, monsieur."

"You know what it is like in the trenches?"

"I was there more than three years, monsieur."

"My wife has been destroyed as a person. She is a living cabbage. A puddle of grief. A pisspot of sorrow."

He put his arm around Madeleine, his shallow brow furrowed.

"Lena is all I have left."

Hector looked at her small shoes showing at the hem of her dress. The kitchen which held an iron cooking stove against the wall opposite the fireplace evidently served also as a living room. No pictures on any of the walls and the stove cold. The sense was not so much of poverty here, not at all, as of tangible despair, evident in a pernicious way even in Lena's shoes. Angela too had small feet. He could not remember anything of Aunt Sammy's. Marcel Gabereau was the same height as M. Trou but nothing near so portly and his craggy face like an unfinished sculpture was clean shaven and his hair cut so short that his jug handle ears were even more pronounced. His small brown eyes were deep-set so that his emotions were for the most part hidden, as it were, in his cranium.

"You are welcome to stay until you have sorted yourselves out. You and your friend. I reckon you have both paid your dues. What good would two more deaths do?"

He smiled sourly at M. Trou and the two older men sat down again at the table. By a summary wave of the hand, Joe was invited to join them.

"Lena will arrange rooms for you. There are plenty of empty ones now. And perhaps she will take you to see her mother."

The three older men, including Uncle Joe, head tilted, fatuously grinning, turned to their drinks and the others gathered round Madeleine. She appeared anxious to visit her mother before anything else.

"Just you, monsieur 'Ector. To begin with. And you can tell maman about...about the things."

Hector shrugged and Tyler winked at him. As he followed her up the carpeted stairs, each step and riser divided by polished rods, a gnawing desire for ordinary domesticity surprised Hector. The rustle of Madeleine's skirt, the dry comfort of the carpet under his worn and cracked boots. He ought to have taken them off. Life on the ranch became suddenly precious. They'd had secret dreams of home, of course, the boys and men in the trenches, but as the years dragged on and the casualties mounted they began to think of it and peace as more and more unattainable. Climbing the stairs after this gentle woman he wondered yet again whether he should have remained loyally with the regiment. But then what the hell use was it being a dead hero? There'd be no homecoming at all in that case, and so it went on, round and round, a circular lunacy. The vexed embarrassment, too, of Aunt Sammy. What a bastard that was. She'd be an old woman by now. He had no Madeleine to return to. What, for crying out loud, allowed him to imagine that this Madeleine would have anything to do with him? Angela Parkes had married and anyhow his father had not been keen on his going out with a girl from the shacks. Fuck his dad. Perhaps not, but they did not know the half of it back at the ranch. He had not thought so much about home for a long time.

"Monsieur."

Madeleine had walked along a passage at the head of the stairs and, standing by a bedroom door was speaking in a whisper.

"Maman would weep for months as the bad news came about each of my brothers. She is very sick. Her world has collapsed." Madeleine looked at him with eyes that were soft but in which compassion was beginning to dry up. She opened the door.

"Are you asleep?"

He would never have believed that grief could be so destructive. Mme. Gabereau was lying in a chaise longue beside a small fire the twin of the one in the kitchen and sharing the same chimney. A blanket was pulled up to her chin, her thin arms in a black bed jacket. Her hair a yellowish white, pinned closely to her head wobbling above the blanket like a pumpkin.

"M. Trou and his family have come, mommy. You know the friend of daddy's. The Boche have taken their farm. And this gentleman has come with them."

Only the eyes of the stricken woman moved. Her lips fixed in a bloodless line, her limbs inert as though paralysed, bones prominent over hollow cheeks. Hector wondered what "things" he was to tell her, what she would hear. It was a spacious room with a large double bed with a canopy over it, but again, no pictures on the walls.

"There was a holy picture of the Sacred Heart at the head of the bed," Madeleine said as though reading Hector's mind. "And a statue of Our Lady on a stand in that corner. Mom used to light candles and put them beside it on feast days. But when the Boche killed my third brother she threw the picture and the statue out of the window and she's been pretty well like this ever since. Guy was her favourite you see. He had fair hair like you."

Despite the wracked face, Hector could imagine that the mother had once had the quiet handsomeness of her daughter. She couldn't be much older than his own mother, and this sent a shudder of apprehension through Hector. Mme. Gabereau seemed to have focused on him and her eyes were beginning to shine in contrast to her dead face. Eerie. Discomfiting. What the hell was happening here—a little life was beginning to twitch and stir in the old lady. He caught a glimpse of himself in the dresser mirror by the window whose blinds were half closed and was startled by his appearance. He had taken off his peasant beret. His blond hair had grown long, his beard jagged at the ends. At home in the Rockies he'd seen half-mad prospectors unkempt like this, returning from years in the wilderness, wild-eyed, talking to themselves, clutching pieces of useless rock.

"She is moving her head. She has taken a fancy to you," Madeleine said.

"Shall I shake hands with her?"

"You can try. It can't do any harm. She hasn't spoken for months and months. I don't know how much she understands."

Hector stepped towards the mother and put out his hand. He lifted hers at the end of the black sleeve, limp, unresponsive. Her eyes burned, moving puzzled from him to her daughter and back again.

"Dad doesn't sleep up here any more. He has an old army cot in the room next to the shop where the flour and dried apricots are stored. That's how it's taken him. You must think we are very strange."

Madeleine appeared to be both relieved and pleased to be talking to someone of her own age.

"I think it's terrible. It's all the fault of this fucking war. Excuse my Dutch, mademoiselle."

She laughed and cocked her head and looked at Hector with tentatively warm eyes.

"There is no need to apologize. Everyone swears at the war. You should just hear my old dad when he gets going."

Hector could feel the faintest pressure from Mme. Gabereau's hand.

"Were any of your brothers married?"

"The eldest only. Paul. His widow didn't waste any time. A few months after we got the awful news she married a master plumber who was years older than she was. Guy had a girl friend, but it was nothing serious."

"You mother is trying to squeeze my hand."

Madeleine shrugged. She walked to one of the bedposts and swung round on it, prettily. Suggestively perhaps. Her ankle showing. An inch of grey stocking.

"And you, monsieur. Have you a wife and children waiting in Canada?"

"I was only a kid when I left."

"So?"

Hector wondered what sort of a monster she would think him if she knew about Aunt Sammy and his tumbling her in the barn and in her room and down by the slough where Aunt Sammy got a poison ivy rash all over her backside. That had not been a good day, a day when a few scales had started to slip from his eyes. Not that Aunt Sammy's magic had disappeared just like that in a puff of smoke, but his erotic and romantic heat had cooled when she showed him her rump covered with red splotches.

The rest of the family had gone to a christening party and out of some kind of amorous bravado he and Aunt Sammy had sneaked down to the slough where the dragonflies skimmed the water. They were mad, he and Bridgie. There was always the risk of one of the hands seeing them and Hector had a feeling that his sister, Michie, was suspicious. She'd looked at him once or twice with latent horror in her eyes.

"How do you know I come from Canada?"

"I heard M. Trou telling daddy about you and that other boy, Teelair."

"Tyler. You know then that we have quit...our army?"

"Yes."

"Deserted?"

"Yes, I do. I think you are sensible." She looked at him as though weighing him up through old and serious eyes. "It must have taken a lot of courage to do that, to leave all the horrible carnage."

Hector could hardly believe his ears, but of course this girl belonged to his, the doomed generation. She had been in the thick of it, four brothers killed. She would not pin a white feather on him as he'd heard society women did on men out of uniform in Piccadilly in London.

In her bedroom the day after she was stung by the poison ivy, Aunt Sammy had bent over coyly and lifted up her dress, the fawn one with the leaf tracery on it. As usual she was not wearing anything under her petticoat.

"Look what that horrible ivy has done to me. It's all your fault, dear boy. Aren't you going to kiss it better."

Normally in this past month the sight of her glossy behind and Bridget's teasing posture would have driven Hector to a frenzy of horniness and desire, but that afternoon the ugly rash and her inviting crouch struck him as ludicrous and he let out a loud adolescent guffaw. Aunt Sammy had dropped the skirt of her dress, straightened up, red-faced and furious and angry and chased him out of the house.

"There's nothing funny about it, you wretched boy."

He'd got on his horse and galloped over to the north end of the ranch where his father and Billy Lilley were fencing off a mud hole, a real sucker when it rained.

"Sorry I'm late, Dad."

His father had grunted, and when they rode back for supper Hector had wondered uneasily what the heck was the matter with himself and where in tarnation it was all going to end.

He found he was still holding Lena's mother's hand and she was staring at him intently. With agonizing effort her lips started to move.

"I think she is trying to say something."

Madeleine let go of the bedpost and walked slowly to the chair in dull resignation. She bent over to catch the hoarse sounds from her mother. As she straightened up she blushed.

"She wants to know if you are my young man."

Hector looked pleased, as though that were the best thing that had been said in a long time.

"She says you should get your hair cut."

"Really!"

"And that I should cut it for you."

## CELINE

"We can't go on the game again, Sue. We just can't. It was different back at the estaminet. We had no choice."

"We haven't much choice here. Tina is sick the whole time and away from school every other day. We can't sponge off these folks for ever, kind as they are. We are absolutely broke. We've got to do something, Celine."

Suzette and Tina and I share one of the dead sons' rooms, Guy's, lot of space for one person, the grocery sure must have done well. We've been here nearly two months and I must say that old jug-ears Gabereau has been very generous. Housing us, feeding us as though the good lord has sent him a new family to take the place of his slaughtered one, though Christ knows there are plenty of folk in Chaubet could do with his help. I think on the whole the people here resent us. They grudge us the pittance of so-called refugee money we get from the Town Hall. They should try living where our farm used to be, the cheap, penny-pinching bastards.

"We can't go on like this. I was talking to one of the local tarts only yesterday outside the butcher's. She says there's plenty of work for everyone who wants it. Anyone who's half passable in the dark and has two legs and a cunt. There's a military depot just down the road and the guys pay very well, especially the sergeants. The trouble would be where could we take them? Maybe after everyone's asleep we could bring them back here."

"Don't talk so fucking crazy, Sue. Are you out of your goddamn mind? If you're determined to go back you'd have to do it up against the barrack wall or in a lousy turnip field. In any case, I don't like you talking such filth. It makes me sick to think of it nowadays. Remember when we were two respectable women."

"I remember you got me on to the game in the first place. Taught me how to turn my first trick."

I am trapped by my past, and honestly I do not believe it is all my own fault. This room is pleasant, in remarkable contrast to the downstairs kitchen, rugs on the floor, pictures, still life, landscapes on the wall here, a comfortable bed which Suzette and I share and Tina has a little cot of her own. She's at school just now where the other kids give her a hard time. It sure would be worse if they knew her mother was a whore. The shop is closed for a couple of hours in the early afternoon. Outside the raw winter lingers on, but occasionally there is a little flowering sign of spring by someone's back door or in a ditch. It won't be too long before the apple trees are in blossom.

"I told Hector a little what our life used to be like before the war. I think he understands. Anyway, he pretends to. I couldn't bear him to know I started whoring all over again."

"For crying out loud, Celine. You told me he was right there in your dad's bar when Tyler screwed the daylights out of you."

"Don't be nasty, Sue. It's not like you."

But she's right and I'd give anything for that not to have happened. I'm not counting those amours in the valley after dad kicked out my husband, Big Red. Something changed in me during those nights in the barns when Hector and I talked till all hours. Before that life was like trudging through a blank grey void, the mindless march of a zombie. I can't say that I have fallen in love with him, can I? There's no future there and in any case I don't think there is any of that kind of love left in me. Apart from anything else those two are in Queer Street, Hector and Tyler. They daren't go to the Town Hall and pretend they are refugees because they'll be found out and handed over to the military and most likely shot by a firing squad. God dammit I couldn't stand the thought of such a thing happening. But the nosy women in Chaubet are getting suspicious. Hector is wearing some of the deceased Guy's clothes. They fit him perfectly. His hair is still long but he's trimmed his beard. Real handsome he is, but there's nothing there for me. Madeleine says her mother's crackers about Hector. Thinks he is some sort of returned Christ come specially for her, even though she threw the statue of the Virgin out of the window. And I don't like the way Madeleine looks at him either, though right now he don't seem so keen on her.

"I thought you were tough, Celine. I thought you could take it. Standing up or lying down."

"Don't be coarse, Sue."

"Oh my!"

"I think we both pretend too much, act as though we don't give a shit. Because that was the only way back there. But now..."

"I can't see how anything's changed much."

"Well, them two boys. They don't treat us like whores no more. Now, do they? They give us respect. And the old man—he's a pretty decent guy even though he doesn't say much. I wonder what dad did for him to make him so kind to us. Even Madeleine is nice, you know. So long as she keeps her snoopy eyes off Hector."

Sue looked at me with a smile full of pity and sadness.

"Don't go dreaming dreams about Hector, Celine. You are only going to hurt yourself."

We are very good friends, Suzette and I, for cousins. Lena, as the family call her, has dug out some of her mother's old clothes for us. She says it's unlikely her mother will ever get dressed again. We are still too fat to get into anything of Madeleine's, though that sodding journey from our old house has knocked kilos off us. In fact Suzette is looking quite smart this afternoon in a fetching gown of Mme. Gabereau's, soft, a deep green, its folds both conceal and enhance her amplitudes. Judging by her clothes, the old lady must have lost a lot of weight. Lena said she was plump and jolly not very long ago. I'll say she's like a skeleton now. And the dresses have transformed us. You wouldn't recognize us from when we arrived in those black, lice-infested sacks we wore then. Once or twice as the weak February sun catches the colour of her borrowed gown, I am reminded of the Suzette I used to know way back. We both work in the shop, it's the only grocer's in Chaubet, and despite wartime restrictions and shortages business is brisk. Of course wily old Marcel gets a lot of stuff from the black market. Hector and Tyler are kept busy fetching and carrying, very much in the background so's they don't come into contact with the public. Come to think of it, old Gabereau has got himself a lot of free labour.

Considering what the last few years have been like, we're not too badly off. I can't think why Sue wants to go whoring again. I suppose it gets into your blood.

ఁ✤ఌ

"There are rumours flying around about you, Celine. Sneaky ones. Not very nice."

I'm positive Suzette was wearing a green dress that day back then, just the very shade of Mme. Gabereau's she has on now, but a more youthful one, its skirt swishing over the yellow buttercups. And I'm sure too that it was apple blossom time, but then when you think back to happiness it always seems to be blue skies and blossoms the fresh rebirth of harmless and innocent things—buds, lambs, you know. There were horrible occurrences in the spring too, but never mind. I wasn't too surprised at what Suzette was telling me. I'd been rash enough recently, but to be quite honest I wasn't ashamed.

"And what rumours are those, dear cousin?"

She was looking so stunning that May morning that I was envious of her, though people did say I wasn't a bad looker myself, not so slim as Sue who was still sylph-like, but then I have always been the sturdier one.

"Well, I don't like to mention it, but they say that since your Jean left you've been...well, you know, careless about your reputation. There's talk about the men you've been seen with."

Suzette had also made a disastrous first marriage, been unhappy practically from day one. She had a lighter skin than mine, more open eyes.

"Who are 'they' darling?"

"Just stories."

"Like me being an easy lay up and down the valley, is that it?"

"Darling one, don't joke about it. Mom's heard something, but she says it's a lot of rotten lies. I hope you're going to tell me she's right."

She sniffed as we walked into the orchard.

"Of course it's none of my business."

It wasn't like Sue to set up in judgement. I was annoyed that gossip had reached the ears of Aunt Claude. I was fond of her and she had always been so kind and understanding in a way that many older people weren't. She was not very lucky with her daughters. Apart from the two who were drowned when they were quite little, she'd had to endure the foul-up and tragedy of Suzette's marriage. It was after church at Whitsun and we were decked out in our Sunday best. Some of the family had come back for a drink and dinner at the farmhouse. Uncle Joe was already playing his accordion in the kitchen, though one of the grandmothers didn't like him playing profane music so soon after church. I'm not claiming that I'm entirely blameless, but I truly did not think that I was a confirmed and branded prostitute. The morning in the barn with Ferdi, just after I'd been bloodied and bruised for the umpteenth time by Big Red, was one of delirious, mindless sexual joy and it marked too the start of a miraculous liberation from the prurient shackles of our river valley and the savagery of my marriage. And I thought I could get away with it. Not a prostitute. A good time girl. I got to call the shots even if I was not always on top physically if you know what I mean. Forgive that bawdy joke. And why not, I argued, so long as one was careful and did not get pregnant? Suzette's husband died when a quarry wall fell in on him.

It was only young handsome men at first. Word had got round, beginning with Ferdi I suppose, and it was wonderful how the news spread that I was a willing and easy lay. A guy would come sniffing up to the farmhouse like a tom-cat—I was surprised my father didn't notice—and there'd be some eyeing and whispering and giggling and an assignation was arranged. Sometimes it happened right there on the spot. The barn was a good place but too chilly in winter. Some of them I told to get lost, I didn't like them and was arrogantly picky. No money changed hands, only a little gift occasionally because most of those boys were not wealthy and some of them got crazy about me and wanted to marry me. But I was not going to fall into a trap like that again.

Most unlike her, Suzette began to nag at me the Whit Sunday some months after her husband was killed by a fall of stone. He was scarcely recognizable when they dug him out. I wasn't prepared to take her criticism lying down simply because she was a recent widow.

"Listen cousin. You know how it was with Jean and me. You know about the beatings. I also know that you were not happy in your marriage because you have told me often enough. Well, I'm sick and tired of us women having to take all this crap."

"That doesn't mean you have to fuck every man in the valley, cherie."

Suzette's language could be as earthy as mine. I don't know how we picked it up, as vulgar as a pair of guttersnipes we were. I think we started talking like that as a dare.

"Not every man, sweet."

But she had a point. It might as well have been every man for all the discrimination I made. I just loved it, craved it as often as possible. The variety and excitement and danger took over my moral sense. The pretending to back off, the chase, the power of seduction. I sometimes excused myself with the fact of my juvenile rape and brutal husband sequence, but my heart was not in that sort of bullshit.

"You know, Sue, you ought to try it. Just once before you dish out any more of that pious mush. I can find you a bloke in two flicks of a lamb's tail."

"How dare you, Celine!"

I remember that Sunday so well. We walked deeper into the orchard to the point where she had left me years before and I was picked up by that sleazy corporal. We could still hear the strains of Joe's accordion coming out of the kitchen door. I was wearing a rather expensive dress for the first time, one that I'd earned. The thrill of a procession of virile young men, their eyes beseeching, passionate, was still attractive to me, but one afternoon when a beau called Maurice was pumping away with an enormous dong he was absurdly proud of I got to thinking. Why only these energetic but poor ones? I bet there's many an older married man along the valley who would pay big bucks for what I am giving away free. When Maurice had finished and was still foolishly showing off his moist penis by flapping it against my tummy, I asked him if he knew anyone of the kind I had in mind. He looked at me oddly and stopped playing with his thing. "I shouldn't if I were you, Celine," he said and I told him to piss off.

Well the soft grey dress I was wearing that Whitsun, of exquisite cut and material but about two years behind the Paris fashions, was the first fruit of my new enterprise, a gift from a fat little draper from V****. He did not take off either his long johns when he was on the job nor his pince-nez because he said he wanted to see my divine tits. He was in a frenzy to get it over with and was terrified that his wife would find out about his moral straying.

"Well it's up to you, Sue, dearest. Just let me know if you change your mind."

As I sit with her in the slain Guy's room in Chaubet I wonder how responsible I am for my cousin's wanting to go on the streets again today. Or how shockingly irresponsible. Yet she's a big girl now, a woman of experience and trial and sorrow. She should not be needing her jollies out of a sordid kind of addiction, should she?

Suzette was miffed as we walked out of the orchard back to the kitchen. Even though I had on this smashing new dress I was still responsible for preparing the Sunday dinner, except that when there was a crowd like today Aunt Claude and Suzette put their aprons on and mucked in. We never rose to the dizzy heights of having a servant in the house. Why should we when there was me around, married or not. I accepted the general expectations of my being head cook and bottle-washer as a matter of course. And a few weeks later Suzette did come to me as I was certain she would.

"You remember what you said, Celie, about you know."

She was embarrassed and practically tongue-tied.

"About what darling?"

"Don't be a tease, Celine. What you were telling me about humping fellows on the sly. Do you really? Is the gossip true?"

"Never mind about me. Would you want to try it, then? Have a bang? Is that what you're asking?"

Without beating about the bush I shot the question right at her. I was grinning maliciously. She traced a circle in the farmyard dust with her toe.

"Sure. If that's what you do. I don't see why not."

We flung our arms around each other, laughing in female complicity, but I could see she was still apprehensive.

"But how do you start? You just can't go up to a guy in the marketplace and say do you want a roll in the hay. Can you?"

My father came round the corner from the stable at that minute. He greeted Suzette and asked whether Aunt Claude's cold was better. One of my lover boys told me that M. Trou was meeting secretly once a month with the wife of a corn factor in a village upstream from us when her husband was away for the day on business. I don't know why, but I was surprised and, for all that I loved my dad, a little disappointed.

"Once it's known you are open for business, cousin, you don't have to do a thing. They'll come buzzing round like horny bluebottles. You better believe me."

☙❧

Since our flight from the estaminet I've given a lot of both nostalgic and guilty thought to the sort of life that Sue and I led during that period of reckless and indiscriminate copulation. Much of my recollection has to do with the unbelievable innocence of Hector. Oh, I realize that in one sense he is a hardened criminal, though not so hardened as Tyler perhaps, which is what the army makes of most young men before it has them butchered. He's whored and he's boozed and he's killed and he's deserted, but for all this there stays with him an indestructible naiveté and guiltlessness. I know that sounds bloody contradictory. Romantic. Stupid. I'll blurt out something even more foolish and say that Hector is essentially a good man. How's that coming from a fat, aging whore? When I was lying in them barns, night after night, by Hector's side, I felt better than I'd done for ages, even as I was crawling out of some dark hole where I'd gradually retreated as the war went on.

Even before my deliberate blacking out of the past, aborting every memory before it could be born, I didn't give a fig for any sort of introspection. I did not for instance inquire into the nature of goodness.

"There's a good girl," my mother would say when I obeyed her or pleased her, and M. Trou carried on with this sort of mindless expression after she died. "That was a good screw, honey," Big Red would say when he was being kind and not beating the shit out of me. The priest did good works in the parish. I became a good time girl and so did Sue. Once she started there was no holding her back. Most of the time as we fucked among the apple trees or on the river bank, there was not a care or serious thought in our heads.

"Listen up, Sue. Those rumours you were talking about. You'll be getting a bad name, too. I think we'd better start to cool it."

The first feller I found for her was no wealthy draper, but a tall, thin weaver, partly bald with a wispy moustache, who used to make his bolts of cloth in a lonely cottage in the back of beyond. He smelt fusty but not obnoxiously so, Sue said. Every few months he's come into town, sell his stuff to an agent and sit in my dad's bar and have a few quiet drinks before setting off back home to hit the loom again. This pick up place was a bit too close to home for my liking, but I'd told one of my boys about wanting a client for another lady and this is what he came up with. When she saw him Sue turned up her nose, but the next day she was not only totally exhausted but full of excitement.

"He must get so charged up stuck away in that cottage that he's fit to bust. Talk about stamina. He's fulla juice. He couldn't get enough. Time and time again it simply spurted out of him, pints of it. He'd always pull it out in time and squirt it all over my tum. I believe he liked looking at it, proud of the goo he'd produced. And ever so gentle he was, Celine."

She wanted to stay with this weaver hero, but I told her it was too dangerous, far safer to spread her favours, keep changing partners. So, I have to confess, there is no doubt about it. I got Suzette started on the game, my game as I literally thought it was, and now, right here in Guy's room in Chaubet, I'm not proud of the fact. Even in my heady days when life was all willing men—not quite all, I still had the farm chores to do—brief fits of remorse would sneak up on me when I thought of Aunt Claude and the way I was leading on her daughter, for you see my conscience and morals had not completely gone. And now, thanks largely to Hector, things have turned completely round and it's Sue who is urging me to go out on the streets.

Not that you could call what Suzette and I were doing in those blessed post-marital days on the farm as "being on the streets". We simply were not professionals in that common, demeaning parlance. We did not stand on street corners hawking our twats. Not then, but we were getting closer to renting out flesh when I took a dress from the baker or when Sue took a pair of shoes and a new hat from a prosperous poultry farmer. It was after a number of purchases like those that we agreed we'd better slow down, be more circumspect.

"Ma is..." Sue moved her head from side to side, "beginning to ask awkward questions. 'Where were you yesterday afternoon?' 'Where did that coat with the fox fur trim come from?' I shouldn't have left it lying around, but where else could I keep it?"

After her husband was killed, Suzette went back to her mother's. The other surviving sister had married and her father was often poorly, so another pair of hands was welcome. It was easier for me with dad being away often, but even so my cousin and I cut down on our capers and tried to behave more like respectable matrons. Terribly dull life became, but the valley was beginning to chatter and so far as I was concerned that insatiable desire I'd had for years was noticeably cooling. Sue eventually married one of her guys, the father of Tina, God knows where he is now, either blown to bits or deserted like Hector and Tyler. One thing's for sure, he hasn't come back. I gradually reduced the number of my men and finally settled for a middle-aged lawyer with an invalid wife. We'd meet once a month and fuck with the utmost decorum in a draughty orangery whilst his bedbound wife would have her afternoon snooze upstairs. I didn't think I was doing anyone any harm.

Later it was different when the war came and the troops trampled over the farm so that nothing would grow and the shells destroyed the apple trees. Shit, it made my heart bleed. Our source of food went, dad couldn't get supplies for the bar, and since the soldiers were only allowed to come at certain times, often the bar was out of bounds to them depending on the whim of the generals. There were precious few customers anyways. Suzette's husband was called up and her parents died when an errant shell hit their house. I was desolated when I heard of Aunt Claude's death, but that was only one of many blows the war brought. Sue and Tina and Uncle Joe, whose carbuncle seemed to double in size overnight, came to live with us. It was a time for desperate measures.

We could have cleared out much earlier and joined the stream of refugees heading west, but Dad was either too stubborn or too rooted to move. The slow fall into degradation is often imperceptible as it happens and one doesn't realize the grievous extent of it until the bottom of the stinking pit is reached. I didn't, that's for sure. Looking back from this bereaved room in Chaubet, a room in which I can nevertheless find a limited, even, don't laugh, a dignified peace, I realize that time can be awesomely compacted, the period especially from when I was sedately humping the orangery lawyer, getting matronly about the hips and the bosom, nodding benevolently to the valley folks as I went to mass with

M. Trou, to the ghastly evening when I was spreadeagled on the old mattress by the bar with Tyler on top of me, wearing a stained dress and tartish black stockings, a smelly old bag whose genitals and mind had become numbed by abuse and indifference. Those years seem to have rushed along like a torrent of diarrhoea. Believe me.

Many people would say that Tyler is some kind of sleazy trench rat, but he has behaved like a perfect gentleman ever since that time of shame on the filthy estaminet mattress, that nadir of casual copulation. He helped me along on our horrendous journey, took my arm at bad moments, gave me a larger tot of rum, was perhaps a little jealous of my devotion to Hector, because that is what it became, devotion, and still is. It's not only Mme. Gabereau who believes Hector's the second Christ. Tyle, as we all now call him, has never once assumed any rights over me because he once paid a few centimes for a quick poke. And as for Hector, who was witness to that shameful exhibition, when any scrap of female dignity was thrown out of the window like Mme. Gabereau's statue of the Virgin, it is as though it never happened. When I was playing the field in those carefree erotic days I got pleasure in the act, more in the tease and the seduction admittedly, but also in the fuck itself, the thrill of admission and penetration. But there was not the slightest pleasure in those bangs in the estaminet when I was trying to earn a few bucks for the family purse. I became inured to the indignity of the passionless routine. The irony is that there was hardly anything to spend the money on where we were, a few miles from the cutting edge of the biggest war on earth.

How did I arrive at such a soulless condition? You might well ask.

Oh, Holy Mother of Mercy it was only too easy. The process of decline is well oiled, especially when there is a lousy war on. A trooper starts to grope me as I'm clearing the dirty glasses off the table and M. Trou turns a blind eye to the molesting of his daughter. Then another gets me in a dark corner and I grapple with him only half-heartedly, and so it builds up feel by feel until the day comes when I'm thrown a few francs for letting a uniformed warrior get the dirty water off his chest. I'm trying not to make piss poor excuses but you must remember the debilitating factors. Hunger was one and boredom was another and fear also. And the sheer shittiness of our situation. Apart from our world falling to bits, the first year of the war wasn't too bad. But I suppose as much out of nerves as anything else, Suzette and I, who both had already become heavier and rounder, began to eat ravenously like pregnant sows, desperately, as though gorging would make the war go away. In no time our attractive plumpness turned to gross and shapeless fat, whore's fat.

Before the first year of this dreadful war was over, our own army had ransacked the farm and commandeered anything on four legs and carted off all the fodder. A real bastard of a sergeant would have commandeered me too, but in those days I gave him a piece of my mind and threatened to cut off his balls with a carving knife and away he went with his tail safe between his legs. That was one of my last acts of human dignity, and from that day on the slide into shame and ignominy began. But I'm kidding myself, aren't I? The slide began long before then.

☙❀❧

"One of us ought to get down to the shop, Suzette."

I am darning one of Mme. Gabereau's petticoats which Lena has bequeathed to me. Sue has moved to the window and is looking down on to the street where we pushed that fucking cart up to the store only two months ago. In a crazy way I became attached to that cart. It represented a solidity in our shifting world, a creaking awkward forlorn hope.

"So you are not going to give it another shot?"

"Nope."

A further irony is that it was Suzette who first became alarmed at our descent into—whatever—morass, degradation, not giving a shit about our appearance or condition. Her husband hadn't yet been posted as missing or killed but she had come to live with us in the farmhouse. Aunt Claude and my uncle had passed away the previous spring and Uncle Joe played his accordion at the funeral tea. Sue said her mother would have liked that.

"We'd better watch ourselves, Celine."

We were sheltering from the misty rain in the lea of the infamous barn where I'd enjoyed many a blissful orgasm in the straw. We had a few fowl left, and they, feathers damp, were scratching about in the mud and wet.

"Just look at you! Look at me! Our gowns are torn and dirty and our stockings are slopping down over our shoes."

"Who cares? What's the point of dressing up, looking good?"

A detachment of soldiers marched, shambled more like, along the lane, stooping, heads down. Not like the first year when they were singing, whistling at any skirt in sight, shouting. Keep your pecker up, mam'selle. The war will be over by Christmas.

"Because we're becoming sluts, Celine."

We did our best to pull ourselves together for a month or two, spruced ourselves up, wore some perfume, but it didn't work out. We were too near the front line. The farmhouse was destroyed by shell-fire and most of our personal things went up in flames. We moved into the estaminet, my obstinate father, Uncle Joe, Suzette, me, Tina. It was a crying shame about Tina. She should have been evacuated ages ago. We all should. The valley was deserted of civilians, the mayor had gone, the miller, my lawyer and his invalid wife had fled their house and the orangery had been blown to smithereens. The lanky weaver with his copious semen, Ferdi who started me on the rosy path, all our young men had enlisted or been conscripted. The roads and lanes had great holes in them. The apple trees were splintered. The buildings started collapsing around us. What was the point of dressing up. Or washing and tidying and combing our hair. A grey fog clouded our minds. Our bodies smelled.

Suzette is still looking down on Chaubet's main street and suddenly she gets agitated.

"Oh my God!"

"What's the matter, Sue?"

"There is a policeman coming towards the shop. And he's got an army corporal with him. A big tall fucker with a red band on his cap. Jesus, Mary and Joseph! You don't think they've come for..."

"Quick. Move your butt, Sue."

My heart stops. I think of firing squads. I rush to the door.

"We've got to warn them two," I scream.

# EIGHT

Hector's son was born to Aunt Sammy, Bridget Plouvier, widow, née Donnelly, without complications, at twenty past two on a Tuesday morning in Winnipeg, but none of these names appeared on the little guy's birth certificate. About three years before his father deserted, probably about the time Hector was waiting to enter his first bad battle, the baby gave his first thin cry after the midwife had cleared the mucus from his nostrils. Bob was Hector's only real buddy in those days, as he was until he was killed. Tyler was in their platoon but nothing special to Hector at that time.

Bridget was not in labour very long, which her sister-in-law said was surprising considering her age and the fact it was a first baby.

"I'm not that old, Marie," Aunt Sammy said in her iciest tones and most disdainful accent. "I'm not at fockin' death's door," she added in Dublin Irish. "Even though this little devil is after kicking me inside clane across the room."

Mr. Chansonnier went for the doctor at tennish the previous evening and from then on Marie Louise's maternal instincts surfaced. She fussed, spilled a basin of hot water, and generally got in everyone's way as she waited the arrival of her grandchild. It was snowing heavily and the doctor, a Catholic friend of their host, had difficulty in getting to the house.

☙❈❧

Hector and Bob were on edge with excitement and fear at the prospect of taking part in a "big push". Bob was blasted by their platoon sergeant who swore he'd blow Bob's bloody head off his fucking neck if he pulled a goddamn stoopid trick like that again. Spring had come to the trenches and the equinoctial sun was drying out the lagoons of mud, but then the March rains would liquefy it the next day.

"This guy I met in the canteen back at L\*\*\* said you could easy tell if Fritz was awake. On his toes, like," Bob said.

"Oh yeah."

Hector was eager to get into a proper fight, go over the top, and he only wished it would happen soon. The battalion had been hanging about, waiting in the trenches for over a week now and he could not get rid of a chronic queasiness in his stomach. It must be like what a woman feels when she's waiting to have a kid, he confided to Bob.

"The feller says you puts your tin hat on the muzzle of your rifle."

Bob took off his helmet and hung it over the foresight of his weapon, the poor bloody infantryman's best friend.

"Then you gets up on the firing step. And you waves your fucking tin hat in the air at the goddamn Hun...like this."

With shattering immediacy half a dozen German machine-guns opened up on the exposed helmet and the boys' faces were filled with wonder and terror. The sickening hammer blows of the guns like a chorus of hellish woodpeckers, the savage buzz of the flying bits of metal as they tore into sandbags and ricocheted off the barbed wire, drove the sergeant berserk and even more so when he realized what had caused the deadly hail, furiously, instantly mounted.

"You crazy cunt, you. You might have give the whole fucking attack away. Why don't you get a megaphone, you dozy boy. And shout into the fucking thing and tell the fucking Hun that we're on our fucking way. Christ! Some poor bleeding mothers have some fucking stoopid sons."

Hector shivered. He couldn't help wondering if one miserable helmet got mangled like that in two seconds flat what would happen when they all went over the top. He soon found out. When his baby was about three hours old he and Bob had managed to get twenty odd yards into no man's land. All hell was let loose. Many of the rest of the company were lying grotesquely around, hardly through their own wire, rigid in death, wishes and prayers gone with them, or squirming and moaning with wounds. The two boys lay flat in the spring mud.

CB ✦ ƏO

Hector's mother, Marie Louise, returned to the ranch shortly after the christening and in due time Aunt Sammy, Angela, and the baby also went back to Higgins Bend. They were surprised at how the blackness of the burned part of the town showed through the streaks of lingering snow. Nick, Marie, and Michelle met them at the train station. After much deliberation the baby was called Richard Samuel Leech—Richard, for the father of Angie's aborted child, Samuel, after Bridgie's former husband, and Leech, Angie's rightful and totally respectable married name. Some cussed irony there, Nick thought, remembering his brother. What had poor old Sam got to do with the coupling of his wife with his nephew.

Whatever the rights and wrongs of the choice of names, not one person in Higgins Bend believed that the baby was Angela's and the father the unfortunate Dickie Leech, but everyone was too timid or too polite to speak out loud and clear.

"It sure makes a feller wonder what the world's coming to," Chuck Turner said in the bunkhouse. He shot a stream of saliva and nicotine at the spittoon.

"What's gotten into your head now?" Billy Lilley asked.

Chuck scratched his long nose and shifted a wad of tobacco from one cheek to the other.

"Well, old buddy, for one thing. Take that young 'un up there at Miz Bridge's. You can't tell me…"

"Now cut that out, willya," Billy Lilley said.

That was about the size of it. Even though folks were curious, gossip was muted partly because the Plouviers were respected and all except Bridget well liked, and Angela, though a hard case, some said, appeared to have done well out of the intrigue, and no one would grudge her that or say a word against the late lamented Dickie Leech. So on the whole the township was prepared to let little lives unfold and mind its own business, not that there wasn't a lot of chatter through pursed lips and behind closed doors.

Part of the deal was that Angie should live with Aunt Sammy and bring the baby up at her ranch house. For three years young Richard throve in the foothills of the Rocky mountains under sun and shower and ice and snow. Angela changed him, fed him, and burped him while the two sisters-in-law, one at once natural mother and great aunt, the other the youthful grandmother, fussed solicitously and jealously on the sidelines.

"I wish Dot Howard hadn't died in that awful fire," Marie said and then could have bitten off her tongue.

"I wish my Dickie hadn't either. But then he did, didn't he? And there's nothing any of us can do about it. Can us?"

"I'm truly sorry, Angela. I shouldn't have said that."

Angela fastened a large safety pin.

"You don't think I can manage him, eh? This little monkey."

She grasped the baby under its armpits and held it up to her face and made raspberry noises at it. Young Richard's head wobbled on his fragile neck.

"Be careful," Bridget said.

03❧80

Hector and Bob risked their own necks in rescuing the badly wounded sergeant who had bawled out Bob before the battle, but they did not get a medal for it, not even mentioned in dispatches, because he died at the regimental aid post and there were no witnesses to their bravery. The thought of winning a medal never entered their heads anyway. They had been pinned down in the mud for hours. A second wave of infantry was sent in and was similarly cut to ribbons. And a third. They'd dragged the sergeant out of a shell-hole after dark and got him back to the aid post where the forearms and apron of the Medical Officer, Captain Tebbins from Toronto, were soaked in blood.

cg ❁ ৪০

One afternoon when the last of the snow had melted, though you could never be certain that it was the last, Angie was giving young Dick a bottle and Aunt Sammy was sitting on the other side of the fireplace with her dog resting its slavering jaw on her knee. It too was jealous of Angela and the baby. Bridget thought how she could well be nursing the baby herself, and at times her breasts were still painful with unwanted milk. Angie was looking particularly pleased with herself and thinking that the child might well have been really hers. Hector had been coming on real strong those nights by the river and she need only to have given him the slightest encouragement instead of mocking him, and then what would these stuck-up Plouviers have said. Couldn't have been worse than screwing your auntie, could it? And getting her in the family way. She laughed aloud, remembering how Hector had stumbled along the river bank trying to hide his erection. She glanced across at Bridget. A lovely lady still, no doubt about it, but for heavens sakes, she was so old...really. A different generation. Lines showing on that beautiful face. How had Hector had the nerve to, you know? He was only a boy and he'd even been terrified of her, Angie, down by the river. Not that she would have let him go all the way. Oh brother, no, not without being married. The scar from the burn on her chin was scarcely noticeable.

Until his father warned him off her he was always getting over-excited, she could tell from the bulge in his pants. They had attended the same one-room school together. He talked different, not only French, which he never used in front of the other kids, but his English. It weren't like his dad's. More proper, la-di-da, like this one's, the real mother's, sitting by the fire here. But he was never too proud with the kids at school and lotsa the time he spoke like them. He was sweet on Angie, and he would have you-know'd her, she was certain about that, if he'd had any idea of how to start, if she'd helped him. Angela smiled secretly as she patted his baby's back.

"Now what are you trying to do, Hector? Don't put your hand there. Them rocks is sticking in my back. Watch it."

The bed of the river as it flowed by Higgins Bend was formed with thousands of smooth round boulders, about the size of curling rocks, and they spread upwards on either bank. You could slip on them when you were fishing, and as for a place for lovers to sport, well forget it. Hector, driven by an inner fury, had tried.

"Would you like to lie down, Angie? Just for a wee while."

"What, on these dumb rocks? Oh boy! You crazy or sump'en? I'd catch my death of cold."

"Naw. It's a warm night, Ange. All I gotta do is move a few of these babies. And put my coat down for you and you'll be as snug as a bug in a rug."

The boulders looked white in the moonlight. Hector worked maniacally, shifting the heavy rocks until he cleared a space about the size of a grave. He'd persuaded Angela to lie down on his jacket.

"Here, you be careful of my dress. My dad ain't no rich rancher, you know."

It was the only half decent dress she had. Hector lay beside her but a couple of feet above her, heroically on the rocks, on the edge of the grave.

"What you think you're doing up there, Hector?"

She'd teased him mercilessly in the short time she'd gone out with him, she realized now, dandling his baby. He had slipped from his perch down on top of her, skinning his knees as he did so. She had received him passionately in a tight embrace. They were only a boy and girl, cowed by parents, but if Angie had not been strong willed that night when the blood was surging and the hormones raging, God knows what could have happened. Beyond their hard breathing they could hear the moonlit waters of the river running seductively by.

"Yes, you little devil," she crooned to the baby. "You could have been mine, that's for sure."

Bridget rose from her chair.

"Come on boy," she said to her dog. "Let's take a hike."

ෆ❀ෂ

Captain Tebbins gave the sergeant a perfunctory examination and shrugged.

"He's just about gone. There's nothing I can do for him. Put him on that stretcher over there."

Hector took the dying shoulders and Bob the feet. The sarge was an awful mess. The two boys hung around trying to clean the mud off their rifles.

"Where do we go, sir?"

The doctor looked as though he were asleep on his feet.

"I don't fucking know. And I don't fucking well care," he shouted.

All around him were the wounded waiting to be attended to. He sat on a camp stool and rinsed his hands in a basin which seemed to be full of blood.

"Sorry, lads." He took off his sodden crimson apron and reached for a fresh one from a wooden chest of bandages and swabs. "It's one monumental screw up. There's not an officer left alive for you to report to, far as I can see. You'd best hang around here and give me a hand."

೦ಬ⚜೮೦

Although she went away, sometimes for long stretches, they were long difficult years for Aunt Sammy watching her baby grow under Angie's mothering. And there was always the war, the heavy, dragging, remote war, and a feeling of being inadequate while the young men suffered and perished. Knitting socks and woollen caps for soldiers was not much of a heroic compensation, bloody boring in fact. She often wondered how she had survived the time between Sam's death and her brief affair with Hector. Of course her nephew and Michelle had been an interest and a delight, took her out of herself, up to the point of that unfortunate madness. She became, slowly and reluctantly, with less hurt and bitterness, used to Angela's arrogant presence and the more attractive young Richard grew the less she regretted not having an abortion. How could she when daily she discovered so much of herself and her past invested in this fragile bundle? And despite herself, her internal agitation, relations were changing. Ever since she'd disclosed her pregnancy the warmth and trust that had existed between her and Marie and Nick had been at risk, but now old loves and loyalties returned and the three lined up against Angie.

She put Mike on a leash when she saw Marie and Chuck Turner in the newly dug garden.

"Isn't it early for planting out? It's weeks to go to Victoria Day."

"Pansies is tough, Miz Bridget. I seed them growing as chipper as could be with frost and ice all around they."

A wonderful day, sun bright in the Alberta blue but a nip in the wind and two snotty rivulets flowed steadily from Chuck's long nose. Mike sniffed at the man's gammy leg and Aunt Sammy pulled her dog back hard so that he stood on his hind legs.

"I'll be off for another barrow load of manure then."

"I shouldn't bother with any more today, Chuck."

The sisters-in-law watched as he pushed the wheelbarrow towards the tool shed, progressing with his obscene limp which threw his back into distressing angles at every step.

"I believe he exaggerates that limp of his more every time I see him."

"Don't be mean, Bridge. Poor Chuck!"

The dog lowered his hindquarters and sat, tongue hanging out, looking contentedly from one woman to the other.

"How's young Richard? Is Angela getting unbroken nights yet?"

"Marie. You were over there this morning. Nothing has changed since then."

Aunt Sammy looked towards Chuck heading for the bunkhouse, but not really seeing him.

"I'm beginning to think, Marie, that your scheme of Angela coming to live with me was not such a good idea after all. Watching my own son grow in someone else's arms."

Mike got up, stretched, licked his chops and pushed his haunch against Aunt Sammy's skirt.

"I'm sorry for you, cherie, you know that. But we have been over all this a thousand times. You remember when you came to me at your wits' end…"

"I know, I know. I agreed. But there was so much I didn't realize. What a little bitch Angela is, for instance."

The indictment was in Bridget's loftiest, most contemptuous voice. She bent down to scratch her dog's ear and he nuzzled up to her.

"I feel fockin' trapped, between the divil and the deep blue sea, as my old mither used to say, poor soul."

ଔ ❀ ଓ

She felt trapped the day after she'd been nearly mauled by a grizzly. And embarrassed, being left in the lodge with Nick and he behaving the way he did. The tall strong rancher was almost in tears for months afterwards begging her not to say anything about it. Since his wife was seven months pregnant with Michelle, Marie had not come with them. Naturally they were all so much younger in those days, but that was still no excuse for what happened.

"Why don't you come with us, old buddy? We won't be all that long away and Marie says she doesn't mind. Glad to get you from under her feet. Dot Howard'll come to see her every day. And we won't be gone more than ten days. At the most."

How different Sam, her husband, had been from his brother. You'd think that they'd been born of different mothers. Where Nick's mouth was set in an uncompromising line Sam's was mobile, thick lipped, feminine. Nick's face a mask, Sam's open, revealing emotions. Nick, tall and lean, Sam shorter, a little, not much, thicker, wavy hair, his eyes caressed women, appraisingly. Conversely women's eyes appraised Nick as he walked aloof and alone, even after he married Marie.

"That's okay by me, darling," Marie had said. "I'm not much fun anyways, lumbering around like a big elephant."

The three of them, Nick, Sam, Bridget set off for Lake Clare riding their own horses, with Nick and Sam taking turns to lead the pack horse. They only needed tentage on the journey because there was a lodge at the lake which the Plouvier brothers had helped finance. The weather in September was always unpredictable, but to begin with this one was exceptionally mild, hot even. As they rode along the trails to Exshaw, Canmore, Banff, they stripped off their outer clothing. It got frosty at night and the mountains brought early shadows, but Bridge was comfortable enough sharing their one tent with the two men. Nick was delicacy itself and got up early in the morning to light a fire and prepare breakfast and give them an opportunity for a holiday embrace.

Maybe we'll hit the jackpot this time, she thought, on the hard ground. Perhaps this'll do the trick and I'll get pregnant. In Ireland girls got in the family way as easy as drinking a glass of water. As they heard Nick chopping wood outside, the tent began to light under the rising sun and soon the smell of wood smoke and frying bacon drifted in as she lay in Sam's arms. It had been a long haul from that tiny room in Dublin where the drunk Michael Donnelly had tried to seduce his daughter, through the county drawing rooms where she'd had to pamper the Lady Icen's whims, through travels with her in Europe, Morocco, Egypt, and finally to Alberta and this blessed hour lying in the early morning on a mountainside. Some of the toffee-nosed bozos she'd dumped along the way would have had fits to see her locked in an embrace with a cowboy.

ଔ❁ଃ

"Come on, Bridie, old girl. I'll race you to the Rufus Stone."

There had been the occasional man who was half decent, did not look down on her, did not think he had the right to fumble her as soon as it got dark. There'd been the beginnings of one wild romance when she was riding in the New Forest. Cecil, was he, Cedric...? Partington, Petworthy. Cecil, she was sure. He called her Bridie, the only one who did, who said he loved her Irish brogue even though she was desperately trying to mask it with his own kind of adenoidal diphthongs. Lady Icen had seen to it that she had lessons from a riding master in Gloucestershire, side-saddle as befitted a lady.

"The chuck wagon's been, you guys," Nick called from outside the tent.

She and Sam looked at each other self-consciously and dried themselves off. Nick was a marvellous cook to have in the back country, and as a matter of course they expected the flapjacks and bacon to be ready for them to eat round the campfire in the melting frost.

"Coming," Bridget shouted, pulling on her clothes. "You are a honey, Nick."

Though he had the drawling vocables of his class, Cecil had been as different as chalk from cheese from Reggie Slatters, the chinless knight, who had bought her for a couple of quid in Dublin, and a slew of other leisured bozos. She remembered as she laced up her boots in the tent that she had been allowed out for once unhampered by the presence and demands of her patron. She remembered the day she had raced Cecil in the New Forest when he'd won easily because he rode astride. He was so different from those others.

"Is that all it is?" she asked when they reached the Rufus memorial. "Do you have to kiss it, like the Blarney Stone?"

"It's very historical, don't you know. One's heritage and all that, Bridie. William the Second. He was killed right here in a hunting accident."

"I thought you said Rupert."

"No, Rufus. Same fellow, Bridie, old sport. William Rufus. Some say he was murdered. What are you laughing at? Dash it all, you Irish have simply no respect."

"I'm so sorry, Cecil." Her face was crimson and contorted.

She jumped down from her horse without waiting for him to help her and leant with her head against an oak, her shoulders shaking in uncontrollable mirth. A grazing forest pony looked round at her. She tried to compose herself. She did not want to ruin this lovely day of freedom, untrammelled by the frightfully formal benevolence of her patron.

"I'm sorry..."

"Not to worry...." He grinned. "I'm not being serious."

"It's just something Lady Icen—"

She burst into peals of unladylike laughter.

"Come on, Bridie. Share it with a chap."

"Oh dear." She rubbed her eyes and looked speculatively at him.

"You see Lady Icen is very proud of this collection of glass ornaments. She keeps them in a precious cabinet in the drawing room." She snorted. "They are called Rupert's Balls."

The pony watched her as she staggered around, holding her stomach and the nice thing about Cecil had been that though looking startled at first he had begun to laugh with her.

"And she said, my lady did, if they get the slightest scratch on them, the balls, they have a little glass tail, they explode.."

They'd flung themselves, hooting with laughter, into each other's arms.

"Exploding balls!"

"A lady shouldn't even know about...dash it. I mean to say."

She had seen her father's once when he was coming at her with his trousers down. Swinging Irish gonads. Tears were streaming down Cecil's cheeks as he held her. It was just as well Lady Icen did not happen along at that moment. They left Wiltshire the next day for Paris and Aunt Sammy never saw Cecil again. For her part, the Lady Icen kept a strict eye on her protegée as they toured the capitals of Europe.

"Come on Sam, lad," Bridget said, tugging at her husband's hand. "Let's get our teeth round that bacon. I'm famished."

ଔ❀ଓ

It snowed quite heavily, wet snow, the afternoon they arrived at the lodge, and though the warm September sun shone as bright as ever the next day it never completely melted the white stuff all the time they were there. The lodge was a remarkable piece of forest architecture to find in such a remote spot, expertly put together with shaped logs, some of them gigantic, far more weather proof than many of the houses in Higgins Bend, or Calgary come to that. A few of the ranchers had clubbed together to build it, a place to get away to without paying pricey hotel bills for cramped rooms and indifferent meals. Of course at the lodge you had to fend for yourself. A hermit trapper, Shortass Frank, kept an eye on it for them when he wasn't drunk or attending his lines.

Bridget kicked the snow off her boots and pushed open the front door. A rudimentary building as yet but with a continuous wooden floor, small but adequate windows, half a dozen bedrooms with doors, roughly walled with logs, iron bedsteads, potential for a second storey. It stood on a tongue of land so that it had Lake Clare on three sides, affording views of mountain and water of infinite and heart-stopping variety.

"This place needs a good clean, Shortass."

"You orta tell me when you is coming over, ma'am."

Frank was a small hunched man, clothes mainly of animal skins, sharp brown eyes looking out of a face covered in bristles like a hedgehog. They paid him a pittance.

"Then I can get 'er all swep' out for yez."

The front door opened into the main room with a large fireplace and a long white pine table running down the middle as in the refectory of a monastery. To the left of the fireplace a doorless opening to a kitchen with utensils, pots, cutlery, tin plates, mugs. Nick was watering the horses —a well had been sunk round the back—and Sam came in with bedding rolls from the pack horse. He dropped them on the monastic table and Bridget embraced him from behind.

"This has got to be the most beautiful place in the world, my dear old Sam. Lovelier than anything I've ever seen, anywhere."

"And you're the one should know, ain't you? The places you bin to...."

Her husband turned to face her, his eyes half-closed, shining in sexual mockery. The snow had still not melted from their clothes. Sam Plouvier still flirted with his wife and she loved him for it.

Cecil had written a couple of letters to Bridget which, she suspected, Lady Icen had steamed open. He had a lovely home in Wiltshire, or his father had, but Cecil would inherit it in the natural order of things. Thinking back, Aunt Sammy wondered why she had not been knifed or poisoned by any number of ambitious mothers in the county. Maybe that was why Lady Icen had steered her adroitly away, opened her letters, stood on guard. She had to protect her own butt in society and it would never do, would it, for her companion, sufficiently pleasant, well-mannered, pretty enough but nowhere near top drawer, to ensnare eligible bachelors wherever she went. Certainly not, my dear. Not on, Penelope. Cecil's letters were warm enough, so far as his imagination allowed, but discreetly decorous so that Lady Icen could allow them through to the person they were addressed to. Bridget always believed that if her lady had let her play her cards right she could have ended up mistress of some bountiful acres adjacent to the New Forest.

They slept the sleep of the just in the mountain air and Bridge was up betimes, foregoing some early dawn passion, to cook the breakfast. The simple fact of being there comprised the holiday. The brothers fished the lake, lazily, not in earnest. They were not as keen as some of the other ranchers on hunting and had not brought their guns, and Bridge was glad about that. The first morning they walked a couple of miles through the spruce and larch forest to a natural clearing where hot springs bubbled from the bowels of the earth.

"With a bit of labour and planning,"Nick said, "we could fix this up and make a bathing spot of it."

The sun lit up the tops of the mountains to the west of them as though they were the backdrop to the world. Yesterday's snow topped the spruce trees and wreathed their sides. A faint smell of rotten eggs rose from the warm water, mixing with the cool of the wilderness.

"We could go in now," Sam said. He looked at his wife. "Skinny-dipping."

"Yahoo," Nick shouted, astonishing them both with a phony cowboy yell. He sat on a boulder with his long legs stretched out towards the springs. His hard face broke into a grin.

"You know what? You're just a couple of lecherous little boys. You won't get me doing any skinny-dipping, I can tell you. Just think what that sulphur will do to you. You'll have sores all over your bodies, like lepers."

Bridge, also sitting on a rock dried by the sun, tugged at her long grey skirt, pulling it above her ankles. It was fairly thick because a cotton dress, or even linen, would be useless for mountain mornings. There would have been no point in bringing her smart riding habit on a journey like this. She'd worn it that day in the New Forest with its exquisitely tailored skirt draped over the soft leather boots. Cecil had commented on it gallantly. Even so, with rougher boots and skirt, a high-necked blouse, a fitted jacket with square shoulders, riding gloves, hat with an Indian feather in it, she looked too smart for a mountain woman. Her patron had said on many occasions that a lady should always keep up appearances. No backsliding, never allow standards to deteriorate.

She was not an unkind woman and Bridget had not led a miserable existence under her tutelage, far from it. She owed her a lot. She had after all plucked her rough as they come from the incestuous stews of Dublin. As Bridget (she had only recently been christened Aunt Sammy in Hector's baby talk) looked at the steam rising from the hot pool, she pondered once again why her lady had taken her under her wing. Her patron liked decorative wealth, fine clothes, food, furniture, pictures. Bridget smiled secretly, fondly, as she remembered precious trivia like Rupert's Balls. And privileged space and elegant architecture to house her possessions and to live in. Lady Icen believed she had a divine right to the titled and the landed, even the brainless ones and no doubt she was pleased to own, without undue ostentation, a pretty companion like Miss Donnelly in constant attendance. But there had never been any untoward hanky-panky, thank God. She had heard on her travels of some quite repugnant practices to which women in her position had been subjected. Governesses had it worse though, dirty minded, precocious little brats, aping their fathers, doing the most disgusting things and then lying about them and putting the blame on the defenceless teacher. Nothing like that in the Icen household.

"Can you see those mountain goats up there?" Sam asked. "By that gap."

Bridge had taken off her hat. She screwed up her eyes against the warming sun.

"Oh yes. Lovely. And I'm jolly glad you are not rushing up to kill them."

When they arrived at the Gloucestershire house after Dublin, she had been astonished at its size and apparently limitless acres. She had been even more astonished to find a Lord Icen, lurking practically like a fugitive in his monied halls, and it took years for the young, raw girl from the Dublin bogs to begin to appreciate what was going on in this marriage. Or rather, what was not going on. Though she shrugged it off like the hardened slum girl she was, she was conscious of the deep sadness and irony of her own mother's marriage, but even so Mrs. Donnelly still shared her bed with her impossible father. The Icens, she soon learned, did not sleep together and for long enough Bridget believed that to have separate bedrooms and as little physical communion as possible was the aristocratic way.

"It was weird," she confided to Sam in the early days of her own marriage, luxuriating in her husband's boisterous love-making. "Lord Icen crept about that enormous place like a fockin' ghost. They hardly spoke more than twenty words a day to each other. Good morning. I trust you slept well, dear. Good evening. That sort of thing. He'd come in to meals and sit silently at the head of the table. A long, long table it was, Sam. All laid with shining glasses, silver knives, forks, dishes. She'd sit a mile away from him at the other end when we had guests and chatter away thirteen to the dozen. You've got to believe it. The poor ladies, though, on either side of her husband, were always embarrassed, not knowing what to say or which way to turn. When we were on our own we'd sit up at his end of the table on either side of him. He would always nod politely to me and then get on with his soup."

"What did he do with himself all day?" Sam asked, lying back on his pillow.

"God knows. He was silent as a wraith wandering round the house and grounds. As spooky as the Kilkenny cats, though I could never see him spitting and fighting in a thousand years. Always dodging out of the way he was, just disappearing round the corner, hiding in the carriage house, the stables, the tool shed. Sometimes when he'd finished his lunch, he always ended it with a piece of cheddar cheese with a spoonful of mustard spread over it as though he were a hedge-cutter in the ditch, then he'd move his lips in a silent grace, give his lady and me a little bow and take off. Often we'd see him by the pig pens sniffing the air as though he enjoyed the stink. The smell of hog shit is really something, as you well know, Sam. He had one of those enormous aristocratic schnozzles and he regularly wore brown leather leggings and corduroy breeches as he went about his estates. A greasy old hat with the brim turned down. You might find him anywhere or not catch a glimpse of him for days apart from meal times. In a cold wind there was always a dew-drop at the end of that great beak of a nose which he'd dab at with an enormous red spotted handkerchief, just like a labourer's. He'd honk into it making a noise like a foghorn as though he were punishing his nose for daring to drip. It's little wonder his wife didn't go to bed with him. Imagine that on the next pillow. Sometimes he'd ride over to inspect the tenants' cottages. Or maybe when my lady and I were taking a turn round the home paddock before tea, beautiful grass it was Sam, we'd catch a glimpse of him in the distance prodding at his herd of Highland cattle. Funny little beasts they are. Have you ever seen them?"

"I've heard of them. Kinda rancher then, was he, your lord?"

"You idiot, Sam." She smiled fondly. "But hold on here. Maybe that's not so crazy as it sounds. I suppose he was in a way, kind of. A fockin' stinkin' rich rancher though, Sammy boy."

She mixed her accents and her idioms when talking to her husband. Sometimes when she was having an orgasm all her slum obscenities and cuss words would come out to Sam's amusement and delight.

"I never know which is the real you, Bridge," he would say.

Lady Icen's asexuality, if that's what it was, did not dawn on the young Bridget for long enough. Over the years, Lady Icen saw to it that a veneer of her sort of culture, a curious mixture of the shires and London, a dash of Paris, was imposed on the slum lore Bridget had assimiliated in the gutters, a low Dublin cunning which embraced most likely an earthier knowledge of carnal matters than Lady Icen was ever to possess. She sprinkled the young girl with a passing appreciation of art, literature, music, horses, hunts, gardening, trees and meadows, the adjuncts of decorative domesticity, food and wines, dress, hair, deportment, manners. But of fucking, nothing. Of breeding of cattle, horses at stud, yes. Of men and women in bed, no.

Information of this sort, intimate details of a world light years removed from the ranch, would delight Sam. He would chuckle in that throaty way which Bridget so loved as they were playing backgammon in the evenings. In their brief marriage they had been sufficient to each other.

"You mean to tell me that your old lord never got his jollies with the missus? Never once? Never one little dippity-doo?" He leered across the card table at his wife.

"I should say from the time I arrived, no. Not once."

"How can you be so flaming certain?"

"Because a flaming woman knows."

On this occasion Bridge was speaking with polished neutrality, her even, detached phrasing totally removed from the sense of her remarks. She might have been talking of mouse droppings by the main larder which the maids complained of to the butler, or the latest tittle-tattle about the hunt ball. But even so she could not conceal the deep musicality of her voice, the plebeian warmth of the Irish coming through in spite of herself.

"Remember I told you when I first met her in that hotel. How I thought she was a saint, a princess, a beautiful lady all rolled into one?" She had fudged some of the detail of her first meeting, omitted altogether the business of the sale and the part played by Sir Reginald Slatters.

"I thought she had everything going for her. She was not very tall, quite a tiny little thing really, but that did not matter. Her complexion was perfect, she did not need half the cosmetics she used. Lovely teeth, no bad breath. I ought to know, I was pretty close to her all those years. She didn't have any body odour. My God, Sam. You should have smelt some of those high-born ladies, the ghastly, decayed pong that came through the pints of perfume they sloshed on themselves. Gamey as rotten meat, enough to make a cat sick."

Sam rolled the dice and Bridget gazed out of their window to the road leading to Nick's and Marie's house.

"Remember that maroon dress I told you about? The one she was wearing when I first set eyes on her? No you don't, but I shall never forget it and that was only one out of hundreds. She was always so careful and clever about her appearance. A great ritual and discussion with me every morning. Shall I wear this, shall I wear that? Will this necklace go with the green gown? But what was it all for, Mr. Plouvier?"

"I guess if she wasn't getting it from the lord, why, there'd be lotsa the guys hoping, eh, buzzing round her like flies round a dead steer."

"That's what I'm trying to tell you Sam. They were, but it wasn't a bit like what you think."

Perhaps because of a repressed horror of her mother's chronically miserable condition or of the abuse of her father or even because of the constant presence of Lady Icen, Bridget never felt undue sexual craving during her days in society, not enough to put her off balance. Normal longings, but never desperate. As she became more self-assured, tuned into language and behaviour, she enjoyed the company and attentions of men that came her way. Quite ironically, despite the depravity of her upbringing, something of the discipline of her church's teaching remained with her, though what with Lady Icen's watchfulness it was mostly not needed. There had been one or two other Cecils whom she might have slept with had her lady been less on guard. The tight rein wasn't because Lady Icen was jealous of her, that was the curious thing. It soon became obvious to Bridget that her mistress received her share of propositioning. The world and his wife gossiped about the marital puzzle of the Icens and, as Sam guessed, there was no shortage of would-be adulterers lining up to take their chance. They, the aspiring courtiers, young and old, did not slaver and scratch their balls, of course not, there was a proper and subtle code to be observed in this sort of casual seduction, but whatever the method they used, however heated or smarmy, they were all turned sweetly away by Lady Icen, politely but firmly with no offence taken or given.

"How can I put this, Sam? She liked the fellers. She loved their company. Gave them the glad eye and would flirt and chew the fat with them, as cool as a cucumber she was in front of their wives, their mothers, their daughters. In front of Lord Misery whenever he was around. But he never paid much attention anyways, and he took off from any social occasion as soon as he could. Do you know I believe she could have undressed and lain down on the Wilton carpet at his feet and screwed with any number of those guys and he would not have batted an eyelid? Of course she wouldn't have. As soon as they came on strong they'd get the heave-ho and they'd totter away looking puzzled and hurt."

"That little lady sounds to me like a goddamn cock-teaser. A real bitch. I would never have thought it of her when she was here."

"But she wasn't, Sam. I don't know what made her behave like that. Some sort of barrier. Maybe some strangeness which made her delight in seeing those poor jerks crawl away. Maybe not all put together, a part missing, I don't know. Perhaps she had a terror of the bed part, but she never gave that impression. I can't imagine Lord Icen courting her or how she came to marry him. There was money and land on both sides, which could explain a lot. We never discussed anything like that, though she sometimes, on the sly, asked me about me and men. She wanted to pry into my experience in Dublin. It was as though no man had ever laid a finger on her, never stroked her hair, let alone patted her on the ass. And it didn't matter how much I denied it she was sure I was some sort of prostitute. I had to be, hadn't I, coming from where I did."

"It sure beats me how you put up with her so long."

"I hadn't much choice to begin with, had I now? But she wasn't bad. I owe her a lot, Sam."

On the walk back from the hot springs they reached the edge of the lake and looked across at the lodge. Bridget stood between the two brothers, slim, the glint of the mountain sun on her raven hair, elegant in rough western clothes, a beauty herself, her whole being slack and receptive to the placidity of the water, to the awesome dignity of the mountain tops, to the nerveless peace and quiet.

಄⚜ೲ

Bridget felt the heat of the grizzly's breath on her cheek and she could smell its rancid odour, a small matter compared with the greater eventuality of dismemberment and death. It made snuffling, grunting noises as it crouched over her. Its savage jaws must only be inches away from her neck. She hoped she had not peed herself, that would be too embarrassing for words. They say that at the point of drowning your whole life passes in front of your eyes. Hers didn't, and she was surely going to die. Only maniacally chosen selections of the past appeared—pictures, memories, regrets—and those only briefly. Most of the time her mind was blank with grey fear. God, it would be ten times worse if she shat herself. But then who would worry about an excrement-fouled, half-eaten corpse. Certainly not Bridget Plouvier. A parching terror prevented her from weeping.

"Never get yourself caught between a sow and her cubs."

So Nick, Sam, Shortass Frank, and ten thousand others had warned. But how were you to know at any fockin' time from one hour to the next where the fockin' cubs were and when they were going to be separated from the fockin' sow. At that moment with the grizzly bent over her as though she were going to rape her, something wrong there, Bridget would have given a fortune to be in the sottish Michael Donnelly's house, even with his pants half down and his braces off his shoulders, his sweaty flannel shirt hanging out and his grey Irish balls dangling. The sow gave her a cuff on the shoulder, and she tried not to cry out with the shock and pain. If she were playing dead it would be no use making a noise.

"If you do get face to face with a grizzly and there's no way of backing off, then you gotta play dead," they said, the fockin' experts.

Wonderful! Why should it matter to a darn great bear, foaming at mouth, whether its next meal were dead or alive.

"They live on berries as a rule. Roots, stuff like that. Maybe small rodents."

Get real, willya, mister. Get yourself under a big fockin' sow who's sizing up which part of you she'll bite and who doesn't seem to care diddly for her cubs. Where were the little bastards anyways?

Bridget fluttered her eyes open for a split second and saw the snow falling silently into Lake Clare. It was their second full day at the lodge and the brothers were busy fixing a new rope on the well and messing about with chores like that, kidding each other. She decided to take a hike on her own. The sun shone and it was still warm.

"I guess you can take care of yourself," Sam said.

There was no path directly round the edge of the lake. It wasn't like taking a stroll on the promenade at Brighton or having a picnic on the banks of the Severn and watching the bore come up. This was wilderness. Cecil would not have fitted in here. A roughly defined track worked its way up and down along one side of the lake, through the spruce and undergrowth, rich and coloured with small leaves and berries, and descending at intervals to the rocky edge of the water. Sometimes the trail was no more than a tricky ledge, twenty feet or more above the lake. Bridget loved being on her own like this, taking in the fragility of the hidden flowers, the secret plants and shapes under the regal trees. She wished she'd brought her puppy with her, but they'd decided to leave him at home at the ranch, not that he would have done much damage to the undergrowth.

Just as well she hadn't, she thought as she lay below the grizzly, her left foot, which the bear had damaged, lying at an awkward angle and hurting like hell. The weather had suddenly changed. She'd got down to the water's edge when the sun disappeared under a mass of grey cloud which had surged over the mountain ridges from nowhere. A sudden wind started whipping wrinkles across the placid face of the lake and soon they changed to angry waves.

"What a nuisance! What an idiot!"

She had not brought a coat or a hat. She stood on a little pebbly clearing by the lake with a tongue of rough sand in which she started to write her name with the toe of her boot. Behind her was a belt of thorny creepers and high grasses and then the trees. A few flakes started to swirl, taking their time to reach the earth and water. She'd got as far as the "d," she remembered with fearful clarity afterwards, when she heard the snarl and looked round to see this great beast waddling deliberately on her hind legs towards her. She collapsed to the sand on her half-finished name more out of terror than design and felt the animal trample on or claw or chew her foot. She must have fainted for a moment, and through some Celtic instinct of survival or obstinacy she "played dead" when she recovered. Unless the cubs were fooling around in the middle of Lake Clare there was no way she could have been caught between the sow and them. It was an unbelievably long long five minutes, ten, thirty, an hour, she had no idea, that she lay rigid in deathly terror, not much acting needed, whilst the fockin' bear snuffled around and the snow fell thicker and thicker and the wind blew icier. Finally she dared to lift her head. There was a fresh pile of shit, not Bridget's thank God, and awesome pawprints in the snow, but no wild animal. She got slowly up, shivering, cramped, and limped slowly back along the trail. It was hard going on the mauled foot, which was now numb, as was her shoulder and the rest of her for that matter. She was shrammed through as her mother would say on a raw Dublin morning.

೧୫୫୦

Sam met her before she had struggled her way along a hundred yards of slippery trail. The paralysing shock was giving way to hysteria. She kept looking fearfully about, and when her husband met her she was crawling like a wild creature, her breast heaving, her throat racked with dry sobs.

"What the heck, Bridge. What the heck has happened?"

He crouched down and gathered her to him, and she winced as he touched her shoulder. She looked up at him with puzzled, wounded eyes.

"A fockin' grizzly. With no fockin' cubs."

She passed out. The snow and wind were intensifying and causing a whiteout so grotesquely different from the late summer afternoon she had set out in. Sam would carry her for twenty yards and stop and ask her if she were warm enough and then on again. After half an hour—was that all it was?—of this slow progress, Nick loomed out of the whiteness and clasped his arms round them both.

"I came as soon as I seed you'd gone. I guessed you'd come searching for her." He looked at Bridget. "Christ, Sam! Is she okay?"

"A bitch of a grizzly mauled her. I can't tell how bad."

Between them they carried her along the slippy switchback trail to the lodge.

"Split some logs, Shortass. Lotsa them. And build the fire right up."

They pulled one of the beds into the main room in front of the fireplace.

"You get her wet things off of her, Sam. I'll go help Shortass. Then we'll take a look at that foot and her shoulder."

"You don't have to be shy, Nick."

"I know that."

They piled the hissing logs on the fire and a huge heat came from it. Shortass made coffee and poured a slug of rye into each mug.

"Here you go. Give the lady some of this. It's better'n no medicine."

The brothers stood at the bottom of the bed where Bridget's injured foot stuck modestly out of a blanket.

"What do you make of this, Shortass?"

The little man peered from his bristly face, serious and solemn. From the bruising and claw marks round the swollen ankle a thin red streak was moving up Bridget's calf.

"Them critters is bung full of poison. In their teeth, their claws. You orta get her down off of this mountain. Pronto."

03❀80

Through the haze of her delirium Bridget had heard bits and pieces of their conversation, just like that in the adventure novels she and Lady Icen had read before they visited the wild west. She could feel the heat of the fire on her flushed face. She did not come to full consciousness when she had fits of waking, scarcely breaking the surface at irregular intervals. She had a vague recollection of Nick fondling her breast but that was stupid. It must have been her husband, Sam, who had every right to fondle at the proper time and place. But why would he be playing games like that at a time like this? Weird. Don't be daft, our Bridgie, her mother would say, you're always imagining. She laughed in her sleep. It must be the rye whisky Shortass put in her coffee. He said something about poison, too, what the devil was that all about. Then she heard them discussing the North-West Mounted Police post. Would the constable be there or not? Why all the fuss? Did it really matter? Nothing mattered except her foot was as sore as hell. She dozed off.

"I wish you'd let me go," Nick said.

"Nope. It's my job. Shortass can take the pack hoss and come with me. He can find his way anywhere, in a storm, in the dark. He knows the country round here like the back of his hand. You stay and take good care of Bridge till we get back with a horse litter. There's got to be a stretcher at the police post. This'll be a lesson. We should always take one with us. Maybe we'll get her out tomorrow."

She distinctly felt her nipple being pinched this time and tried to remove the intruding hand and hadn't the energy to do so and slipped back into her half consciousness. If the chinless bastard Sir Reginald

Slatters or any of his slimy kind wanted to grope down the front of a scullery maid's dress, he did so, and there was nothing the poor girl could do about his impudence. If she had complained to her mistress, that ineffable sleaze would have alleged, like Potiphar's wife, that the maid was trying to seduce him and she would have been sacked on the spot. That had been the way of the sexes ever since the first caveman had clubbed his mate before copulating with her. But if jawless fockin' Reggie had tried a similar trick with a lady of breeding, a genuine product of the top drawer, his action would in most cases have been judged a gross liberty and he would have been drummed out of society and most likely been challenged to a duel. To that limited extent the female lot, the privileged crust of it, had improved over the millennia.

During her time with Lady Icen she'd come across a number of would-be bosom dippers and ass gropers, but after the attempted improprieties of her dad, Michael Donnelly, on her own person when she was a kid in the slums, their cavalier attempts were as chicken feed. Moral: if you wanted to learn how to defend yourself from male insults get yourself an abusive father. You betcha. But Nick? Her brother-in-law taking advantage of her? Hell no! She was gradually assimilating a third language, cowboy English, but only when talking to herself or to Sam. Lying feverish under the rough blanket she had to admit that there were times when Nick stood nearer to her than was necessary. Very close. My brother's very fond of you, Sam said.

◌❀◌

"We've really got to get to know each other, cherie," Marie Louise had said as soon as they became sisters-in-law. "Stand by each other. Support each other. Is that not so?"

The slough was equidistant to the north from the two ranch houses and its water level depended on the seasons. Some years it would dry up altogether. Bridget hadn't been married long to Sam and she and Marie had been walking round the pond when Marie had made her declaration of unqualified love for her husband and her assumption of his for her. No monkey business on either side, no backsliding.

"I must tell you, darling. Nick would hate me to say things like that about him because he is the strong silent man, is it not so? He doesn't like to be praised. I just hope you are as 'appy with Sam."

The water was fringed with bulrushes and reeds, and red-winged blackbirds—aggressive birds who would fly directly at humans to protect their young—were mating and nest building. The greening of the brown grass, the filling out of the trees with leaves, those which lose them in the fall, is not completed in Big Hill country until June when the sun is almost at its highest point.

"It is wonderful how Nick and I met. I never expected to meet my dream knight out here." She gestured lightly with open palm to indicate the slough, the ranch, the mountains, the sky. "He has no eyes for any other woman. At least," she smiled, "I want to believe that. Because if I don't there is something terribly wrong...."

ଓଞ୍ଚ୍ୟୋ

Bridget twisted uneasily under the hot blanket, and this time she grabbed a hand which was between her legs and looked up into Nick's face. The manly jaw was slack, the grim mouth hanging open, his eyes burning as intensely as the log fire, brimming with a passion that both frightened and excited her. It must be some bad dream. She pulled his hand slowly from her crotch. There was no knowing how she might have reacted next except that Nick, with a melodramatic sob, lurched away towards the dining table, stumbled through the front door into the whirling snow.

ଓଞ୍ଚ୍ୟୋ

"I feel fockin' trapped," she said to her sister-in-law.

That was years and years afterwards, an eternity later as they stood by the newly planted pansies in the early springtime, after her son had been handed over to Angela. Mike, her dog, yawned so wide that it looked as though his jaws were going to split at the hinges.

Nick, Sam, Shortass and a North-West Mounted Policeman, had got her out of the mountains with heroic effort. It had been a slow, painful journey and she'd had to go into the Calgary hospital for weeks. Her picture appeared in The Herald. She was swathed in bandages and the news item was headed TERROR IN THE OUTBACK: RANCHER'S WIFE MAULED BY GRIZZLY. Nick had come back that evening out of the snow and made her some cocoa. He would not look her in the eye. The others and the constable had returned with the stretcher and another horse at noon the following day. The storm had stopped as quickly as it had risen and the September sun warmed the angles and clefts of the mountains. Michelle was born whilst Bridget was in hospital and she was happy for Marie Louise. There was no sign of a child for Sam and her, and before there was he had to go and get himself killed on that stupid frozen slough.

If Lady Icen had been alive she would have packed her bags and gone back to Gloucestershire. Nick and Marie were wonderful, Nick atoning perhaps. They took her to their hearts with a spontaneous sympathy. At first stunned and then working out her gnawing grief, Aunt Sammy turned for consolation to Marie's children. Hector was a lovely little guy now, cheeky, grubby at times like any other kid, but filling a raw gulf with his infantile love. He and Michelle brightened the long empty years which were to culminate in that lunacy with her favourite and beloved nephew. The bliss. The aggravation. The humiliation. Now her own child was taken over completely by a regular bitch of a foster mother. Fockin' trapped. She must have been out of her fockin' mind to have agreed to this insane arrangement.

☙❀❧

For three years her son grew in sun and shower, protected from the icy blasts in winter by a jealously devoted Angie. The war years dragged on, the remote war, young men dying, the feeling of inadequacy, the fockin' woolly caps. Many of the wounded had filtered back west and they could be seen wearing their ill-fitting blue suits in the streets of Calgary. Men without arms, legs, eyes, without balls. Letters came irregularly from Hector to his parents. Once he sent Aunt Sammy a picture postcard of a Parisian street scene and asked on the back if she recognized it. Not surprisingly she did. She'd strolled along the Champs Élysées with Lady Icen. Sometimes he ended his letters: Say hi to everyone. Sometimes it was: Love to Michie and Aunt Sammy. Bridget was always given them to read. Nick would occasionally bring one to her and hand it to her with a look of sad irony.

"He doesn't say much, does he?"

"No."

"What is there to say? I try to imagine what it must be like for him and I'm sick to my stomach."

Nick was standing close to her as usual.

"You can't blame yourself. You tried to join up, remember."

"That doesn't help that poor boy much."

"He's a man now, Nick." Bridget blushed. "I should know."

Little Richard grew for three years before her eyes, in her own house, with Angie the important mom, assuming all the maternal airs and graces, and exclusive parental concerns so that at times Bridget could have screamed. She watched, helpless, often with unbearable anguish. During this period the boy's soldier father attacked and retreated over random stretches of French mud. Much of the time he just sat on his ass in a hole in the ground. When Richard began to talk he imitated Michelle and called Bridget Aunt Sammy. The first time she deciphered this name among his childish babble she thought her heart would burst.

Then one chilly January Bridget had been visiting Marie and was standing by the front door on her way out when she saw a tow-haired kid from Higgins Bend haring up the track by the slough.

"What's that youngster in such a hurry for, I wonder?" Marie asked.

A breathless, freckle-faced boy came running up past the Sick Barn.

"Mr. Jenkins says I oughter bring this to you. Damn fast, he says. Move your butt, he says."

"Oh, my God," Bridget said. "It's a telegram."

The war and the harsh climate were marking the faces of the two women, skin drying, worry lines, darkness under the eyes.

"Thanks, son," Marie said. "Thank Mr. Jenkins for me."

The boy stayed where he was.

"Well, ma'am. Aren'tcha going to read her? Mebbe there's a reply"

Marie opened the buff envelope, her hands trembling a little as she read, mouthing the words. She shook her head.

"There isn't a reply."

The breath of all three came out as clouds of vapour in the freezing air. Marie turned to Aunt Sammy and their faces reflected each other's horror.

The battle from which Hector had deserted had swayed to and fro until through sheer exhaustion on both sides it petered out into yet another static confrontation. The Allies had regained some ground, ground which was covered in mud and decaying dead. It was impossible to identify many of the slain, friend or foe, as they were all shovelled together and buried in a mass grave. Those whose ghoulish job it was to try to put some bureaucratic order into the detritus of war—padres, orderlies—managed to collect some identity tabs. Other accounting authorities made calculations from roll calls of the pathetically few survivors in hospitals, transfers to other battalions, to rear echelons. In many cases they could not make definite pronouncements. Something had to be sent out to next of kin, however, especially if the soldiers' letters home ceased to arrive.

MISSING STOP BELIEVED KILLED IN ACTION STOP

Marie read the message out to Aunt Sammy and the boy started back to Mr. Jenkins. Angie came along the garden path holding Richard by the hand. He was well wrapped up against the winter's cold.

# NINE

Hector was aware that when one of the feller's number came up and he was no longer for this world because of a bullet through his brain or a belly full of shrapnel, the military authorities would inform his nearest and dearest of his death. He'd agonized about it ever since gathering his wits together after the desertion. Day after day as they pushed the unwieldy cart, night after night as he'd talked to Celine in the barns, this extra bit of shittiness lurked at the back of his mind. It became more important when he and Tyler were cornered by a big military policeman and a thin doleful gendarme in Marcel Gabereau's storeroom. Celine had come rushing downstairs just too late.

"The police, Hector. You two had better…"

The fugitives had been moving sacks of dried beans from the back of the basement store to a flight of wooden steps leading up to the shop.

"Excuse me, madam. We should like un mot with these two gentlemen, if you please."

The gendarme was politeness itself, his features set in unhappiness, boredom, his nose chapped and red, his pill-box hat the worse for wear, his baton resting on a great wheel of cheese. Before anyone could reply there was a shouting from above.

"Who do you think you are? What do you think you are doing? Bursting into my house like this?"

M. Gabereau came thumping down the stairs at a remarkable speed for a man of his age and bulk, M. Trou at his heels. The military policeman took off his hat and scratched his bristled head.

"Arf a mo, gents all," he said in English. He was from Essex and no one took any notice of him.

"Have you got a warrant?" M. Gabereau demanded. He was panting, cheeks going in and out like bellows, jug ears flushed.

"What insolence!" M. Trou added. "You'd think they owned the store."

"Please calm yourself, monsieurs. With your permission we simply wish to ask these two young gentlemen to show us their papers. Just routine, my friends."

"Four of my sons have been killed in this dog shit obscenity of a war."

Gabereau's face was full of anger. He waved his arms. "Who asked you to come and push your nose in here? I'm surprised at you, Bernard."

The gendarme took off his cap and wiped his fingers round the inside of the brim as though it were summer and he was sweating. He was bald with neatly trimmed patches of black hair above his ears.

"Monsieur Gabereau. The citizens have been complaining."

"God damn the citizens to hell! I thought you would have more respect for my family, Bernard."

"I have the greatest respect, monsieur. But the citizens say..."

"Blast the citizens!"

Bernard looked woebegone and tapped the side of his leg with his baton.

"They say there are rumours. They suspect that these fellows are English tommies. That they are deserters."

Hector listened to the accusations with dread, sick apprehension. Yet part of him wanted to get it over, to face the music, to be marched in front of a firing squad. No blindfold. The explosion of the rifles. The thought of his parents thinking he was dead had become more persistent and nauseating. Not to mention Aunt Sammy. He'd grown a lot since that business with her, become a man and looked back on that past, that boyish escapade, as a rueful indulgence. Unfucking believable. He did not know the precise drill for a military execution but he'd heard that one member of the killing detail was issued with a blank round, the idea being that any one of the guys could believe himself possibly innocent of the slaying. The only fault with that was that any soldier worth his salt knew when he was firing a blank and when a live round. Then again, which would be worse for his father? Learning that his son had been killed in action in the war to end all wars or that Hector had been court-martialled round the drumhead and shot as a deserter. Hector would be dead in either event. He waited docilely, head bent, as his benefactor argued the toss with the gendarme.

"So you are prepared to listen to the chatter of a bunch of old wives, a gaggle of jealous cretins, before coming to me. Is that so, Bernard?"

The gendarme looked more disconsolate and the English corporal more and more impatient, stamping his enormous boots on the store-room floor.

"I do not, monsieur. But if you would only allow my colleague here to ask them a few questions in English...."

Gabereau looked up at the military policeman in disgust.

"Listen, Bernard. This man," he pointed at Hector, "has completely lost his memory. They both have if you really want to know. And is it surprising, Bernard? If you'd been in that hell, in that hell for months, years,

Bernard, you'd have lost more than your memory."

"What line of bull is the old geezer coming up with mate?"

The gendarme translated for the Brit in halting English.

"Oh, bloody marvellous. That's what they all say. How very convenient. It don't matter about leaving your comrades in shit street, do it?"

"You remember my son Paul, Bernard? One of the four who has been killed? The one who used to go out with your niece till she dumped him? Well this boy is a friend of Paul. They were in the same regiment and Paul brought him back on leave one time. His name is Plouvier, a goddam French name, Bernard, you would agree. I don't know why those old cows should think these boys are tommies. A lot of rot."

Hector was astounded and embarrassingly moved by the lies old Gabereau was telling on his behalf.

"That's why he came back here. He must have found his way by instinct, to sanctuary, poor boy, with his mind all shattered. And now what do you wretches want to do with him? Torture him? Send him back to hell? Shoot him like a dog?"

Hector could sense that this was a critical moment for him in more ways than being a matter of possible life and death, though that sucker was important enough in the short run. So thoroughly had he immersed himself in his own living lie that he was beginning to wonder whether his reason were turning. The Jesus like appearance he had affected, the long hair, the beard, his semblance of piety, were becoming more than a disguise for a brutalized soldier. "You don't have to be kidding the troops all the time, old buddy," Tyler had said. "Loosen up. Be your old self, for Chrissake." An angel from Mons. He would like to think he was wandering around the world helping out as he was heaving sacks of whatever dried goods from one corner to another. Madeleine Gabereau took him up regularly to see her stricken mother. Madeleine said Hector did her mother a power of good.

The grocer snatched off his beret and threw it down by the cheese.

"Go ahead then. Ask them what you like. But here in front of us."

"No sneaking off behind our backs," added M. Trou. He lit his clay pipe and blew the foul fumes in the direction of the Essex corporal.

The unhappy Bernard nodded at his companion, who immediately marched with heavy tread towards Hector and Tyler.

"Right then, you two. Pay attention. Name and number and your paybooks. Now, you horrible men. Now. Not tomorrer," he shouted in English.

There was an agonizing silence until Tyler could not contain himself longer. "Get lost, you big bastard," he muttered almost inaudibly.

"There. What d'I tell you?" the English policeman screamed.

"Caught the bleeder red-handed. Gave his bleeding self away he did. Din he?"

Hector interposed himself between Tyler and the corporal and started to speak in voluble French, some of it rubbish talk, some of it alluding to his friend's hallucinating, holding out his arms, Christ-like in supplication, occasionally touching his forehead with his fingers. Celine took her cue and harassed the gendarme with a thousand reasons of pity and charity for not pursuing the matter any further. Suzette joined in, wagging her plump finger in front of the Englishman's nose.

"What's this? A fucking madhouse?" he said. He had a long, clean-shaven upper lip, squat nose, flattened between his cheekbones like a chimpanzee's.

Oh, you great fucking fool, Tyle, Hector was thinking to himself underneath all the posturing and the hollering. You can't keep your mouth shut, can you? How stupid can you get? Now that arrest seemed imminent, the firing squad had no attraction for him at all. This ambush was going to be a bitch to get out of, was it ever.

"Worrer tell yer? The bleeder knows English 'swell as I do. Why? Cos he is English, that's why. I knows a deserter when I sees one. And if this horrible little man ain't no deserter I'll eat my fucking hat, that I will."

The corporal was bending forward from the waist, back still rigid, eyes glaring from under the peak of his cap in patriotic indignation.

M. Gabereau retrieved his beret from the dusty floor and flapped it against his knee. "What's this monster braying about?"

"He says..."

"Tell him to shut his foul mouth. All our brave poilus, and you well know this, Bernard, have picked up scraps of English here and there. Because of this rat shit of a war we all have learned a bit. Even so I can't understand a word that big fool of yours is saying."

"I am spikking ze anglais," said Celine, and Tyler winked at her. He was puffing at his pipe, not a care in the world.

"The poor boy's mind has gone," Gabereau yelled. "Totally deranged. He should be in hospital, they both should be by rights, if the hospitals weren't too full already."

To atone for his indiscretion Tyler began to act the fool. He laid his hot pipe on a sack of lentils. He inserted his forefingers at each corner of his mouth and pulled it apart so that his moustache stretched thinly across his upper lip. He crossed his eyes. He danced around like a monkey on a string and made a gibbering squeal after every leap. Even the gloomy gendarme smiled, and everyone else, with the exception of the infuriated

Essex corporal, burst out laughing. Uncle Joe, who had slipped in from the yard, laughed the loudest. Christ, thought Hector, caught up in the hilarity despite himself, he sure has guts, old Tyle. But he's one crazy bozo. He's overplayed his hand again. Hector tugged at his blond beard. He really must shave it off, but not with M. Trou's open razor.

Bernard shrugged his shoulders and started to move towards the wooden stairs.

"We shall have to discuss this later, M. Gabereau," he said quietly, gloomily. "When everyone is calmer. I am sorry, very sorry. But, as you know my friend, I have my duty to do."

"I think my sons had their duty to do."

"You have suffered a tragic loss. I will grant you that. No man has suffered more."

The gendarme led away his fellow policeman, snorting, red-faced.

"You'll hear more about this, you lot. Just you wait. We'll get you yet."

ఴ❀ఴ

They got Tyler very soon after this fruitless visit. He simply disappeared. They did not even allow him to return to the grocer's to pick up his few belongings. One of the prostitutes Suzette had made friends with provided the only information.

"They arrested him on the corner of St. Anthony Street, not a hundred metres from the store," Suzette said. "Fifi saw them take him to the barracks, and he went without a murmur. An English officer there questioned him and said he was a Yank and he's been taken off to the American Army."

"Fifi?"

"That's her street name." Suzette grinned at Hector. She was cheerier, more forthcoming these days.

Old Gabereau, accompanied by M. Trou, went storming to the police station and demanded to speak to Bernard and to Bernard's superior, a kindly man who had been to school with Gabereau. Both denied any complicity in the affair. It was the military, they said, who had taken matters completely out of their hands.

"But you brave fellows started it, didn't you? When those nosy women complained? Malicious sows."

"Yes, sadly. We had to. But we did not finish it. I assure you, my old friend. Bernard was most upset when he got back from you."

"That bastard British army copper wasn't, I wager."

"No."

When they returned to the shop, Gabereau called a family council. The grocer, Hector, Trou, and Uncle Joe sat round the kitchen table with glasses of apple brandy. Madeleine, Celine and Suzette, both looking fetching in Mme. Gabereau's gowns, stood behind the men while the lady of the house stayed upstairs in her own cruel silence. Gabereau spoke first to Hector, lugubriously, each word heavily burdened as though he had lost another son.

"I think our friend is up the creek."

He took a sip of brandy after every short sentence and wiped his lips with the back of his hand.

"But at least it seems he will not be charged with desertion and shot. If they think he's a Yankee he may well end up in the American army."

"Poor blighter."

"I think that Mister Teelair..." Gabereau spoke even more slowly. "I do believe that he wanted something to happen. He was getting bored here."

"You could be right at that. But he don't need no more fighting. He's had it up to here. If Tyle has to go into another battle he'll darn well take off again, just like that."

Hector flicked his thumb and middle finger. Madeleine refilled her father's glass. He looked hard at Hector as though denying any effeminate favouritism on his part.

"Meantime we have been warned to lay low. Keep our asses down. Otherwise we could lose you as well."

Hector was once again immensely touched at the way this old man had without any hesitation taken them into his paternal care. He was beginning to feel more affection, love perhaps, for Gabereau than he had had for his own father. But, come on, that was not fair. He was ashamed that such an idea should come into his mind. The situation was as different as apples from oranges. This old man, Gabereau, had himself been partly knocked off his emotional perch by repeated shock. That would explain a lot.

"So, my old friend," the grocer nodded in the direction of Trou, "he and I have decided you should go to Babette's till the fuss dies down. Lena can go with you. She needs a break. And perhaps you two mesdames," he turned round to face Celine and Suzette, "will do a little extra in the house and the store."

"Without doubt," Celine said, but she did not look happy with the arrangement. She smoothed down the front of Mme. Gabereau's dress.

"Certainly," Suzette said. She was only too grateful. She'd been persuaded by Celine that there was no need to go hawking her body again.

Hector looked round the pictureless walls. An old clock, which was always kept half an hour fast, stood high on a corner cupboard and for a time nothing was heard other than its loud tick.

"Who is Babette?"

"A cousin. She lives in a village. A few houses, hardly a village. She and her husband were in the market gardening business. They started it themselves and were doing very well. Then he volunteered for the army and….We think he has gone west, done for, kaput. Babette won`t believe it. She manages the best she can. Perhaps you can give her a hand while you are there."

"Perhaps I should just take off on my own," Hector said. "And then I wouldn't be bringing trouble down on you folks no more."

Gabereau and Trou looked at each other. They drained their glasses. The grocer thumped the table with his clenched hand.

"We're damned if we're going to listen to such talk, son. And we ain't got much time if we are going to get you off before the police come snooping round here again."

C3❀80

Hector and Madeleine travelled in an open four wheeled wagon, the two wheels at the front, which turned left or right independently from the rear pair, being smaller. They carried a modest load of supplies from the grocery for Babette. The horse's ribs showed through its hide and the wretched beast had a peculiar gait because of a stiff hind leg. We'da shot that critter on the ranch, Hector thought, put her out of her misery. Drizzle and a chill wind as they set off, a becoming flush rising on Madeleine's cheeks.

"I can't get no fodder for the old hoss," the wagoner said. "And business is trickier nor a ferret's ass what with the war and that." He looked as though he could do with some fodder himself, Hector thought. His thin body was wrapped in a discarded army greatcoat, hat pulled down over ears and brow, a blue scarf round his neck and chin. Grey stubble. "We're dead lucky, mind, that the army hasn't took her."

"How far is it, Jules?" Hector asked.

"Bout twenty kilometres to the turn-off past P****, then eight, ten maybe, down the side lane."

"That road will be terrible at this time of the year," Madeleine said. "Full of potholes. Deep ruts."

Hector had had his hair cut short by Madeleine.

"I used to trim my brothers' hair. Paul said it was a waste of money going to the barber's. So none of the others would go to one either."

As he sat on a chair in the kitchen near the back door so that his blond locks could be swept conveniently into the yard, and as Lena, as the family called this marvellously composed woman, combed and clipped expertly, Hector could sense the calm and pleasant nearness of her with an excitement and tingling that was not a raging lust. It had been the same with Celine in the barns. Perhaps the act of desertion had a bromide effect, though in the case of Celine, fond as he had grown of her, there had not been much in the way of seductiveness in her neglected and abused body. Yet she had certainly changed, he noticed, Celine, in the last month or so, reshaping, skin glowing. Both Gabereau and Trou had urged him to have a haircut.

"We don't want you drawing attention to yourself more than necessary. The war has begotten quite a few crazies and if they're loose and wandering around the police generally give them the once over. You can keep your beard if you want. Makes you look less like a soldier, that does."

If Madeleine remembered the hair clippings falling from the heads of her dead brothers, she had given no indication of it and she had made a neat job of Hector's hair. Now as they sat on some sacking immediately behind the old wagoner, their backs to him, huddled together for warmth, Hector's cropped head was covered with a shapeless hat, brim pulled well down. Droplets of drizzle gleamed on his blond beard. She was so easy to talk to, so difficult to get to know. It was pleasant, goddamn serenity itself, having a woman like her so close, but nothing disturbingly erotic about it. Even bundled up in winter clothes she seemed slim and elegant stretched out beside him. A long beige overcoat with its collar trimmed with pink velvet, a quiet, subdued pink. Soft leather boots peeping below the hem of her coat, so dainty along side his clomping army ones. There was something about Frenchwomen.... But come to think of it, how many did he know apart from a scattering of camp-followers and Celine, no longer a whore in his book, and now Madeleine. Come to think of it, how many women had he really known in his life, and he, a sceptical warrior, at the peak of manhood, rising twenty now. The war stole so much from a fellow. Yet if he had stayed in Higgins Bend, what then? Apart from his sister, Michie, she'd nipped any adolescent groping in the bud, taught him an early lesson and no mistake, and his mom, and his Aunt Sammy, crikey, bring her into mind later, not now, there had been Angela Parkes. Dear Angie. One night by the Bow River he had almost got it up her in a bed of fucking rocks. After he'd seen her home to the family shack that night he'd had to jerk himself off in the shadow of the brickworks, out of the glare of the moonlight.

Madeleine sat placidly beside him as the wagon bumped and

bounced. This was the good road. Hector would be the first to admit that he was pig ignorant about women. As a farm boy he learned at an early age the basics of animal reproduction, bitches, cows and mares in heat, their being served and so on, but then when he tried to transfer this knowledge to girls and women in his everyday life he floundered. Last week Madeleine had been pale and listless. Did this mean she had been, well, bleeding. His sister had become very private about this sort of thing. Of course, he and the other boys sniggered about it at school and he was told in the most vulgar and explicit terms all sorts of genital stories from the married guys, and the single ones, in the trenches. Though after a while he began to take such tales with a grain of salt, they were enough to turn a guy off women for life. Shit. A lot of those fellers were dead meat already. If Angie had let him get it in that night by the Bow would he be a father by now, for instance? A heifer seemed to get pregnant first shot under the bull, but that did not appear necessarily so with human females. He wondered how Madeleine would react if she knew what he was thinking.

"You visit with Babette a lot?" he asked.

Their shoulders were touching and when she turned to face him her mouth was so near he could feel her breath. She smiled gently, yet she was not a passive woman. Not at all, Hector thought. An enigma, a paragon, a delightful, unobtrusive presence but very much her own woman.

"Not very often. She's very nice, Babette, bright, a cheerful little body. You'll like her."

"I like your family, all of you." He realized that he was skating on thin ice here, that if he were not careful he could make some fucking clumsy remark about the brothers. He felt, however, he could share her bereavement, that in some weird way he had come to know the dead siblings.

"I love you," he said, the battle-hardened soldier, "you and your father and mother. I can't believe how kind you all are. Even your mother. And you are taking such big risks for me."

Madeleine, Hector preferred her longer name, turned and shrugged slightly. In the barns Celine had asked about his speaking French, his home, the mountains, the farm. But Madeleine seemed totally uninterested in his past, or at least she had not questioned him so far. In an approximate way he recognized in her an innate good taste, polite reserve, a quality which even as an inarticulate boy he had been aware of in Aunt Sammy, even when they were indulging in those rapturous bouts in the hay and she was crying out in joy. Another mystery about Aunt Sammy which had occasionally in the past tied knots in his guts was why had she not become pregnant. Obviously she hadn't or there'd have been all hell raised. The fellers in the trenches had told him there were ways of preventing a woman getting in the family way. They shove something up their cunts, he was told. Presumably Aunt Sammy knew all about that.

"You've made me feel at home, as though I were one of the family."

"We are supposed to be brother and sister, remember, if anyone questions us. That's papa's idea. I am to say that you have been very sick in hospital. And that you still have a few screws loose up here."

Lena tapped her head and laughed. Gloves on her slim hands. A cloche hat, very French.

"I'm taking you into the country to recuperate. That's our story." Merriment in her eyes.

"Who's going to be dumb enough to believe that sort of baloney?"

Once again she smiled and shrugged. It was all very well, in his continual self-analysis—perhaps he was examining himself too often and too closely—to conclude that women had little physical attraction for him since his desertion, but, chivalrous as he intended to be towards Madeleine he could sense that her constant proximity, simply through her gentleness which was in stark opposition to the obscene killing of her brothers, might well change his present attitude. He had talked his abstinence over with Tyler before his arrest. "Get real," Tyler had said. "Your prick's had one hell of a shock, pal. Like you. That's all there is to it. You'll be poking every little piece which happens along in no time. And another thing." Tyler had looked at him earnestly. "You are taking this Jesus bit too far, I tell you. Your brain's going soft." He wondered if Madeleine knew men talked like that. Did her brothers? No reason to suppose that soldiers in the French army were any different. Naturally he would not talk like that in front of Michie. He wondered what his sister was doing now, how she was.

There was some truth in what Tyle has said. His present sexual continence had more to do with his running away from the war than with any of the dirty trench stories of female anatomy. Yet it wasn't all shock, Tyle. His long hair, for instance, and desire to help people had nothing to do with any sudden religious conversion or seeing the light or the angels flapping over that incredible slaughter. If anything, it was the other way round. Although he respected the few padres he'd come across in the army, his campaign experiences had turned him against religion. God couldn't be on both sides at once. If he were all powerful, why did God let the massacre and maiming go on so long? That sort of fucking obvious question perplexed him and turned him away. And other, subtler things troubled him too. His defence for a long time was a cynical hardening of body and heart and mind. But when he escaped from the blood and snot, ran away from it if you like, he stumbled over the Trous, civilian victims this time, non-combatants, especially Celine, and his cynicism began to slough off him, leaving him both sadder and more vulnerable, but to a small degree morally more robust.

The grey sky was low above the wagon, the road eerily deserted as they creaked along between leafless hedgerows and occasionally a row of stark poplars on one side of the road only. Apart from a crow or two, there were very few birds. You would never dream there was a maniacal war being waged a short distance to the east of them. Though his nerves were still taut and he had to resist the impulse to throw himself on the floor when he heard a loud noise, Hector felt immensely at ease in Lena's company at Chaubet and delightfully relaxed sitting close to her in the back of a farm cart.

"Look."

She touched his knee and pointed. A fox ran across the road behind the wagon.

"Are there many round here."

"Quite a few. Can you see his beautiful tail?"

"We have coyotes at the ranch. Sometimes wolves. We shoot them. They worry the cattle."

Lena did not appear to be particularly interested, and they rolled creakily on away from the dog fox which went sniffing along the ditch. Rather than anything spiritual, his beard was more the consequence of his fear of M. Trou's cut-throat razor, but he admitted that he had come to like his facial hair as a token of defiance of all things military. And also, because it made him look older, he felt more mature, more confident in facing, say, Madeleine or her parents. The fresh complexioned, clean shaven prairie boy was history.

He used to get news of his sister in his mother's letters, and once in a blue moon Michie would add half a page of big writing at the end of her mother's. His father never wrote. Marie posted a letter religiously once a month, but sometimes they would arrive in bundles of four or five. She wrote in a beautiful hand which she had learned from the nuns in Montreal, quite unlike the scratchy, illegible French writing. Hector often wondered as the war went on whether letters from home were good for morale or not. Some of the troops would receive letters from prurient well-wishers telling them that their wives or sweethearts were getting tired of waiting for them and were seeking, and getting, local solace.

"I'll strangle that woman of mine when I get home, so help me. The disgusting bitch."

"But listen up, Barney. Can you honestly say that you've been true to her all the time you've been away?" the officer or the padre would ask.

"That's different, sir."

Thank goodness Hector, like a lot of the fellers, had no one to remain faithful to. At the beginning—and now he could laugh about this—he used to think of himself as being true to Aunt Sammy. Once he'd nearly told his old buddy, Bob, about her. Thank God he hadn't, though Bob wouldn't have mocked him or told tales on him and he certainly couldn't now, poor blighter. It was upsetting all round when the mail orderly brought letters and parcels up to the trenches. The guys who got nothing would pretend they did not care a shit, while the recipients would be in various states of thought, nostalgia, misery, simulated joy, a brief transition to another life, another place and time and then the grim realization that they were all still in the fucking front line with lice and mud and stinking latrines and God forsaken years, for all they knew, still to go.

His mother wrote last year that Michie was getting bored on the ranch and was pestering her parents to let her go to Calgary to train as a nurse. So far Dad won't let her go. Some nurses are being sent overseas and Dad's afraid that Michie might try to do that. You know how impulsive she is, dear boy. He says one child of his abroad is enough. Hector thought he should tell his father that the Gabereaus had lost four sons. He would get ideas like this and then realize with dismay that he could no longer write home, not unless he wanted to make a clean breast of it and tell them that he had run away from the army. How would he mail the letter anyway?

Some time ago his mother had written him about a curious arrangement at home, but she did not tell him until he had been gone for two years or more. Apparently there'd been a big fire in Higgins Bend, perhaps even before he'd left Canada, the recruits never got to read the Ontario newspapers much in the infantry training depot, and the husband of Angela Parkes that was, Dickie Leech, the kid with the flat feet, had died in this fire. Dot Howard, also. Hector was sorry about her whom he remembered with great fondness. He was sorry about Dickie for that matter, though by the time his mother wrote him this news guys were dropping like flies about him and life had become very cheap. But this was the funny thing. Angie had been pregnant—they hadn't wasted any time had they, she and Dickie?—and had herself been burned in the fire and nearly lost the baby. All very sad, but, he had to read the letter twice at this point, Aunt Sammy had taken pity on her and now Angie and her kid were living at Aunt Sammy's ranch house. Holy mackerel! At times he felt jealous about Angie and the baby as though they were usurping

Hector's special position at Aunt Sammy's. What if there were some hanky panky going on and Angela were being kept as a prospective wife for him when he got home? Naw, they'd never do a thing like that, not one of them. What was he going to do, anyways? It was a nagging dilemma. Just stop writing altogether. Let them think he was dead. They'd be hearing officially soon that he was "missing" or worse if they hadn't already. Why should he worry about Angela's baby if he were not going home?

When the wagon got to P**** the driver stopped to give the splayed horse a drink, and Hector and Madeleine walked along the cobbled street. She took his arm.

03✾80

"What's he say his name is, sarge?"

"Tyler Brown."

"Funny way of speaking he has. Never heard no one talk like that before. Can't understand him sometimes."

"None of the guys can. Guess he's from Maine, Vermont, somewhere up there. He never says."

"May be at that, though he ain't no country hick."

"Not from Kansas, that's for sure. Like the rest of our fellers."

"Naw. He ain't no Corn Belt boy."

"Officer says he lost his memory. Can't recall the name of his last outfit. I don't know how they figured he was in this man's army anyways. But let me tell you something, Billie Joe. That feller's bin in action afore, I just knows he has. You can't tell him nothing about no infantry weapons, rifles and grenades, like. He can look after himself, that one."

"Keeps hisself to hisself though."

"Yup. Sometimes he seems as if he's gone and lost something and he's given up searching for it. Or him or her. Course, it could be a buddy killed or a girl friend cheated on him. This war do strange things to a man. You just watch him, Billie, setting over by that heap of old ammo there, real cool, him and his little moustache, you don't see many doughboys with moustaches, and that goddam stinking pipe. He don't give a cuss whether we're talking about him or not, do he? Never says a word about his family or nothing."

"But he's okay, sarge. He helps the young fellows out over this and that. Shows them a thing or two, but he's not a smart ass. No sir."

"Officer says we got us the big one coming up soon. We'll see how he shapes up then."

"What's it like, sarge? Scrapping? To tell the truth I gets shit scared at times, thinking on it."

"You'll be all right, Billie Joe. Trust me."

ᚳ ❀ ᛉ

A message came to Babette's from old Marcel Gabereau that it was necessary for Hector to stay away from Chaubet for a much longer period. His old schoolmate, the police chief, had warned him that the truculent town gossips, many of them widows or mothers of absent sons, were not satisfied with the sacrifice of only one of the young men who had appeared so mysteriously at the grocer's. No one had guessed the exact whereabouts of Hector, the wagoner having been both threatened and bribed by Marcel, but some of the women were suspicious. They were fairly certain that Hector had not been arrested along with Tyler and oddly enough not one of them had put two and two together and associated the absence of Madeleine Gabereau with absence of the man they believed was a deserter, a British tommy. The military and civil authorities too, Gabereau was informed, were in the middle of a round-up frenzy, just as though the deserters, the sick, the shell-shocked, the vagabonds, the malingerers, the blind, the beggars, the mad, the cunning, the human detritus of a long war were so many ornery steers running wild on the range. Lena could go back if she wanted, her father said, but that was up to her since Celine and Suzette were doing a dandy job helping out at the store. Madeleine decided to stay with Hector at Babette's.

"I wish I had my old hoss, Mad. A mare she was, a quarter horse, no good for heavy farm work but great for running around the ranch."

"Please don't call me Mad. How would you like to be called Hec."

"I am. Most of the folks do back home. I thought you didn't like Lena."

"I don't except for my dad. I know he's being loving when he calls me Lena and I'm in trouble when it's Madeleine. My brother, Guy, started it. When he was little he couldn't say Madeleine."

Shades of Aunt Sammy. They had slipped into spring, a busy time for market gardeners. Hector's back ached from bending over sowing radishes, lettuce, chard, onions. The dirt was different here from that in the foothills of the Rocky Mountains, heavier, richer.

"What do you want a horse for? To gallop up and down the back lane? You couldn't have a horse charging all over the carrots and the beets, now could you, cowboy?"

The relationship has changed between them. She came at him more strongly, challenging, teasing yet keeping one foot on her protective base of calm non-commitment. Her attitude both worried and pleased Hector. Most astounding of all had been her reaction to his discovery of Willi Schmidt. In their second week at Babette's, Hector had found the German hiding behind some barrels in the potato store. He had heard a noise and thought it was one of Babette's pride of cats—gingers, tabbies, strays, toms, pregnant moms, striped, furtive, slinky, all over the place. Kittens chasing balls of dust, scraps of torn paper. A fat old male snarling and spitting when disturbed. Two younger males waiting their chances. A cat smell throughout the house and outbuildings.

"I'll be darned. Who are you?"

The tall fugitive came out from behind the barrels, unfolding his length and raising his arms above his head so that he touched the ceiling of the root store. Young, younger perhaps than Hector, same blond hair, long jaw line, vulnerable in a boxing ring, distinguished Roman nose, also vulnerable to a right cross. Hollows in his cheeks. He was wearing nondescript farm clothes but Hector knew a German soldier when he saw one, even out of uniform.

"Here I am staying," the fugitive had said in rough, barely serviceable French. There was a gap between the bottom of his shirt and the top of his pants. "Please not to let the dog out of the bag."

"The match, mister whoever-you-are. Uncover the match, the French say...give you away. And put your arms down for God's sake."

"So you have found Willi."

Hector turned his head. Babette had appeared in the doorway to the store which led off the basement of the main house.

"He is as much French as German. He comes from Alsace. He has relatives in France. If you tell on me I shall be the disgrace of the neighbourhood and Willi shall be taken away and shot."

Babette was a short woman, well rounded at bust and hips, black hair cut straight across her forehead. She was a good deal shorter than Hector, Willi half a head taller.

"I don't think he'll be shot. He'll be put in a prisoner of war camp. He would be shot for desertion if the Germans got hold of him again." Hector sounded righteous.

"Very well then, just as I said. And I shall be shot. For harbouring the enemy."

"But why should I tell on you, Babette. Me of all people." Hector laughed.

He was sure that Madeleine had told Babette about his own position as soon as they had arrived, but both here and at the grocer's he found an admirable restraint about his act of desertion, an ignoring of it as though it were no one else's business but his, as though he had a cleft palate or a club foot which it was impolite to notice. As though too there was a growing civil conspiracy against the war, everyone, the victims of political circumstance or something more pernicious, fed up to the back teeth with the whole shebang. It was remarkable how neither he nor Madeleine had stumbled on Willi earlier, especially when they discovered that he had been sharing Babette's bed.

"I'll be blessed," he said to Madeleine later. He would have expressed it differently to Tyler. It was a constant struggle in her company to muffle his oaths, to temper his language.

"What's the matter?"

Without a wink or a nod or sly look, Babette had given them adjoining bedrooms, half in the roof, with little attic windows sporting chintz curtains and looking across the meadow and the arable land where the salad and vegetables were cultivated. Until arriving at Chaubet where he'd shared with Tyler, Hector hadn't slept in a civilized bedroom for years. He felt rough and awkward. He would finger the sheets, pat the pillow. He would recall Aunt Sammy's bedroom. He and Madeleine had slipped into an amiable routine. He worked in the yard and the fields, she about the house with Babette, sometimes in the greenhouse or the potting sheds. They wondered how Babette had managed on her own, though there were fewer chores to get through in the winter. In the evening, before supper, they would share an aperitif in one or other of the bedrooms just like a brother and sister. In the army you attacked a meal when you could get it, gobbled it quickly down before the next salvo of shells.

"This crazy jerk, Willi. Where did Babette pick him up?"

Madeleine looked at him thoughtfully as she took a sip from her glass that had a crack down one side which caught the light.

"What is this 'crazy jerk'?"

"Come on, Mad, don't give me that. I mean, would you expect your cousin to be sleeping around with a goddamn Hun? I mean does she even know for sure if her husband has been killed? He may be out there some place wounded, shell-shocked, waiting for her."

Hector was sitting on his own bed which was tucked under the slope of the roof so that he had to be careful not to bang his head in the mornings. He'd taken off his muddy boots at the back door and was wearing Babette's husband's leather slippers. Lena was sitting on a wicker chair by the open door, her long legs stretched out under the folds of a workaday dress that was loose fitting and oddly becoming.

"You astonish me saying things like that. You really do."

"For Chrissake, think of your brothers. Those bastard Germans killed your brothers, Madeleine."

She rose slowly and placed her unfinished drink on a white painted dresser. She crossed her arms and held her elbows tightly. He had never before seen her looking angry. She turned and began to walk down the short passage, arms still locked in front of her under her bosom.

"Hey, Madeleine, don't go. Holy-moly what've I done now?"

Babette had inherited part of the acreage from a childless uncle who had died in this house unvisited on his death bed by any relatives. Before her good fortune she scarcely knew of his existence. She and her husband, Georges, had started their married life here, borrowed from the bank, rented some adjoining land, and got the business going after much strife and many mistakes. They worked hard, happily together until the Germans invaded. Hector learned all this from Babette over suppers. Once again he had been made undeservedly welcome, this time by this short woman of boundless energy and merry eyes who seemed to live for the day. After he had stumbled across Willi in the potato store the German deserter appeared openly at the supper table. Babette still reminisced about life with her husband, but Willi didn't seem to understand much. Hector wondered what they talked about in bed, or how much. He supposed it didn't matter, there had not been much conversation between him and Aunt Sammy.

"Please come back and finish your drink," he begged.

He'd rushed after Madeleine and taken her hesitantly by the shoulders. Her eyelashes were wet. He was bound to say something real dumb about the brothers, some time or other and now he had. So far she had been to him a companiable, soothing presence, intangibly good. Perhaps he had discounted her femaleness.

"How can you say such things?"

Close up she became more humanly identifiable, faint dark hairs on her upper lip, angry nostrils. Apart from when they were huddled together in the cart he had instinctively avoided this sort of nearness. Her eyes grave, her face thinner, a narrower oval than Angela's, but it had its strength as well as fragility and understanding. God knows how her looks compared with Aunt Sammy's, it just did not seem possible to bring the two of them into plausible comparison. She was no Angela, no Aunt Sammy, but she was here, she was sharing this fucking war in Europe, and she was precious. He did not wish to lose her friendship, or whatever it was that may be more complex.

"I've always wanted to ask you about your brothers but I never liked to. I thought it would be rude. And now I've said the wrong thing."

He led her gently back to the room, sat her down and handed her the unfinished drink.

"I think it might rain tonight," she said, "or early tomorrow morning." She smiled.

Spring was certainly on its way. You could feel it in the air and on the soil as well as see it in the hedgerows. And with the spring came spring offensives. Again. And they said this was the war to end all wars.

"I'm sorry," Hector said. "I shouldn't have sounded off like I did about Babette. I can't talk about nobody. I should keep my big stupid mouth closed forever, especially when I think of those poor fucking soldiers…" He looked at Madeleine and she returned his gaze steadily. "…still fighting in all that crap. Make darn sure you have a round up the spout, men. Fix your goddamn bayonets. I wonder what the hell Tyle is doing."

☙❀❧

"That guy just volunteers for everything, Billie Joe. He thrives on it. You'd think he was wanting to get hisself shot."

"Who's that, sarge? Tyler Brown."

"That's the man. The officer ask me ain't there no one else in the goddamn platoon, in the goddamn company, to go on them patrols. Ain't you got no other fucking heroes, sergeant, 'cept private Brown."

"What you say, sarge?"

"I said lotsa the guys are willing, captain. Not exactly crazy about it but they'll go. This feller Brown is different, captain, I says. The patrol commanders like to have him there, right on the spot. And the rest of the fellers feel good with him."

"And what the officer say to that?"

"He said aw what the hell, sergeant. Do it your way. So long as we're getting us good results, and we are doing just that. The colonel says that this squad is doing a mighty fine job. Even Dogface cracked a smile at us catching that Kraut having a shit last night. And bringing him in with his pants down. They squeezed that soldier like a wet rag before they give him a pair of G.I. trousers, that's for sure. Colonel Dogface says I gotta tell you guys he's proud of you all. Specially since this is your first time in Bulletsville."

"The officer says all that?"

"The officer says that the Colonel says all that, Billie Joe."

"Does the Colonel know Tyler Brown captured that bozo all on his ownsome, just about. Corporal Stuyvesant will tell ya straight out, sarge, and he was in charge of the patrol."

"He knows it, son. The brass makes a note of the heroes for when they is dishing out the medals."

"I don't think Brown is looking for no medals."
"You're darn right, Billie Joe."
"Sarge."
"Yup."
"When they interrogates a feller who's been caught like..."
"Having a shit?"
"That's right. What sort of stuff do they ask him? Like what do they want to find out?"
"Well I guess they wants to know which Fritz regiment is out there, if it's some big league outfit, stuff like that. For when we attack. And that's gonna be darn soon, believe me."
"What good'll that do us, sarge? Knowing who they are? I mean them sons of bitches all got rifles and machine guns, don't they? They can all fucking shoot, can't they? Every goddamn mother's son of them."
"Now you're talking like an old soldier, Billie Joe."

ଓଙ୍କ

Tyler Brown was pissed off when they tricked him into speaking English at Chaubet, but he thought he'd better take his lumps and try to keep Hector out of the mess he himself had walked into. He still played out his loss of memory act when they were trying to trace him through records, but made no objection when the British Intelligence officer who couldn't tell the difference between a Canadian and American accent accused him of being a damn Yankee. An undeclared compromise with his interrogators was eventually arrived at. Tyler lucked out, for he might well have been put summarily before a firing squad. He agreed, as though in a daze, he would join a U.S. infantry division and in return would not be charged with desertion. He could have risked continuing to play dumb, they had no proof at all that he had deserted, but he wanted to move the heat away from Chaubet and the grocer's store. Tyler would have laughed to scorn anyone who accused him of acting through selfless gallantry. The hard-nosed Torontonian or whatever would have argued with a diminishing sneer that it was he who persuaded Hector to desert in the first place. So what the heck, brother. Forget it.

Tyler was also determined, come hell or high water, that in no way was he going to take part in another mass murderous offensive. He decided to play the percentages. Tyler's experience had destroyed any vestige of self-delusion. He believed he was no more heroic or no more cowardly than the rest of the infantry, and he also believed by his reckoning that he had more than done his duty to his king and country, not that he was ever burning with patriotic fervour like some of the guys. He often wondered why Hector had been in such a hurry to enlist. He calculated that on a reccie or even fighting patrol a soldier had a sporting chance of coming back alive, unlike the odds in mass attacks which was just like fucking sheep going to slaughter. On the other hand he did not want to be shot for desertion. He had got away with it once and may not be so lucky another time. Another factor in his plan, not necessary for survival but important in the matter of his guarded feelings, was that he did not want to make close attachments with any of these American kids. He'd lost too many buddies in war and he did not want any more of that grief, thanks a million.

So part of Plan A was to keep himself to himself. Be amiable, okay, but none of those deep friendships that develop between men in constant danger. This was not too easy because these Kansas boys, many of the unit seemed to come from the same part of the state, looked up to him and were a real friendly bunch. They would come over and hunker down, chew the fat, offer him American tobacco for his pipe, say what a swell moustache he had there, betcha all the broads fall for that piece of spinach, huh, Tyle. It was like turning away a puppy dog.

He also kept squeaky clean in the matter of military discipline. No pilfering goodies from the quartermaster's store, no dodging drills or sentry duty, no giving lip or the finger to corporals. Above all, he volunteered for all the patrols which military commanders in their chateaux considered necessary for any number of specious reasons before a big "push". After a time, some of the guys for all their friendliness began to look at him suspiciously as though he were some sort of smartass trying to show them up, but that couldn't be helped. It was part of the penalty for sticking to his plan. No man's land on this sector was unusually deep, more than half a mile—Tyler had known times when it had been less than fifty yards—so, to the delight of the colonels and the generals there was ample scope to send their troops out patrolling, test our boys under real fire, Hyram, wadya say. Way to go. Coming back through the wire after his umpteenth patrol, Private Brown tore his arm on one of those jagged protrusions with which barbed wire is adorned. When he got into the trench he made a point of showing the gash to Corporal Stuyvesant.

"You wanna get that baby fixed, Tyle. It could go poison on ya."

"It's just a scratch."

Since the enemy was comparatively distant the troops did not have to shit in a corner of their trench but had some field latrines set further to the rear. Tyler Brown chose a time when none of the other soldiers were emptying their bowels, and taking his bayonet with him sat on the wooden pole which served as a seat. He worked on the gash with the point of the bayonet, deepening it, filled it with dirt, boot blacking, excrement even, and bound it tightly with a khaki strip of cloth torn from the tail of his shirt. It hurt like hell, but he gritted his teeth.

Coming back to the shelter of friendly trenches after patrols set off a weird nostalgia. An indeterminate feeling, horror present and fear, but also a perverse attraction for the familiar sights and sounds, however vile. He had first noticed this demonic ambiguity as he'd marched towards the fields of glory with his new American comrades, very few of whom had been under fire before. A kind of satanic homecoming. The noise first, the muffled thunder and growl in the east, gradually identifying itself into the whine and screech of shells and bombs from cannon, howitzers, mortars, whizz-bangs, the rattle of machine guns. At night the lights of war sporadically illuminated its grisly arena. Smells of the earth and mud and decomposing corpses, cordite, rat shit, cold steel. Tyler half expected old faces waiting to greet him, comrades of earlier campaigns, familiar grins and grunts and scowls, bitter mockery, sentimental recall. But Hector was in Chaubet—he deserved a break, that kid—and most of the rest of the fellers were either repatriated cripples or buried in eternal rest in the slime further along the line.

He fastened the dirty bandage with a safety pin. Old soldiers had to learn about buttons and pins as well as rifles. He just hoped the timing of this mutilation was right.

ᛯ ❦ ᛰ

It was warm enough to be hatless and the west wind blew through Hector's beard, across the fields, sending the few white clouds racing towards the trenches where the soldiers on both sides would gaze up at them with apathetic and jaundiced eyes. He was hoeing beets, working down towards Babette's house and moving up in his direction in an adjacent row was Willi Schmidt, until recently of the Wehrmacht, who Hector discovered was born in a rural village in Alsace. No twittering of birds, no buzz of insects, the two seemed to be almost alone in the world with no other sign of human life apart from the occasional flash of Madeleine's green turban as she flitted from the back door to one of the outbuildings. She wore this unusual but, to Hector's mind, fetching headdress to cover her hair when she was doing what she called "dirty work". The wind was so strong that it would whip words and sentences away so that the two men scarcely spoke to each other except briefly when they crossed.

The insanity of the situation was not lost on Hector. The presence of

Schmidt was embarrassing to him, belittling the gesture of his desertion. That is what his running away from battle was becoming to mean, less a matter of instinctive self-preservation, more a shaking of his puny fist at the madness of the system. And, oh brother, so selfish when you really thought it out. And now he had collided with one of the enemy running away too and they had to meet in the middle of a goddamned beet field. As the wind stirred the drying soil about the tiny leaves he entertained idiot fancies of the solution to it all. Take a colossal vegetable farm, the biggest in the whole world, stretching as far as the eye could see and issue all the allied soldiers with hoes to work from, say, north to south. And then get the fucking Boche with their rifles also turned in for garden tools working from south to north in a vast agricultural armistice, just as he and Willi were doing. Horseshit.

He'd better watch these crazy notions or they'd be carting him off to the loony bin. He hadn't mentioned it to a soul, but before setting out to come here, before the arrest of Tyler, he had some weird conversations with old Mme. Gabereau, Madeleine's mother, who was supposed to have been struck dumb with grief, or near as dammit, as her sons disappeared one by one into the sacrificial pot.

"Maman asks for you every day. 'When is he coming up to see me?' she asks. I believe sometimes she is confusing you with one of her sons." Madeleine kept pushing him. "And then sometimes she asks for her Canadian boy. I'm sorry. It's not really your worry, but she gives me no peace."

"She doesn't say anything when I go up. Just holds my hand, with her eyes closed half the time. It can get spooky."

"I know. I think she is talking to you in her own way, Hector. She has changed since you arrived. You could be her salvation."

"Good God!"

"You could be. Don't underestimate yourself."

Hector used to visit her room reluctantly. He could not help reminding himself that Guy and Paul and the other two had not run away from the enemy, perhaps they never got the chance. He was disturbed by their absences in their mother's room as her emaciated mind stretched out for them in vain misery. Yet she would smile a ghost of a smile occasionally and unclutch his hand. A further upsetting fancy was that she was of the same generation as Aunt Sammy, a year or two older perhaps, and it was disconcerting to think of this wretched shell of a woman lifting her skirts and showing him the poison ivy rash on her ass. He had to work hard to obliterate such images from his mind.

One afternoon when Hector was stiff and dirty from unloading sacks of flour—he'd caught Madeleine's beseeching eye and gone straight up to the cheerless bedroom—Mme. Gabereau miraculously started to talk as though she'd been forgiven for throwing the statue and the holy picture into the yard. As if from the bottom of a noisome well, thin, reedy syllables strongly accented with the regional patois came bubbling out, yet as Hector bent forward he could understand her clearly enough.

"Let me tell you something about women, my boy. About marriage. About men."

Suddenly, unexpectedly the sentence came out. Frowning, gazing perplexed through narrowed eyes, she stroked Hector's beard and then clutched his wrist with an invalid's intensity. Her tongue and mind may have been partially freed from the paralysis of sorrow but there was still confusion in identifying her listener.

"I wish to tell you this, Paul, before you marry...what is that girl's name? Oh yes, a nice girl, no doubt. But you can't be too careful. Her eyes are set too close together."

Schmidt and Hector passed each other in the beet field with only brief nods this time. The German had made a sly remark the other evening at supper, suggestive, conspiratorial, as though Hector and Madeleine were sleeping together, as the Boche was with Babette. What had irritated Hector was that Madeleine had blushed and she and Babette had laughed in a stupid women's way, knowing, mocking.

"Hazel, isn't it, her name? Are there not enough saints' names, my son?" Mme. Gabereau asked. "Why does she have to be called after a nut?"

It soon became apparent that she was confusing two men in her unsteady mind, her eldest son Paul and Hector, and was also mixing up two women, the local girl whom Paul had married and her own daughter, Lena.

"You will be driven crazy at first by what my mother used to call the flesh. By that, my boy, she meant love-making and all its works. All lumped together, no differences. A piece of beef, a thigh, a mouth, a breast. Making babies. I can tell you something about them all right. Making them and having them. Both are revolting."

The blanket which the old lady used to keep tight under her chin was slipping down, revealing an elegantly embroidered nightgown, an irony on this wasted body. Her hair, her crowning glory, was combed austerely back, fastened in a tight bun. She was not all that old, for Crissake, Aunt Sammy's age.

"At the beginning you will think that bed will be the be all and end all. But there will soon be trouble in Paradise if you don't watch out. He will want to do it more often than you."

At certain points in her confidences, which were spoken hurriedly as though her renewed power of speech may be snuffed out again at any moment, she was apparently addressing the female of the pair, either her Lena or Paul's intended. She never named the latter in her admonitory discourse. She was simply her or that woman.

"My husband, Marcel, had his good and bad qualities. Who hasn't? Yet he always insisted on what he called his rights. Willing and immediate obedience which he said I'd promised at the altar at any time of night or day, whether it suited me or not. Get up them stairs quick and on my lousy back and open them legs whenever he snapped his fingers. Headaches were no excuse nor time of the month. Did I ever tell you he tricked me into marrying him? He was a shyster in his way. He was after my father's grocery business and of course he got it, didn't he? Time for a little crumpet, he'd say, and I'd have to put down what I was doing and go up to the bedroom. Not this room for the first year we were married because my parents were still alive and sleeping here. He had a smooth tongue all right and I was a naive Chaubet girl who obeyed her husband as a matter of course.

That's why at first I thought it was such a filthy business, lovemaking. And I was always a little disgusted both before and afterwards. When he was finished Marcel would roll off me and go to sleep or return downstairs to the store if it was daytime to get on with whatever he was doing before he got a rush of blood to the loins. And leave me to clean up the mess. I used to be very religious and believed I was being a dutiful wife according to the teachings of St. Paul."

Hector was astounded at the ideas and language that this meek, bedridden woman came out with. It must be another hidden self speaking. He looked across at the table where the statue of the Virgin had been. The hurling out of that precious symbol must have been the act of a woman driven by the deepest despair. Yesterday Madeleine had put a vase of catkins on the Virgin's table. He wondered if the seasons meant anything more now to the grieving mother than religion did. He looked back at the huge four poster bed with its canopy and feather mattress, presumably where Mme. Gabereau herself had been born and later her own children conceived, at least the last four, according to St. Paul. He speculated what time of day the conceptions had taken place. During a break from slicing up cheeses?

"My five children came like that—pouff!" She opened and closed her fingers. "Every year. Is it surprising?"

Her revelations, confessions, advice, did not all emerge fluently at one session. After a time she would tire and her thoughts come out scrambled and she finally withdrew into her mute and chronic pain. Hector worried about telling Madeleine. No doubt she would be overjoyed at her mother's speaking again, but would she really like to hear all the shocking and intimate stuff about her parents. Hector for sure wouldn't want to know details like those about his own parents. Christ, surely the cases weren't comparable. They couldn't be, but then if you took into account his antics with his aunt where'd you get to?

He banished such foolhardy conjecture. As he stood prodding at the beet he caught a glimpse of Madeleine's hat and realised he had not yet told her about her mother. He was waiting for a time, a right mood, when he could broach the subject delicately, cutting out all the embarrassing crap. She waved to him from the yard. He could have told her in the wagon on their way here.

"Mind you, I'm not saying there was no joy," Mme. Gabereau had said, "that it was all horrible and defiling. That's what you will have to remember when you marry Lena, my boy." Hector could repeat that bit, could he, if he were to tell Madeleine anything at all. When she got into her stride the mother spoke very fast, as though the thin piping voice were racing against time.

"Even Marcel could be tender at times, and he was devoted to the babies when they arrived. A model father. I could love him even though he was so domineering. I was a doormat. He is a fiery tempered man as you can see, and he got so he hadn't many other interests beyond the grocery business and drinking brandy with his cronies. One got used to it and life went along as it does. And I loved my babies. This set her off into agonizing sobs, weeping tearlessly as though her eyes were desiccated.

"Perhaps you should rest now, madame."

She nodded, and Hector helped her pull the blanket up under her chin.

"I shall never forget the day Marcel was introduced to me," she began the next time Madeleine bullied him to go up. Hector was getting used to the unprefaced bursts of reminiscence as with a brave, wavering smile she greeted him. Her head didn't wobble so much and perhaps the hair was not drawn so tightly back. There were few repetitions but still the confusion of identity. She insisted on holding his hand. She refused all offers of food or drink. He couldn't think what she lived on. On this evening she'd got her daughter to fetch from her wardrobe a shawl of knitted browns and ochres and yellows which was thrown round her shoulder and over the protective blanket.

"There you are. Maman's all dressed up for her beau," Madeleine had said as she left them together.

"My mother had taken me to some soirée or other—we were all very proper in those days. Boys and girls weren't allowed to meet in country lanes or at the street corners. Everything had to be above board. Anyway, there was this young man turned up, I don't know to this day how he'd talked his way in. He was very handsome then, slim, hair flattened with pomade, stiff white collar. He had a way with the girls. He comes from that place, where's it, where your M. Trou has his estaminet." She knew more of present events, obviously, than she let on.

"I fell for him like a ton of bricks. He had such merry eyes and such a sly way with him. I never knew he was on the make, that underneath all his flattery he had his eyes more on the store than on me. Maybe that's wrong. Maybe he had set his heart on both of us. And I certainly set my cap for him, so far as I could. He took my mother in, too, and my father, made out to be much more of a man of means than he was. When we married he hadn't a penny to his name if the truth be told."

At noon Hector and Willi Schmidt stopped for lunch. If it were too wet or cold they would eat in the kitchen of the main building where there was a wood fire. This day however, with the winds bringing the new season's warmth from the Atlantic, they sat on a bench in one of the greenhouses where it was quite hot out of the stiff breeze and the sun shining through the glass. Willi had rolled up his English Balaklava helmet and it perched rakishly on the top of his blond head. His long nose was red and shiny from the wind. Babette brought them sausage, crusty bread and apples, and a carafe of water.

"Beer there is not, darlink?" Willi asked. His French was German accented and structured.

Hector could not stand the bovine, sensuously demanding look the German gave to Babette nor, to be frank, the stupid moist-eyed way she returned his gaze. Hand on jutting hip, waggling her ass. What the fuck, there was something really revolting about this crazy affair with the enemy. How could a respectable Frenchwoman like her give herself with such obvious joy to a fucking Hun! God damn them all to hell!

"Willi, my dear," Babette said, patting her lover's cheek, "don't forget there's a war on, as though you don't know, darling. There are only old men left at the brewery and they are working short time. But we have a little beer left in the cellar, or there's plenty of wine if you like."

Underneath her apron she was wearing a fresh white blouse which gave her a skittish, flirty look. The erotic curves were emphasized on her short torso. Hector watched as the Kraut ran his long goddamn hand down her rump, pulled her towards him and kissed her forehead. Hector chewed stolidly at his bread and sausage. He much preferred the time when he and Madeleine were here on their own, even though all the while this lousy Boche had been in hiding. It must have been a shock for Babette when she heard he and Mad were coming, must have put a spoke in her little game.

The day Mme. Gabereau started relating the story of her marriage to Hector, or sometimes to a resurrected Paul, she suddenly took her hand from Hector's and began toying with her coloured shawl.

"It's pretty, isn't it? I love pretty things, clothes. You know, my son, everyone should wear clothes—even at night—from your neck to the tips of your toes. Unless you are perfectly shaped men or women and don't smell, and don't have a lot of hairs and blotches or knock knees or bandy legs, or a bum too near the ground, or flaky skin and are no more than twenty, then you should never be seen without nice clothes on. Most men and women are horrendous when they are naked, don't you see."

A faint smile came to the thin lips, a simper, a clearing of the clouded eyes with a flash of knowingness and yet no hint of prudery in the thin voice.

"You may think that woman of yours is beautiful and you are besotted by her figure." She was now apparently addressing her dead son, Paul, but Hector couldn't help but eavesdrop as she clutched his hand again and pressed it with distempered urgency.

"But listen to your mother. All your lovemaking should be in the dark with the candles out and the curtains drawn tight. Pitch black everywhere." Would she have talked like this in real life to her son on the brink of marriage, before she was stricken, when she herself was a dutiful wife in a familiar world? Hector found it hard to believe that she would.

"Marcel had one virtue going for him, my boy." She was talking to Hector now, and her voice was weakening, starting to whine. "There was no snooping or prying or wanting to see my private places. He'd follow me into this bedroom and before I started to undress, he would go over to the window and draw the curtains and he wouldn't look at me until I was under the covers. Yet often I would catch a glimpse of all those body hairs coming at me and the belly and the loins not to mention that great purple knob.... Oh dear! Whenever will this ghastly, ghastly pain go away?"

Willi went off with Babette to look for beer and he did not reappear that afternoon. As Hector was coming out of the greenhouse, he met Madeleine.

"Have you seen Schmidt? There's a ton of work to be done still. Goofing off again, is he?"

"How would I know?"

Madeleine tossed her head and blushed. She had taken the green turban from her thick glossy hair. As always she looked fresh, clear skinned, though in the daylight the little hairs on her upper lip were more pronounced. So far as he could remember his sister Michie hadn't any there, nor Aunt Sammy. Celine, however, had a regular moustache. Madeleine had not been her amiable, placid self since he had criticized Babette. As he eased past her they heard a woman's laugh coming from an upstairs window. After an accusatory glance at Madeleine, as though she were to blame for Willi's philandering, Hector collected his hoe and trudged off to the fields.

That had been the last time Mme. Gabereau had spoken to him, and as far as he knew she had not spoken at all to anyone else otherwise the house would be buzzing with surprise and joy. He'd made a point of visiting her to say goodbye before setting off in the wagon. Madeleine had gone upstairs to the bedroom with him but her mother was again in the same state as when Hector had first met her, rigid, uncommunicative, grief-racked. Blanket up to her chin, no pretty shawl.

"Oh dear," Madeleine said. "And she seemed to be coming along so well. Perhaps she knows you are leaving and that has set her back."

Hector loosened the soil around the young beets. He wondered whether the old lady was still as silent as the grave and what she would think of Babette spending the afternoon bedded in the arms of a German deserter. He was also worried about Madeleine. Perhaps he was in no position to moralize about her cousin's shameless affair with Schmidt. What the hell! Why should he worry about any of them? Shit, he knew he didn't mean to think that. It was a senseless bit of bravado. He was devoted and grateful to all the Gabereaus, and he even liked Babette despite her fucking a Kraut. Even so, remoter ties and loyalties would keep creeping into his consciousness, the more so now that Tyler had gone. As each day went by it was becoming more difficult to remedy the past if that is what he was going to do. Previously in sinking, helpless moods he'd turned to Tyler, brash, ironic, reassuring. He had hoped that in a very different way from Tyler, Madeleine would take his place, be someone he could go to for comfort.

He looked down the row that Willi should have been working instead of humping his mistress on this lovely afternoon in springtime. One of the things that stuck in Hector's craw was the realization that that lover boy with his long arms and legs and nose, snuffling about in Babette's bedroom, was in exactly the same military dilemma as Hector himself. What possible future was there for Willi? Presumably they shot deserters in the German army. But if Germany lost the war, as it had to, eventually, God knew when though, Willi would be herded back with all the prisoners of war and no one need ever know that he had deserted. In Hector's case there was no way that he could pretend he had been a prisoner.

The old lady had been right. Men and women were better with their clothes on, though there had been a time when a naked Aunt Sammy could drive him to distraction. And by and large the bare-assed young were not nauseating. He and a bunch of kids from school had many a time gone skinny dipping in a stream that ran into the Bow. They felt a bit silly sometimes about their little willies and shrivelled balls and they'd laugh at any guy that got an erection, though the water was so cold that rarely happened. Yes, old mother Gabereau was right, twenty was the maximum age for human nudity in public or private. Clothes were part of civilization. If you didn't believe that you should join the army.

The wind blowing over the beet field had eased considerably. Hector took off the jersey, dark blue almost black in some lights, that belonged to Babette's husband and looked like a fisherman's. He tied it round his waist. He still wore the thick shirt he'd been given by the Trous after he and Tyler had trashed their uniforms. One of the women washed it for him once a week. In the army you saw some awful sights in the barracks, in tents, in the trenches. You started with row on row of shining young men on parade, the regimental band playing martial airs, drums rattling away, caps on straight, jackets and trousers pressed, puttees meticulously bound, boots rigorously polished with elbow grease. They looked like civilized soldiers, the nation's pride, walking out with their best girls or with the local whores. Wonderful. But after they'd been herded together for years in durance vile, as had Hector and his comrades, they saw the pathetic underside. Degraded men in a state of undress, hairy bums, sweaty armpits, discarded underwear soiled with piss and semen, shit sometimes, after a bad battle.

Not only soldiers. Everywhere, people looked better when they were clothed, his father, mother, the cowhands, especially them. He'd never seen Madeleine or Celine undressed unless you count the time Tyler fucked Celine in the estaminet, and that was a ghastly memory best erased.

In the distance, Hector suddenly noticed, a cloud of dust arose, and as it approached he realized that it was stirred up by the wagon from Chaubet. The old horse was making what speed it could with its stiff leg, and Jules the wagoner was crouched forward and slapping the horse's flank with the reins. He reached Babette's house and disappeared inside. A few minutes later Hector heard Madeleine calling his name and soon saw her, green turban on, racing through the young beets towards him. When she reached him she flung her arms round him, her face in anguish, her heart throbbing against his chest.

"Take it easy, Mad." He pushed the turban gently back on her head and stroked her thick hair.

"It's maman."

She could not go on for a while, gulping for breath, sobbing into his shoulder.

"Take it easy, Mad."

He could feel her stiffen. She stood away from him, her face grave but composed, a wet patch on her cheek gleaming in the sunlight.

"Jules has just come from Chaubet with terrible news. Maman threw herself out of the bedroom window."

"For Crissake!"

He put his arm round her and they headed for the house. When they got to the yard, Willi Schmidt came out of the back door of the main house fastening up his trouser buttons.

"First it was the boys, one by one," Madeleine said. "And now this. I don't know how much more I can take."

## MADELEINE

Papa and I are the only two left now, and it seems only yesterday that there were seven of us. Mom used to say when she was in the kitchen baking, sleeves rolled up, flour up to her elbows, busy as ever, "When the stork kept on bringing those brothers of yours I believed I would never have a daughter." She rolled out a lump of pastry into a thin flap and placed it across a pie dish. I was getting to the age when I was beginning to have some little doubts about the stork story. Some of the girls at school would roll their eyes and giggle whenever it was mentioned.

"Then the good Lord was kind and our little Lena arrived."

She tapped me on the nose with a floury forefinger. The kitchen was a cheerful place in those days, and I loved being alone with her by the busy table and the hot oven. She trimmed off the excess pastry and gave it to me to make a little man with currants for eyes. He would go in the oven with the pie. I thought about that the other night and cried myself to sleep. In the morning I determined not to cry again, although I don't want anyone to think our maman was not worth weeping for.

When Jules the wagoner brought the news of mother's suicide to Babette's, I thought it was the end of the world. I said to him it must have been an accident, and he wouldn't answer. He did tell us that my father said that it was still far too dangerous for Hector to return to Chaubet.

"Balls!" Hector said, using some such army expression or other. It

doesn't bother me, really, I got so used to the bad language of Paul and Guy and the other two after they joined the army, not to mention the occasional cuss word as they were growing up and showing off, but I must say not one of them ever swore in front of Mom. Dad would curse under his breath now and then when he was mad. I couldn't bring myself to speak one of those dirty words to save my life.
"Of course I'm going back with you. To pay my respects."
Hector didn't tell me till much later about maman getting her speech back and chatting away to him on all sorts of subjects.
"You won't be able to pay any respects if you get yourself arrested like Tyler."
"We'll watch out for that, Mad."
"And what about Babette and all the work here?"
I can't think why I was trying to stop him because I badly wanted him to come with me. I suppose my mind was not working properly because of the shock, either that or subconsciously I wanted to protect him. I couldn't bear to think of his being shot.
"What about it? If only this bone lazy Schmidt would get off his butt in the afternoons."
"Hector, please."
The comments that Hector made about Willi made me uneasy for some unaccountable reason, because in my heart of hearts I too was surprised at Babette's behaviour. But then I've never been to bed with a man. No one expects a girl in my position to have been, least of all my parents who would have been grievously shocked at my even thinking about it. There was a boy once, whom Guy brought to our house, but that never got further than our holding hands and him giving me a chaste peck on the cheek. My father didn't approve of my going out with soldiers from the barracks and that was that. What I'm trying say is that Babette had all those years of marriage when she and her husband built up the business, and as far as we knew in Chaubet they were happy together. True, there were no kids, but then some couples are unlucky, aren't they? Even so, however much she missed him.... I have a married friend of my age who is always on about it and says once you get used to it, the bed thingy, you miss it an awful lot when you can't get it. I find it hard to believe that Babette would throw herself at a German deserter she found hiding in her potato store, but as I say being as ignorant as I am who knows how much she was driven into doing things she wouldn't do in normal life, with no war on. I'm having to think hard about the effect this other deserter is having on me. So far I haven't given Hector the slightest encouragement and that's not only because I can't see any future with him. Dad likes him a lot, I admit. A son come back, maybe.

Eventually I agreed Hector should go to Chaubet for a few days. He hid at the bottom of the wagon as we neared the town and kept indoors all the time he was there. We were both shocked at dad's appearance. He was almost in the same state that mom had been all those ghastly months, silent, staring into space, not moving from his chair at the kitchen table, sipping brandy. M. Trou was a tower of strength, jollying along his old friend, keeping the store going. We tried to reassure dad that miserable as everyone was, terribly sad and shocked, it was a merciful release for mom, although we could not give much consolation to him over the horrible way she died.

"Do you think she was, you know, making up for throwing that statue out of the window?" Hector asked me as we stood looking at her pallid sweet face in her coffin in the best front room.

I couldn't answer him. This war has made us all very confused, whatever the priest says. I used to go to mass, confession, communion, say my prayers, as a matter of habit without thinking too much about it. I still do. But I must say that when mom hurled the virgin into the yard I wasn't all that surprised. Shocked at first, yes. For a woman brought up in the faith as she was, as all of us were, she must have been, I don't know, I was going to say desperate. Everyone says the war is going to be over this year. I hope so, but every time we make a big push and gain some ground then it seems we are further back than we were before it.

Dad thought it was not safe for Hector to show his face at my mother's funeral. Despite the military commandeering every animal that could run, kick or jump, the Chaubet undertaker had managed to hang on to two black horses to draw his hearse and when they arrived outside our house with black plumes nodding above their heads Hector stared at them curiously from an upstairs window. He had never seen anything like that. He also said that he hated funerals anyway but would have attended in honour of maman. Dad was pleased at the impressive turnout of mourners from the town, including the women who had accused us of harbouring a British deserter. Little did they guess that Hector was hiding in the main bedroom. He wanted to stay on and help with the store, but dad had made a miraculous recovery, pulling himself out of his paralysing grief. He said he and his friend Trou could manage. He looked fondly at Hector.

"Besides," he added enigmatically, "we can't afford to lose another one, can we?"

I felt my face going hot when he said this. My father is a man of wayward passion as all of his children had experienced from time to time, and there was little question that he had taken a strong fancy to Hector, to what end I found it embarrassing to guess. Did he, and that was why I blushed, think of him as a prospective son-in-law? I can take things equably as a rule, but I resented this kind of hint and manoeuvre, if it were true. I was having enough difficulty analysing my own feelings about Hector, thank you very much.

"You are far safer at Babette's, son," my father said.

So off Hector went once more in the wagon with Jules. The understanding was that I would join him there in two or three weeks. That was my father's plan, not mine. When Jules returned he brought the news that Willi had been captured.

## BABETTE

"Bonjour, Babette. Comment ça va?"

Hector jumps off the wagon and comes forward, arms outstretched, to embrace me just as though he were a proper Frenchman. His face is fresh, guileless, his hair ruffled (he is not wearing a cap on this mild spring day), his smile diffident and I see him through eyes, clouded with misery, as though I'd never noticed him much before. Of course I haven't, since I've been totally absorbed body and soul with Willi Schmidt. I have a feeling that Hector disapproved of my carrying on with Willi. And who, sacred blue, does Hector think he is?

"Hey, Madame Babette, what is the matter with you?"

I cannot help myself. I bury my face in his chest. He is so tall this foreign soldier from across the ocean and his muscles are as hard as iron. Quite a guy. But he is gentle and he strokes my cheek and looks down into my face. His accent is different from ours, naturally, but his French is truly amazing, far better than Willi's. As I think of Willi's bad French I start to howl.

"There there, Babette."

The hard lines which overlay the boy's face are softening and his beard which is browner than his fair hair makes him look like the picture of Jesus in my old Sunday school book. I am almost ashamed to tell him what is causing my grief, but then I think that after all he too must have doubts, mixed loyalties, mustn't he? He too is up the creek without a paddle.

"They came yesterday and took Willi away."

I press my forehead into his jacket. It looks and smells like an old one of cousin Gabereau's.

"Who came?"

"An army officer and two soldiers. Some kind neighbour must have betrayed me. I thought perhaps at first they were looking for you."

"Christ! They did not say anything about me?"
"Oh no."
"But they were French army?"
"Of course."

That oaf Jules is taking it all in, standing like a bag of bones between us and his wagon. I'm too miserable to bother about hiding anything from him but I wouldn't be at all surprised if he knows about Willi and me. I wonder if they told cousin Gabereau. I don't think Madeleine would have done so and this Hector can't very well go shooting his mouth off, seeing what he's done himself.

"I happened to look out of the upstairs window and saw the three of them marching down the lane as ferociously as though they were going into the Battle of the Somme."

It was afternoon and Willi was bored with hoeing beets and was insisting on making love. I asked him why not wait until night but he'd already pulled off his trousers. I turned from the window in horror and told Willi to get his pants back on. I don't mention this part to Hector.

"I screamed at Willi to get himself down to the potato store as quickly as he could and hide himself under the old sacks. You remember where you found him. It's dark there and a good hiding place as Willi well knew. Then they came hammering at the door as though they owned the place."

"Come on, let's go inside," Hector says and puts his arm round my shoulders and leads me into the kitchen and shuts the door on Jules. I start my foolish crying again and Hector wants to get me a drink.

"No, no, thank you." I go to the tap and wash my face. I look at myself in the little oval mirror above the sink. My hair's a mess.

"Of course they find Willi in no time and he pretends he has just arrived and broken into the house and that he doesn't know me. Bless him. The officer looks disappointed. An older man with a pasty face and a pot belly, he didn't seem to me like a fighting soldier. He obviously doesn't believe a word and there's no way Willi looks as though he's been sleeping in hedge backs. Someone had obviously told him that Willi was..." I blush and Hector looks embarrassed, "..more to me than he should be. You could see the way the gallant officer's dirty mind was working, hoping that here was a chance for the villagers to shave my hair off."

"Shave your hair off?"

"Yes. That's what they do if a woman has any..." I blush again, "is suspected of having a German lover."

I said a moment ago that I don't care what Jules the carter thinks, but that's just whistling in the dark. For some infuriating, unaccountable reason I do care what Hector thinks, and I want him to have a good opinion of me. When the men were working out in the fields Lena and I used to chat about them, naturally, as women will. I asked her if she had a soft spot for Hector and she said she didn't really know. I suppose, if I'm honest, I was on the defensive about Willi and me, half wanting her to admit to some bizarre relationship, a weakness, something a bit off limits. She is so proper, a darling, but proper. She said her heart was full of pity for him, for them all, when they'd arrived pulling that cart from the battlefield and even when her father told her that Hector was a deserter she felt sorry for him, even liked him more. Well, there you are. In my opinion Lena is probably fond of him but she is a very undemanding as well as virtuous girl, very much under cousin Gabereau's thumb. I'm not necessarily saying her father's a harsh man, but there are stories among the relatives about the way he treated his wife. His changing the name of the grocery store, for instance, shows which way the wind blew. Very assertive, very much the boss in that house. They say one of the boys took after him, but Lena is his exact opposite.

"But that's barbaric, I can't believe it. I suppose it grows back again in time. The hair?"

I smile wetly at Hector. He doesn't seem to get it and yet he's not stupid by a long chalk. I'm pretty sure he isn't.

"It's the shame, Hector. The shame. Most people have lost a lot in this perishing war, I don't have to tell you that. Some have lost everything, possessions, homes, husbands, sons. If a Frenchwoman sleeps with one of the enemy they think she is a traitor. And she deserves all she gets."

Hector has been bending over me, humouring me, being the big strong man. Suddenly his face alters, the firm features and lines disintegrate.

"I'm just as bad as you, Babette. In my own way, perhaps worse. And here I've been...shit!"

"What?"

"Judging you. I ought to go and fuck myself."

I know that Godforsaken, helpless feeling, don't I just.

"I'm sorry for the cussing," Hector says.

My husband, Georges, and I spent long hard years building up this business and we got on very well together, considering. He had large smelly feet and never cut his toenails properly but, my God, I'm not making a big deal out of that, even though my ankles and shins were covered with scratches and cuts. My pet name for him was Sol. Although we weren't always billing and cooing you could say that as we worked side by side there existed a deep love and respect for each other. And if anyone had suggested that I would let a damned Boche into Sol's bed, well,

I would have knocked their filthy blocks off. I suddenly find myself confessing, explaining to Hector in my kitchen, in Sol's and my kitchen.

"We were just beginning to show a half decent profit when this rotten war came and before you could say Jack Robinson Sol got his call up papers and off he had to go."

There's a knock on the door. It's that wizened old pain in the ass, Jules.

"The boss says I gorra get back tonight and I hafta be in Chaubet afore dark. These brave soldiers'll steal the wheels offen your wagon if you aren't careful and what would Mister Gabereau say to that, eh? He'd tear his hair out I can tell you. And mine as well, more like."

I feel as miserable as a wet hen and guilty as the devil about leaving Jules out in the yard like that. My head's spinning. All the old agonies of Sol's being dragged off into the army are coming back with a vengeance. And the shock of the arrest of Willi is mixed up with love and treachery. I jump up from the table, nearly bumping Hector's chin with my head.

"Come in Jules, come in. Sorry to keep you waiting, my old one. You must have a drink and I'll get you something for you to eat on the way back, that is if you really must go now."

"That I should, missus."

"The wine's in its usual place," I say to Hector. "Could you pour him...use the big mug over there."

I put together some bread and garlic sausage and a piece of cold sweet pudding I know he likes.

"You sure you can't stay and eat here?"

"Best be getting along, missus."

Hector asks if I want some wine and I nod without thinking. If Jules hadn't knocked on the door just then I was going to tell Hector about the state I'm in. I don't know whether it's better to keep it to myself. And I don't quite know how I'd put it in words he would understand. I was about to protest to Hector that I am not a cheap tart, that I did not lie down for Willi as hot as a fiddler's bitch, but you know that is exactly what I did do. I don't want to go blaming it all on Willi. He's just an ordinary guy, with a guy's wants, pressed into the army, starved of women. I'm sure if I'd said no or even frowned he would not have laid a finger on me. I drink some of the wine. It's sharp, this wartime stuff, but I suppose we're lucky to have any at all. Jules gulps his down at one go and wipes his mouth with the back of his hand and we see him on his way. Hector and I return to the kitchen and he pours more wine.

"How are they all now at Chaubet? After the funeral? I should have asked before this. Forgive me. I'm so confused. I didn't sleep a wink last night."

"Madeleine's taken it worse than she lets on. I guess she's relieved that her mother's suffering is over. I thought her father was going to be another basket case at first. There's only M. Gabereau and Madeleine left now out of all that family, course you know that. The people I came with, the Trous, did not know madame except as a human cabbage. I think M. Trou was taken up to the room one time or the other but the rest did not even see her."

"But you did?"

"Oh yes."

"Lena told me the mother took a fancy to you."

"Perhaps. It was agony to see her like that, destroyed by grief."

"She lost her voice completely, and all interest in life, Lena says."

"Almost. Mad could understand some of the things she tried to say."

I can see that he is on the brink of telling me something else about Mme. Gabereau and then he decides against it. Even though he is cruelly young he is the sort of man a woman can confide in. And trust. His eyes have obviously witnessed much pain but now there is a kindness and comfort in them. It's strange that a boy like him should be able to cope with the horrors like that. It helps me even in my raw state. He is embarrassed at the moment.

"M. Gabereau thought I should come back here...to give you a hand. But also for my own safety. That gentleman does so much for me. I hope it's all right, my coming. I mean, we didn't know about Willi."

I can't help laughing in a bleak way. I put my hand on his, which is small for a man of his build. Sol had big hands as well as big feet.

"Hector, my friend. You and Lena caught me in a bad, wicked situation. I've being trying to summon up the courage to explain how it happened, the loneliness and so on. But that's all excuses."

Hector looks out of those compassionate eyes and you can almost see the scar of grief in them. I all but falter.

"What I'm telling you is that I am not a whore. I don't jump into bed with every man who comes to this house."

"Yeah...well."

"I'm glad Cousin Gabereau sent you. You know how much I need help."

"That's all right then, Babette," Hector says. "For both of us, eh? Let's get into them fields."

He takes his coat off and looks around for the hoe. I laugh and say, "Wait a minute big feller. You'd better get something to eat first." I'm still in a misery of grief and shock but there is a glimmer of light on the horizon. I hope I mean what I say about not jumping into bed, but surely I do, I couldn't. Devices and desires are whirling round in my head. It's obvious that Cousin Gabereau intends Hector for Lena.

# TEN

## MARIE LOUISE

Of course it felt like the end of the world when I got that telegram from Ottawa. Bridget took it from me, holding it between her thumb and forefinger as though it were something she'd pulled out of the john and silently handed it to Angela who appeared genuinely moved and tears came.

"I'm sorry, Marie," she said and sniffed and dabbed her eyes.

Not so long ago, when she was living in the shacks, she would not have dared to call me Marie. Irreverently I wondered what shenanigans went on between her and Hector and then was instantly ashamed of my foul thoughts. At that baleful time malicious bits of garbage, strewn in my head, were surfacing. Jenkins's boy was walking slowly away, shoulders hunched, down the road. A wind came whistling down from the Rockies and I tried to pull my blouse tighter round my throat. The earth was unsteady. A huge knot of vain fear filled my stomach but my mind was not yet numb. On the contrary it was flashing with pictures and memories of Hector at all his stages, as a mother's does in times of pride or anxiety. Richard tugged at my skirt.

"Are you all right, Annie Lou?"

Because of my scheming we obviously had to surrender our real relationship of mother and grandmother and we'd all agreed that Bridget and I would be aunts to the little boy. Lou was easier for his baby tongue than bridging the "r" in "Marie." Nick was Unca Nick. Oh dear, I don't feel old enough to be a granny. I remembered the breathless, wonderful night when Hector was conceived with a blizzard raging outside in Winnipeg. I remembered the time he was Richard's age. The ground beneath my feet seemed to be exploding and melting at the same time.

"I think we'd better go inside," Bridget said.

We three women trooped in, Angela holding Richard's hand, and Bridget set about making some coffee. This was the room where Hector had been born and dear old Dot Howard had been such a help. We got through that awful day somehow. Michelle was in Calgary and had to be told. Nick was out on the ranch. After a shock like that thumps you and knocks all the breath out of your body, the paralysing grief sets in. Later I began to wonder who I was being sorry for. My son? Before Nick came back that day, we sent Billy Lilley out for him. I believe I was afraid of showing him the wretched telegram. Even though I was sick to death myself I had a dread anticipation of his reaction. And my fears proved only too true. My beloved Stoneface was shattered.

"When did this come?"

Bridget and Angela and Richard had gone back home.

"Jenkins's kid brought it an hour ago."

They say that if you live intimately with someone day in and day out you are least likely to notice any marked changes in that person, but at that grievous moment I could see how the war years had drastically altered my husband's appearance. The normal toll of the years had trebled, the lines about his eyes and nose had deepened, the severity of his countenance become rigid. I confess that I've mocked him for putting on such a grim uncompromising appearance, although he would lighten up with me, not so much recently, not really in the war years, but I don't want to see again the total collapse of a strong man's face. As he read the telegram in our front room, the one where Hector was born and which looks out on the flower beds, the lineaments of his face, so firm and unflinching, disintegrated as though the head bones were melting. His lips were drawn back in a ghastly snarl. He did not weep and perhaps that would have been better than his dry-eyed distress. I was glad Bridget and the others were not present to witness this searing, humiliating exhibition.

"Don't, Nick. I can't bear it."

I embraced him and his fingers dug into my shoulders and back as though he would tear me apart. He pulled away from me and sat in my old nursing chair which for sentimental reasons I still kept in that room. He sat in awkward misery, his long legs folded, his knees jutting sideways, his hands hanging loose almost to the floor, head down so all I could see was the crown where his hair was starting to grey. Slowly his features began to recompose.

Anxious as I had been I would never have believed that he would have taken the news of Hector's death so much to heart. He had taken off his hat and thick leather jacket as he came storming through the kitchen. He was wearing a black and red plaid shirt which I should have thrown out years ago. I looked down on him in silence. It was better not to say anything just yet. I went to the kitchen to fetch a mug of stewed coffee.

Nick's being knocked out like that helped me to inch back to normality, though at that stage I felt nothing could be ever steadied and ordered again. The shock of Bridget's pregnancy was nothing compared to the finality of this flimsy notice of death. Hers, however shameful and profoundly disturbing, had after all been an announcement of a new life, bizarre as it was. Now one of the begetters of that new life, and how delighted we all were with Richard now, was slain on foreign soil. Foreign. Despite my ancestry I can feel no attachment to France. Nick stands up as I bring in the coffee. He will not look at me.

"I'm going to take off, missy."

I want to throw my arms about him, hold him here to share our loss, but I know my Nicholas, not all but a lot of him. Better not to. He grabs his jacket and hat. He leaves the back door open and I hear him muttering to his horse, Jacky, and then the drumming of the hooves in the back yard as they gallop off.

I was dead certain that Stoneface was riding out to see Clarence Manythumbs. Nick thinks I'm totally ignorant of the drunken Indian he visits once in a blue moon somewhere out on one of the reserves but round here nothing can be kept secret for long. I don't sneak around eavesdropping, believe me, but if you keep your ears open you can pick up all sorts of interesting information and maybe some things you don't want to hear. Often the hands give the game away inadvertently, and that scoundrel Chuck Turner tells me the wildest things when he is sucking up to me.

"I saw that Indian friend of the boss's in town, Miz Marie. Last night. Me and Billy was down there, like. Rolling around real bad he were. Dunno what brought him in."

"Oh."

We were planting out pansy seedlings. Tough as old boots, pansies, frost or no frost. Chuck had prepared the ground and I was putting the plants into little holes and watering them in, a job I love doing. My grandson, Richard, was just about one year old, I can't remember whether we'd celebrated his first birthday or not.

"Which Indian is this, Chuck?"

"A crazy feller called Clarence. The white kids mock him something cruel. Folks say he was a hotshot hunter at one time but the liquor got to him. It does to all of them."

"Pass me that watering can will you Chuck?"

I don't wear gloves for gardening. I like the feel of the soil and getting my fingers all dirty.

"The boss has knowed him since they were young 'uns."

The little roots of one plant are intertwined with another and you've got to separate them carefully or there's a chance they won't take, though pansies can stand a lot of punishment.

"You've talked about this Indian before, you know, Chuck. Is there anything special you want to tell me this time?"

"No, miz. Just happened to see him, like."

I don't know how much malice there was in Chuck's gossip, probably little, and there may have been a naïve but touching concern that I should be kept informed. It didn't much matter. I figured out over the years enough of Nick's mysterious relationship and didn't want to learn any more. Sufficient unto the day is the evil thereof. Not long before Sam died in that terrible accident—he was a sweet man for all his faults—he let drop a few hints when he was drunk one night about Nick having a problem in the past with an Indian girl, or a half Indian, but I left that buried in the back of my mind. The French can be both practical and sagacious as well as passionate and jealous in affairs of the heart. Mind you he'd have got the rough edge of my tongue and more if I caught him fooling around with an Indian or any other girl after we were married and yet, after Hector, Bridge, Richard, we have no longer any basis for moral values. Even so, I firmly believe that Nick has been utterly faithful to me, true blue Stoneface, and that is a comfort.

I guessed that day the telegram came that he was galloping off to search out crazy Clarence or whatever the drunk was called. And if he could get any consolation from a chronically pissed Indian that was all right by me. There were many days and months ahead when we could mourn together. The last occasion, that I knew of at any rate, when he'd gone off like that was after the Sunday dinner when we'd broken the news to him about Bridget's pregnancy. I used to think we were a lucky and happy family. That was the day of the fire in Higgins Bend when Dicky Leech was burned alive and Nick pulled Angie out of the flames.

There was a knock at the back door and I realized I was still standing like a zombie by the nursing chair. Billy Lilley was there when I opened the door, his filthy hat in his hand, his grey hair, it had got so much greyer, almost white, catching the afternoon sun which had broken out fitfully.

"I seed the boss riding off like the devil, ma'am."

When I sent Billy to get Nick, Billy just happened to have come back with the wagon from Calgary. I didn't tell him anything about Hector. I didn't want Nick to get the news that way.

"Is there some bother, ma'am? Is there ought I can do?"

"Come right in, Billy."

"My boots is dirty ma'am."

I almost screamed at the good old man.

"Come in, Billy. It doesn't matter. You can smoke that disgusting old pipe of yours if you like. And spit. Spit all over the fucking kitchen."

"Ma'am?"

Billy looked bewildered and stood his ground at the back door. He rubbed the bristles on his square chin apologetically. Then out of nowhere Chuck Turner, bobbing up and down with his ghastly limp, loomed up behind him and I saw a few of the hands riding in from the ranch up to the bunkhouse.

"I'm sorry, Billy. Come on in the pair of you."

They advanced a few steps into the kitchen, a couple of Nick's faithful cowhands, the long and the short, Chuck, taller, ungainly on his bad leg, Billy Lilley, compact, kind inquiring eyes. I guessed they knew something terrible had happened. I picked up the telegram and read it out to them.

"We sure is sorry ma'am. I guess all the fellers will be."

Billy's eyes were gazing into an unknown distance as he muttered his slow condolence. It was getting to be more than I could bear.

"Would you like a drink? Rye?"

"No thank yer ma'am."

Chuck tapped his long nose. His bad leg trembled as though he had the shakes.

"Well mebbe, Miz Marie, just a small..."

Billy kicked Chuck's good leg. He thought I didn't see him do it.

"Get outa here, willya."

It was Billy Lilley who took me to see Dot Howard that night, three years ago was it, of the Higgins Bend fire.

ଔ☙

Later historians were to say, never having been there but plump and comfortable in their little towers and with the lofty assurance of hindsight, that danger, disease, frustration, weather extremes, heartbreaking disappointment, finance, stamina, courage or the absence of the last three, crop failures, stock infestation, were all daunting factors in settling the west, but that perhaps the most devastating and unforgiving of all was fire. Shacks and bigger wooden buildings, huddled together in unplanned proximity, were ready fuel for ravaging flames accidentally or sometimes deliberately started. Through their research the historians discovered that the many of the early communities had been partially or totally destroyed by fire. Even an isolated ranch house could be burned down in an hour or two.

Higgins Bend was no exception. When Nick rode off into the west carrying the burden of his new knowledge, the unbearable fact of his son and sister-in-law fornicating and creating a child, Christ, how dumb could they get, Marie and Bridge sat together for long hours that gloomy afternoon, sisters-in-law, confederates in womanly misery, saying very little. Shortly after dark, Billy Lilley came to the house. Marie had never seen him so perturbed.

"Where's the boss, ma'am?"

"He's out. What's the rush, Billy?"

"There's a fire in the town. A big one by the looks of her."

Marie and Bridget admitted to each other afterwards, when they got over the shock of the destruction and the deaths, that they almost welcomed Billy's news, catastrophic as it was. It gave them something to do. It shook them out of their apathy and diverted and neutralized for a time their self pity.

"I don't believe I've ever been so depressed as I was that afternoon," Bridge said often in later days.

The church was in a part of the town untouched by the fire and there, together with the local doctor who broke commendably out of his usual alcoholic stupor, they set up a place of refuge for the injured and the homeless. They were helped by other wives whilst the men fought the fire.

"Where's Dot Howard?" Marie asked.

"Haven't seen her all night."

"You seen her, doc?"

"Nope."

No doubt she'll be along soon, Marie thought. She was invaluable in a crisis, whooping cough epidemic, measles, drownings, farm accidents. Always there when needed. Gradually the stricken walked or were carried in. Some badly burned, some choking from the foul smoke. One kid had broken his leg when his mother threw him out of the window and another old guy had a heart attack, not too serious according to the doctor. A man who worked in the brickyard was caught with his pants down in the outhouse and had the skin scorched off his buttocks. The rest of his home was untouched. He refused to let Bridget care for him. For all her present self recrimination Aunt Sammy remained an attractive woman as she helped the burned and the battered in the church. Her high necked green blouse was fastened by a scarab brooch which Lady Icen had given her and she'd tied an apron round her long dark skirt. Her black hair had shaken loose and a lock fell across her broad forehead as she looked questioningly at the man from the brickyard.

"I gotta see him, the doc, Mrs. Sam. I hardly dares tell you where I got myself burned," he said. "Begging your pardon, like."

He told the doctor he wanted to be treated in private where all the world and his wife couldn't see him naked as the day he was born.

"Where, for Pete's sake, man?" The doctor spat out the small cigar he was smoking. "Just you tell me where we can be private in all this. You're not the only one, you know. If you don't pull your pants down right now you can get your ass out of here blisters and all."

Some of the burns were sickening. Under the doctor's instruction the women dabbed them gently with a boracic lotion and bandaged them wherever it was possible. Late in the evening when no more injured seemed to be coming in and Nick had already taken Angela up to the ranch, Billy Lilley, face blackened, jacket torn and scorched, came into the church and went straight to Marie.

"I think you'd best come with me, ma'am. If you're not too tired like."

"Is the fire finished, Billy?"

"She's just about burned herself out. A few hot spots by the river and that's it."

Marie finished tying up the sprained ankle of a little girl, Emma, from a large family of Wilkinsons and gave her a smile and a pat on the cheek. The dull ache and bewilderment of the afternoon were still there, but the fire and its demands had taken her out of herself. She looked around the church. Most of the people who had to stay had stoically settled down, but there was not room for everyone who had lost their homes and some accommodation would have to be found for them. Folks would rally round okay, but someone had to make sure that no one was left out.

"Can't it wait, Billy?"

He'd taken off his hat and stood solidly, square, before her. He must shave sometimes, Marie thought, otherwise he'd have a beard. But when, she speculated inconsequentially, the bristles on his chin seemed always of a given length, not very attractive. His eyes as always were gentle.

"It's Dot Howard, ma'am."

"Oh no."

She grabbed her coat and hat and followed Billy down the blackened streets, acrid with the smell of smoke. Now that the fire had passed, it was like a ghost town. They reached a familiar house.

"Isn't this Dot's place?"

"Sure is. Hardly been touched, eh? But I guess Dot must of gone to help a neighbour."

They walked to a burned out shell a couple of dwellings further along and the sick apprehension of the afternoon returned to Marie. Dot was lying inside an open front door, her nurse's bag on the ground just out of reach of her outstretched hand. Debris of the fire littered the interior, some of it still smouldering, but the body of Dot appeared mostly unmarked.

"I can't think what happened to her, nor where the folk are what lived here. It's a mystery. Seems as though she bin struck down by sump'en, but then there's no sign of no beam or nothing like that."

"But she's...?"

"Dead as a doornail, ma'am."

☙❦❧

I was reminded of that sad night when I read out the telegram to Billy and Chuck. For one thing, Nick had gone riding off to see Clarence Whosit and for another, Billy had come to tell me about the fire and later in the church about Dot. When we sorted everyone out, incidentally, we counted only two deaths in that terrifying blaze, Dot's and Dicky Leech's. Lucky for most of us. I was mortified over Dot, I think the whole township was. It's ironic how things work out. I mean, if Dicky hadn't died that night we wouldn't have had Angela bringing up Richard. I'm not sure we would have had Richard. In that case we'd have lost an awful lot of joy.

We weren't to know the day the telegram came, but the war had not much longer to grind on to the eleventh hour of the eleventh day of the eleventh month. Some poor fellows were killed on the tenth day, and some were killed in August 1914, some mothers' sons. Nick came home that night looking neither the better nor the worse for his encounter with his aboriginal friend, and we were united in our grief though we each tried not to make a big deal of it outwardly.

# ELEVEN

"Sarge."

"What is it, Billie Joe?"

"I is shit scared, sarge."

"That's nothing to be ashamed of. Every goddamn mother's son is and if he says he ain't he's telling a goddamn lie."

"I wish Tyler was with us."

"Me too. He sure would steady everyone down. He was as sick as a dog when that arm went bad on him. He oughta of reported it before he got hisself poisoned up like he did, but I guess he didn't want to miss this goddamn attack. Crazy guy that one. Great guy. I think he's gonna lose that arm of his."

"Corporal Stuyvesant said he was suffering real terrible, moaning in his sleep, like."

"I never seen such a mess as that there sore. Cut it on the wire, he said, and didn't think nothing of it. Stinking it was. Youda thought he'd of noticed the smell."

"Them guns sure is making one helluva din. A feller can't hear hisself speak."

"Just you think what them Kraut bastards is feeling, Billie Joe. All that shit's falling on them."

"I keep thinking of that, sarge. And I keep thinking that soon the shit's gonna be falling on us."

"We'll be all right. You just wait."

"What time is it, sarge?"

"Not long now, son. You got that old bayonet fixed on good and tight?"

"You bet."

ଔ✥ଈ

At about the time that the infantry regiment from Kansas was taking part in the spring offensive in which the doughboys marched like lambs to the slaughter and which Tyler escaped by the skin of his teeth, and about the time that Nick and Marie Plouvier were consumed in parental mourning, their son Hector was sitting with Babette at the foot of a lone poplar on the edge of a field further along the lane from the beets he and Willi had worked. He'd been planting potatoes all morning and a back breaking never-ending job it was. Give him his hoss and the ranch and fence mending any day, but he could do without those thoughts or comparisons. Babette's and Sol's original design was for lettuce, radish, spring greens sown there, but the authorities ordered them what to plant these days and they demanded solider stuff for the troops, spuds and beets, no salady frills.

"Just the usual grub. Nothing very exciting," Babette said as she bounced up wearing a dirndl dress, the hem of which scarcely reached the top of her boots. She'd brought out lunch in a basket with a brown check cloth on top.

"I could have come to the house."

"Yes, but it's such a lovely day. Let's go over to that tree. The grass is quite dry. Do you like raw onion?"

She was roguish, hips swaying in front of him.

"Sure do."

Of the two of them, paradoxically, it seemed that Hector missed Willi more, though not a great deal more, as a man about whom it being the way the ironies of war shaped up, a fellow outcast prodding away at the good earth, one he could identify with, a man about whom he could say he's just as screwed up as I am. When he and Babette sat down, she bent over and took his face in her hands and stroked his beard.

"How soft it is. What a dear you are, Hector."

Her fondling may well have held no amorous suggestion, but Hector was not so sure. She had made an astonishing recovery from Willi's arrest. She bubbled with a natural vitality that made suspect her lamentation for both Sol, her husband, and Willi, her very recent lover. Apart from beard stroking, which Hector had to admit he liked, she had made no very obvious coy or seductive moves, but Hector was sure it would not be difficult, if he wished, to do a Willi and exchange the potato sowing that afternoon for Babette's bed. But perhaps that was being shitty and unfair to her.

"You don't have to work your fingers to the bone you know, Hector."

Hector took a bite of buttered bread and then a bite of red cheese and then gnawed at the onion. It made his eyes water.

"I've got to do something for a living, something to repay you folks for looking after me and risking God knows what if you're caught."

"I don't know about that. There isn't any real risk, is there?"

"What about getting your hair shaved off?"
"Oh that's different. You're not a German, silly man."

Babette was wriggling around on her seat. Even when she was sitting down her head came only up to his shoulder. Hector was not unhappy here in the peace and isolation of a little corner of French countryside so near to that pitiful and fearful war and yet curiously removed from it. Sometimes, through half-closed eyes, he fancied himself back on the ranch and that probably partly accounted for the sick bouts of guilt and sorrow that punctuated his day. He tried not to think of Aunt Sammy, and Angela hardly ever entered his daily consciousness. In battle, in the long tedious weeks in and out of the trenches, a soldier could develop an artificial neutrality towards his nearest and dearest, kin he may never see again and who, in Hector's case, now probably believed him dead. He could, and sometimes did, set up a mock indifference to them, chase them from his memory or at least distort their images. Their way was no longer his which was concerned solely with survival from hour to hour. Nevertheless, after the shock of his monstrous act of desertion had eased somewhat, their forgotten shapes would come back to haunt him, lacerating his peace of mind in their mute and urgent affection. The natural first of his kin had to be his mother, the woman whose body had given him his body, his heart, his liver, his balls. Marie Louise. His conscience. She was the most difficult to banish from nagging thought, although a subtle change had come in their love and regard for each other during the frenzy of his adolescent affair with Aunt Sammy.

"I don't know how you can eat an onion like that," Babette said and waggled the toes of her boots. An early cabbage butterfly fluttered past in tipsy flight.

"My Sol never could eat a raw onion. He had to be careful, you see. His stomach gets upset so easily."

As his infatuation for Aunt Sammy had intensified, Hector imagined there had been a change in his relationship with both his parents, but they had never said a word even if they had suspected anything. It was an intuitive inkling of growing up on his part perhaps, an unconscious foray from the nest, from family binding. His mother had always been there to turn to emotionally and his father had, well, he'd taught him to ride a horse among other things. Under the poplar tree with Babette Hector wondered whether his father had ever—before his marriage of course—dipped his wick into some willing prairie maiden, whether his granite face cracked into a smile when he did so and then Hector tried to switch such a thought off because it was too embarrassing to think of one's father in gross situations. That was not the easiest thing to do either because there was more to his grim faced pa than riding lessons and mending the fucking fence posts. A masculine bond existed between him and his father, indestructible so far at least, of pride and emulation which was as strong in its own way as any umbilical cord. Dear old dad, God damn you.

"I should have brought something to sit on," Babette said. "The ground is not as dry as it looks."

The poplar had already shed some of its sticky buds and one or two were clinging to her dress.

"You're very quiet today, Mister Hector. What gives? Has the cat got your tongue?"

"I was thinking about my parents. They've likely been told by now that I've been killed. In action, in a battle."

"Oh. That's terrible. Terrible. Terrible."

She turned to him in horror, her fingers touching his beard.

"Can't you let them know? Can't you do anything?"

These French women were too kind. They were smothering him with compassion.

"Napoo. Sweet Fanny Adams. Not unless I want to get myself shot. And then they'd be no better off than they are now. Worse, I think. I certainly would be worse off, I suppose."

Aunt Sammy was kin too, very much so, even if not by blood. Hector gnawed at the onion and tears came to his eyes. He had been banishing and reinstating Aunt Sammy ever since he got on the train an eternity ago for the infantry depot in Ontario. It was about time, wasn't it, after living for years with men in daily peril of extinction or mutilation, of whizz-bangs and star-shells and corpses hanging on the wire, to stop thinking of her as Aunt Sammy. He was no longer a callow nephew to have his prick pulled out in a barn with only a sick steer looking on, shitting intermittently. Old Mme. Gabereau, for Chrissake, who had lost four fucking sons, count them, dad, one, two, three and four, shot to fucking ribbons in the trenches, looked up to him as a saviour, was devoted to him. No sir, he was his own man now. And if Angela—who the heck was she?—and Bridget and his mom and dad were upset well that was no skin off his nose.

"Holy Mary! Who is this crowd?"

Babette jumped to her feet as they heard the creaking of Jules's wagon coming down the lane. She shook her dress, picking the buds off it.

"It looks as though the whole of Chaubet's come visiting."

They had expected Madeleine to return soon to Babette's and she was indeed on the cart as demure as ever and also, waving excitedly, were her father, his bat ears obvious from this distance, and Celine and Uncle Joe who presumably had come for the ride. My God, Hector thought uncharitably, Celine, the big-hearted whore. He'd been forgetting her in his permutations.

☙❀❧

"Okay, Billie Joe, here we go. There's the whistle. Get your butt up this here ladder."

"The fucking moon's fucking bright tonight, sarge. Like a fucking searchlight."

"Yup. That's the idea, so's we don't get ourselves lost when we're kicking ass off of them Kraut."

"But it means they can fucking see us coming a mile off."

"Come on, kiddo."

"I wish Tyler was with us."

"Keep your place. I'll be right with you as soon as we get over the top, stay real close behind me."

"I can't hardly hear a word you says, sarge, because of this goddamn noise."

"Here we are then, Billie Joe. Here's the gap in the wire. Now just run forward, crouching, easy does it, just like when we was training. Billie Joe. BILLIE. Oh Christ no.... Oh you murdering assholes. Oh no...."

☙❀❧

Hector did his best to live up to M. Gabereau's expectations, tried determinedly to stoke up his feelings to the necessary level for loving Madeleine and wanting to marry her. After all, there were just the two Gabereaus left out of a family of seven. What a crock! In a sense her father had saved his life, and was still protecting him.

"You can put us up for the night, Cousine Babette?" Gabereau asked as he clambered down stiffly from the cart.

"Yes, certainly. I am so sorry about madame...."

He waved her condolences aside. It was obvious to Hector that his wife's death was just one more horror to be consigned to his overflowing pit of misery as quickly as was decently possible. For the moment Gabereau appeared to have cheerier intentions in his mind. He was a tough old bird and no mistake.

"You can fix up Jules in the stables. He won't mind."

"I think we can find him somewhere better than that, cousin."

Throughout that spring and summer of 1918 the blossom came and went, the insects did their stuff, the fruit formed as nature moved in her replenishing cycle. To the east the guns were never silent, barking intermittently at all hours and every month or so rising to murderous crescendoes. Hector and Madeleine walked together in the evenings like lovers past the scattering of houses. In the garden of one widow a lilac bloomed mauve, and as it sent out to them its romantic scent he would glance speculatively at her face and shoulders. Often she would wear a pale yellow shawl, intricately crocheted, which she said belonged to her mother. He may well have been prompted in his conscientious courting by his debt of gratitude to her father, but there was no denying either that she was an attractive woman and pleasant company. Celine had caused him some embarrassment the night she stayed at Babette's. It wasn't anything she said or did, but she had become part of his haunting past or, more accurately, she represented a bridge between military discipline and its connotations of death and civil nostalgia on the far side of his desertion and, on this side, the "freedom" and guilt of his present existence. Yet despite his outcast dilemma he had discovered an astonishing kindness and love from these two French families. Whichever way you kicked the can, Celine comprised yet another importunate debt.

Marcel Gabereau had set about making it a night of celebration, as if daring Hector and Madeleine not to anticipate future joy.

"No more work today, my son," he said to Hector.

For many the war had cancelled the old strict periods of mourning. There was so much to grieve for one thing, but even so Babette whispered that she was surprised at the way her cousin was acting. Uncle Joe had found in the attic of the Chaubet house a concertina which had belonged to one of the dead sons and he brought it along triumphantly in the wagon. It was not as grand as his old accordion but it would do. He had also acquired a white scarf which he wrapped around his neck to conceal his monstrous growth.

They had all walked from the wagon back to the house.

"There must be joy tonight," Marcel declared in the yard. "For everyone. We shall have lots to eat and drink. I have it on the best authority that the war will be over in two months."

"I believe the poor old fellow has lost it," Babette said quietly to Hector. "The agony has been too much for him. It's not surprising, really."

"He used to be so silent at the store," Hector said. "Hardly spoke a word all the time I was there when his wife was alive."

"Hurrah!" Uncle Joe shouted unexpectedly, waving the concertina in the air and then squeezing out a few bars of a saucy ballad. Marcel

Gabereau had sent him to an old doctor friend in Chaubet who was treating the growth on his neck with poultices. Joe would proudly tell Celine and Suzette that the horrible boil was beginning to shrink a little.

M. Gabereau's celebratory meal was not a wild success. It caught them all emotionally off guard. They'd brought cooked meats which Madeleine had prepared at Chaubet and some bottles of Calvados of which Gabereau seemed to have an inexhaustible supply. The first thing he did was to open one of these on the kitchen table and drain a couple of liqueur glasses himself. The others, except for Uncle Joe, refused a drink.

"And now, my boy," the grocer said, taking Hector by the arm and blowing brandy fumes into his face, "you and I will take a walk round the fields and you can show me what you have been doing."

With his cropped head, veined bulbous nose and short stature he resembled Lena as little as possible.

"Wait for me," cried Uncle Joe.

The women were left to sort out the sleeping accommodation and to get Cousin Marcel's impromptu dinner together.

As the three men reached the beet field Gabereau turned his bullet head to make sure they were out of earshot. He had changed out of his workday clothes and was wearing a charcoal suit with high stiff white collar and tie.

"You know that Babette's husband, Sol, is dead."

"Well fuck me," Hector said. "Pardon me, monsieur. Yours is a very sad family. So many deaths."

"It's like that all over France, my son."

"But..." Hector kicked at a clod of earth.

"Yes?"

"Does she know about this? Babette?"

"Oh, she knows all right. She tries to pretend it never happened."

೦ಶ⚜ಶಿ

At the dinner Hector sat between Madeleine and Celine. He believed that the latter was indeed losing weight. When she had related bits of her history those nights in the barns he'd found it difficult to reconcile the young girl of the apple orchards with the grotesque cynical whore lying by his side in the cold damp straw. They all tried their best to make a go of the evening, especially Madeleine who looked fondly at her father. After some stiff shots of brandy, he ignored the wine which Babette provided, Uncle Joe got a little pie-eyed and started dancing around the kitchen playing old songs, one of which Celine sang solo in strong, sure voice.

"I didn't know you could sing like that."

Her whispers in the barns had not held any suggestion of a melodious voice. They'd been like any old whore's in an estaminet or a knocking shop, rasping, hoarse and in sardonic contrast to the tales of her young life.

Marcel sat at the head of the table, elbows on the shining cloth Babette had laid, napkin tucked into his hard white collar, knife in his right hand held aloft like a conductor's baton, perspiration on his brow.

"What's he trying to prove?" asked Babette.

"Well done!" the grocer beamed at Celine. In his dour reclusive days he had scarcely noticed her. "Now let's have more music, Joe. Choruses we can all sing to."

Madeleine smiled gently at him and put her hand on his arm and pulled it down along with the knife.

"Be careful, papa. Or you'll be chopping someone's head off."

Hector ate his dinner voraciously. The women had cooked hot vegetables to go with the cold ham and beef. I don't know whether I've figured this right, he thought as he ate and Joe played and Gabereau was getting as tight as a tick, but if I have I sure don't know what in hell to do about it. Even Babette, married to a dead husband, was looking at him now with secret promise and hope in her eyes. Maybe that was part of it. So many of their men had been killed and they were looking for husbands. Even a deserter would do. He took a sip of the red wine, dry and harsh. He did not drink much these days. Knock it off, he admonished himself. He looked round the table, beaming. It's about time you pulled your lousy wits together and stopped thinking you're the rat's ass with half the female population of France wanting to marry you, you insufferable jerk. You are imagining all this about three decent women. Uncle Joe was sitting by the window pumping out a thin melody of something or somebody lost and a hush came over the table, even the noise of the cutlery was stilled. Who do you think you are, Hector? Some kind of shithead.

03 ❀ 80

At a United States Army field hospital housed in a chateau where once a promiscuous count gave scandalous parties, an army surgeon stood over Tyler Brown.

"We had to take your arm off, soldier. We couldn't wait. The infection was spreading fast. I don't know how you got it in such a goddamn stinking mess. It must have given you hell."

Tyler was lying among rows of other wounded on a patch of what had once been the floor of the great dining hall. His usually trim moustache had grown long and unkempt, making him look much older.

"We'll get you out of here as soon as we can and back Stateside. Where'd you come from, soldier. What's your name?" He glanced down at his clipboard. "Brown, right? Tyler Brown, it says on your chart."

"Yessir."

"And your home?"

"Kansas, sir."

"And your outfit?"

Tyler told him.

"There's a guy from that regiment just over here by the old fireplace. I'll get you moved next to him if we can find an orderly who's not chasing his tail in circles."

"Thank you, sir."

The surgeon hung around, almost asleep on his feet. His face was grey. He wore a military cap and a bloodstained apron.

"They'll fix you up with a prosthesis in the States. You know what that is, Brown?"

"No sir."

"A wooden arm. We were able to leave you a stump below the elbow and they'll fix a leather socket and the new arm and the wrist and the hand to it, the stump. It's a real dandy piece of work. You'll be able to move the thumb."

"Thank you, sir. Sir."

"Yes."

"Do you think I could have a smoke?"

"Sure thing. Here take my pack of cigarettes."

"I smoke a pipe, sir. But I need to get it filled."

They moved him that afternoon near the fireplace. The wounded man had been in his squad but Tyler hardly recognized him with his head half swathed in bandages.

"Hi Herm."

"Christ it's Tyler. Still got your old stinking pipe?"

"You betcha. How're you doing."

"Oh, I guess I'm gonna lose this eye. But boy, am I ever lucky"

"How come?"

"You not heard, then?"

"Not a fucking thing."

"I'm the only one to get out so far as I know. The sarge and Billie Joe both snuffed out as soon as they got to the top of the ladder. None of the guys got more than a few yards. Corporal Stuyvesant got a burst in the gut that just about cut him in half. You left just in time, Tyle."

"Shit."

"You lose that arm o' yourn?"

"I guess."

"Tough. Better'n being dead though, right, buddy?"

෬෯෨

The spring and the summer and the fall stretched out their tedious length to the peace of November. Tyler Brown had played his percentages accurately and had exchanged a hand and an arm from below the elbow for his life. On more than one occasion, however, his fellow deserter, Hector, had decided to surrender to the military authorities and then had drawn back from the brink. The day after Gabereau's dinner, which fizzled out after a few more drinks and tunes from Uncle Joe, the visitors returned to Chaubet and Hector remained at Babette's place with the two women. It was both a flattering and embarrassing period for him and did not help him one bit in his disturbing uncertainty, the constant gnawing at his conscience. Delightful as it was in many ways, the situation was a strain and, he thought, undignified for the two women, even though Babette was well aware that Madeleine and he had stayed on the express wish of Gabereau. We can't leave Babette stranded out here on her own, he'd argued, although before the arrival of Willi about whom the grocer knew nothing she had been left struggling alone for months on end.

All three worked in the fields and got dusty and hot and tired. Either Babette or Madeleine or both would go back early to prepare the dinner. Before eating, the three of them would sit in the kitchen and drink some wine before the meal. Gabereau had said he could manage at the store with Celine and Suzette, both of whom he knew were as strong as horses.

One evening when a cold wind had got up and a light rain set in, Babette had placed a glass of wine in front of him according to the daily ritual.

"I think I'll go tomorrow."

Madeleine was still upstairs, washing, changing into a fresh dress.

"Go where, dear?"

The "dear" didn't mean much. She and Madeleine were too decent or too proud to compete for him in open hostile rivalry.

"Tomorrow, or when Jules next comes with the wagon."

Madeleine came downstairs looking cool and as fresh as a daisy for all her day's toil.

"Yes, but where?"

"What's this all about?" Madeleine asked.

Hector looked up at her. She was always a delight to the eyes and the spirit and he wondered why he was so perverse about her.

"I think I'll have to go and turn myself in at the barracks at Chaubet. Finally. They're desperate for men. Maybe they'll let me go and fight instead of shooting me."

"And maybe cows will fly," said Babette.

Madeleine took a seat and looked at him thoughtfully.

"It's not easy, Hector."

"You can say that again."

"It's not easy for the relatives, either."

"Oh Christ, don't I know that too. For yours. For mine..."

Babette went to stir the rabbit stew simmering on the stove. She tasted the gravy with a large ladle and screwed up her face when she burned her tongue.

# TWELVE

The former infantryman, compact, shoulders well back, more fleshed out, cheeks less hollow than when he was lying on the floor in the field hospital, walked up the street from Higgins Bend train station towards the coffee shop which was opposite the War Memorial. The sun was shining, the sky blue and cloudless, the tops of the mountains glistening in the west. He'd never seen the Rockies before, though Hector had talked about them often enough. He was wearing a smart American suit, brown tweed, narrow pants, the height of male fashion in Larkin Rock, Kansas. He had a trim black moustache and his derby, also brown, was perched at a jaunty angle on his head. His shoes, brown—what else?—were highly polished. He passed the bend of the river which was flowing swiftly, reflecting the sun. Despite the glory of the day, the streets and buildings of the little town looked down at heels, drab. He went into the coffee shop and sat at a table near the window through which he could see the Memorial. The owner's wife came over to take his order.

"You must be a stranger here, mister."

"Sure am."

She brought him a coffee and a piece of apple pie.

"You come a long way, then. From the States, are you?"

"You could say that."

"Ernie's got a sister and brother-in-law lives in Montana. Nowheres near there, eh?"

"Nah."

"Billings. Two nice kids they got."

"Montana's a big state, lady. Takes a good day and a half to get from top to bottom."

"I knows that. What d'you take me for?"

She retired to the cash register, miffed.

Tyler Brown pulled out a little comb from an inside pocket and, cupping his wooden hand over the bridge of his nose, surreptitiously groomed his moustache. He kept his derby on his head. He stared across at the Memorial and wondered whether Hector's name would be written there among the war dead. For all he knew Hector might well have died one way or another. Ever since he'd been discharged, three years ago already, he'd been meaning to write to the grocer's at Chaubet but hadn't got round to it. It would have to be in English anyway and perhaps that was not a smart thing to do. He turned to the coffee shop owner's wife.

"Ma'am!"

She scowled at him.

"This is Higgins Bend, right?"

"Has been ever since I was born here."

"You know a family by the name of Plouvier?"

Mollified, she got off her stool and moved ponderously to his table, a large sturdy woman, as much muscle as fat, a blue work coat covering her amplitudes, a matching turban on her head. She looked more as though she were some sort of cleaner rather than waitress.

"Rose is the name, mister."

"Hi!" He raised himself a little from the chair and lifted his hat an inch off his head. "Tyler. Tyler Brown."

"Pleased to meetcha. Plouviers is ranchers round here."

The United States Army had done Tyler proud up to a point. They'd shipped him back to a veterans' hospital in New England and there he'd been fitted out, as the field surgeon had promised, with a prosthesis. The fingers of his new wooden hand were half-closed, permanently, but the thumb pivoted and through a system of metal and rubber bands stretching to the opposite shoulder could be moved minimally. Tyler quickly learned how to hold a box of matches in the artificial hand, strike one with the good hand and light his pipe safely clamped in his jaws. Filling the pipe with tobacco took more practice.

When it came to his being discharged there was confusion over the paper work. "We don't seem to have any records of you, soldier, before that last battle you were in. Seems they wanted to recommend you for some sort of medal, except most of the fellers in your outfit was killed. We could try to investigate if you like. I've got to tell you it could take months." Tyler said not to bother thank you and murmured something about losing his memory. They were very busy in the office and couldn't spend too much time on him. They gave him an American identity, an honourable discharge, his back pay plus a hundred dollars and a train ticket to his home town. He said he came from Larkin Rock, Kansas.

"Them Plouviers sure is one unlucky family."

Rose refilled Tyler's coffee cup.

"How come?"

"Well, I guess lots of folk lost someone in the war, but somehow them up there don't seem too happy, even now. Always seems a cloud like is over that family. Course it's a crazy setup they got, them two houses. Nick Plouvier, he's the boss man, rides into town looking like thunder. Mind you, he wasn't very cheerful even before his son got killed. Would you like some more pie?"

"Thanks. It's good pie. You bake it, Rose?"

"I do all my own baking."

"What two houses?"

"You see the spread originally belongs to Nick's father, some says he was French, had to be with a name like that, didn't he? The two sons, Nick and Sam, come into the land when the old man died and live in the old ranch house. Then Nick marries a real Frenchie from Quebec and later when Sam marries he and his new bride move into a split new ranch house. Very hoity toity, up your nose, Mrs. Sam is, though she's always been nice enough to me when she come in here. She better be, I says to Ernie. I don't stand for no nonsense like. I won't have folk looking down on me, I can tell you. No matter who they are."

Rose cut a fresh piece of pie and placed it in front of Tyler.

"Then Sam goes and gets himself killed."

"In the war?"

"Good Lord, no. Years before it. Skating on a slough. Smashed his head in or someone did it for him."

"They had no kids?"

"Not one."

"The widow never married again then?"

Rose looked at her customer with a questioning archness.

"Mrs. Sam? Never. She got very fond of her nephew and niece."

Tyler tapped his match-box on his wooden hand.

"Okay. And then what, Rose? You said they were always unlucky."

"Well, like I told you, there was Nick's son, Hector. He got killed in France a few months before the Armistice. Oh and there's been trouble on and off up at the ranch. Say, what's the matter with your hand, Mr. Brown?"

珞 ❦ 珞

Larkin Rock, not a hundred miles from Kansas City, was the home town of Corporal Stuyvesant. Just before Tyler was evacuated from the trenches with his poisoned arm, Corporal Stuyvesant had given him a scrap of paper with his address written on it in indelible pencil. Tyler had folded it and kept it in his tobacco tin. Bits of the writing had smudged purple where it had got wet.

"If we ever gets out of this fucking war alive, Tyle, and if you is ever down Kansas way, why don't you drop by? You'd be mighty welcome. I'd sure like you to meet my folks."

Mr. Stuyvesant Senior was typical of the father who had made the supreme sacrifice and wouldn't hear anything from his wife about his son's death being a waste. Ron had his duty to do, Edith, and he did it like a man. He was entirely bald apart from a grey wisp of hair arching round each ear. He had a strong straight nose, pitted with little craters as he grew older, and the fierce bristles of his moustache hanging over his mouth. He had opened the door of a house bigger than most of its neighbours, more imposing than the Gabereaus' in Chaubet. He was a good six inches taller than Tyler.

"Mr. Stuyvesant?"

"That's me." He looked down suspiciously as though Tyler were trying to sell him a bill of goods. In a way Tyler was.

"I guess I knew your son, sir. I was in his platoon."

Tyler produced the piece of paper from his tobacco tin.

"Just before the last battle he give me this."

The older man took the creased and stained paper. Tyler watched as surprise, joy, and pain succeeded each other across the father's face.

"That's Ronald's writing all right. So you were in his squad! Well, can you beat that. Come right in. What did you say your name was?"

Tyler followed him down a short passage into a spacious living room with large windows facing a back yard. In a corner near the window was an upright piano with a bowl of cut flowers on top of it, daisies perhaps.

"Edith."

A small woman with greying hair, large anxious eyes, haunted look, every soldier's mother, put down her knitting and got up from a chesterfield which was covered in bright chintz. Beside her was an attractive woman in her twenties, face a little pudgy but slim figure. She smiled shyly.

"This is Tyler Brown. He was with Ron just before...."

The mother grasped her throat and tears threatened in her large eyes.

"My wife, Edith. My daughter, Nancy."

The girl stayed on the sofa but smiled gently, unaffectedly. She looked significantly at their visitor's wooden hand.

"I'm sorry about your arm, Mr. Brown. Looks as though you have problems too."

"Not to worry, miss. You got sharp eyes, don't you. I guess I lucked out really."

"Gee I never noticed that," Mr. Stuyvesant said. "I suppose you lost it at..."

"Yes. Same time."

Edith shook his good hand.

"It's good of you to take the trouble to come, Mr. Brown. We sure appreciate it even though it's a shock at first, you coming. It brings it all back. You can understand?"

"Sure do, ma'am."

She glanced over at the piano. By the vase of flowers in a gilt frame was a photo of Corporal Stuyvesant looking very serious in dress uniform. The picture brought it all back for Tyler too, the trenches, the wire, the half-blinded soldier in the field hospital who had told him about the corporal's death.

"He was a great guy," Tyler said to the three of them. "The fellers would do anything for him."

03 ❀ 80

"You're asking a lot of questions about the Plouviers, Mr. Brown, if you'll pardon me saying it. You know the family, like?"

"Knew of them."

"In the army, eh? I betcha met Hector Plouvier in your travels."

"Yeah. You said it."

"There you go. I guessed that's what it was all about. You know what you ought to do. You ought to get yourself up to the ranch and introduce yourself. Only don't say nothing I've been telling you, not but what it's God's truth. The folks'd be real pleased to talk to you, someone what knew their beloved Hector. They took it bad, you know. Hector's death."

"Nah, nah. I don't want to do that."

"Why ever not, Mr. Brown?"

"I have my reasons."

"Suit yourself. It's like I said. Always some crazy deal coming up about that family."

"How come crazy?"

"Keep your hair on. I'm not saying you was crazy. Have another piece of pie?"

Rose unfolded her arms and brushed down the front of her blue coat. Her eyes and mouth were small in a big pasty face. She looked quizzically at Tyler as though speculating how far she could go.

"Well perhaps weird more that crazy, what's the difference? There's that Angie Leech, for instance, what lives up with Mrs. Sam and is all full of airs and graces. She's no better than what me and Ernie is. Born in a shack she was. And lived in another after she got married to that poor Dicky Leech. And it got burned down in the big fire, like. And her husband killed in it wasn't he. Roasted to a cinder, poor man. And she pregnant and that's a story in itself."

"Tell me about it."

Rose pulled out the other chair at Tyler's table and sat down. She put her elbows on the table and bent her large head towards him in a gesture of conspiracy. Tyler filled his pipe expertly, one handed.

"Real neat the way you do that."

He listened patiently. He, the big city man, had got used to the twists and innuendoes of small town gossip in Larkin Rock. It was ironic, though. Life was good down there, the most stable he'd ever been in his life thanks to the generosity of the Stuyvesants, but even though he'd adapted to his circumstances, he'd be a fool not to, and didn't want to give it up, he felt stifled from time to time with the sheer goodness of the Kansas family. Of all his experiences of war, its dishonesties, heroics, deprivations, he would never forget that hike out of an unbearable hell with Hector and the Trou family and the fucking cart. He remembered uneasily, this man without a conscience, how he screwed Celine on that filthy bed. Tyler had laid his share of whores in Canada and France but he wasn't too proud of that one, especially when Celine became a sort of comrade. Funny the way Hector had gone soft on her on the journey. In Kansas he thought of them all, on and off, so when a rare opportunity came to head north to Canada and although he had only the vaguest idea of what he was going to do or find he jumped at it. The irony was that to discover anything he had to endure more small town gossip, this time from Rose. He certainly was not going head to head with the Plouviers.

"You listening, mister?"

"Sure. Sure thing. Go ahead."

He lit his pipe and held the match box over the bowl to draw it. Clouds of smoke billowed over the table and Rose coughed.

"Where was I up to? Angela. Some say that Hector Plouvier and her went out together, but he was such a kid at the time. Mind he was only a kid when he joined the army."

"Musta been, Rose."

She looked round the shop to make sure it was empty.

"Here's the funny part. When Nick Plouvier saves Angie from the fire she's supposed to be pregnant see. They makes a darn great fuss over her and she goes to live with Mrs. Sam. Course she's been a widow a long time by then and living on her own. Half the town was burned down but we all thought it was strange that Angie should be picked out, a real wilful girl that one, to go and live up there. I mean there was more deserving folk what lost their homes. Then what do you think happens?"

"What happens, Rose?"

"The next thing is that she's off on the train to Winnipeg with Mrs. Sam and Mrs. Marie. Well, people in this town were busting themselves with curiosity and then Mrs. Marie, Nick's wife, come back on her own and tells us that Angie's had a baby boy in Winnipeg and she is all smiles and looks very chuffed. I mean why should she be excited about Angie's kid? I tell you, folks is chattering away like crazy." Rose held up a plump hand and beat her fingers against her thumb.

"So what was wrong with that, Rose?"

"You might ask that. And you might be right. But why did those two women have to go with her and why hundreds of miles from here, eh? Why did Mrs. Sam have to stay behind in Winnipeg? There's a guy called Chuck Turner who's a hand up at the ranch and he can tell you a few tales about Mrs. Sam. You ought to talk to him before you go, that's for sure. And why did Angela and the kid have to live up there with her and still does. Mind you, he's turned out a nice boy...."

"I don't see what you're driving at, Rose."

ଔ☙

Perhaps Tyler didn't want to understand what Rose was driving at. He'd been working down in the Gabereau basement with Hector the week or so before his arrest when Hector was in the depths of depression. He thought his friend had been recovering well, gaining back sanity and health, partly through his Jesus beard and his new do-good attitude. Admittedly he had black moods which did not last long and which Tyler put down to the horror of his desertion, an act about which Tyler had little guilt. Well, nothing so agonizing as Hector's.

After all, he'd paid his dues to King George V, hadn't he, all those years in the trenches. But Hector would go on picking at his guilt, his goofing off, moaning about the shame of it, whatever would people think. They hadn't much to do that afternoon, a day when the sun would come out for half an hour, shine promisingly and then the sky would cloud over. They'd unloaded a few sacks of rice and dried beans from Jules's wagon and Hector was sitting on the dusty floor, his back propped up against the wall.

"Cheer up, old buddy. It can't last for ever."

Hector slowly focused on his fellow exile.

"It's not the war this time, Tyle."

"What is it then? Because we got out of the goddamn army? Because we went absent without leave?"

"Nah."

"Firing squad blues?"

"The hell with the firing squad."

"What then? Tell me. Instead of looking like death warmed up."

Hector flipped his beard up with the back of his hand and was silent for what seemed ages. They had not been allowed to grow beards in the trenches in case they got lice. They got lice on other parts of their bodies. Tyler sat down beside him.

"What would you say if I told you I'd fucked my aunt?"

"You what?"

"Fucked my Aunt Sammy."

"You serious?"

"Dead serious."

Tyler turned to look at him and started to laugh, great guffaws of salacious merriment.

"Jumped your aunt?" he asked with tears in his eyes. "Where?"

"Whadya mean where, you dumb asshole. Between her fucking legs, where else?"

Another gust of laughter from Tyler. He was holding his sides. "I mean where was you when you done it?"

"In the goddamn cowshed. Hidden in the bulrushes down by the slough. In her own bed. Any lousy place, what does that matter..."

Hector glared at his friend, but gradually he caught the infectious laughing and a slow grin turned into hysterical mirth.

"How old were you?"

"Seventeen."

They both roared at that.

"I guess she didn't object. She gave out all right?"

They quietened down, wiped their eyes. Hector wondered if anywhere in the world there was a more treacherous shit than himself.

"Aw, come on, Tyle. It's no laughing matter."

"Is that why you ran away to join the army?"

"May be. How the fuck would I know?"

Tyler helped his friend up off the floor and silently they started stacking the rice in a corner next to the coffee beans. That was the last full and clear picture he remembered of Hector, his fair hair, his ruffled beard, his eyes wet with laughter, shining as though some demon had been released.

"How come you called her Aunt Sammy?"

☙❦❧

Rose's gossipy insinuations had brought back the memory of Hector's confession, although it had lodged in the back of his mind when much else was forgotten. Tyler got up and went over to the till and paid for his coffee and pie.

"You figuring on staying here a while?"

"I don't know, Rose."

"There's a nice hotel a block further down. Nothing wonderful, but clean. And we do hot dinners right here."

"Thanks, Rose. I gotta think about it."

He walked across the road and stood before the simple monument to the glorious dead. There were far too many names on it, in alphabetical order, for such a small town. The plinth was set in a square of grass, green and fresh in the sunlight, tidily mown. A narrow gravel path ran across it to the base of the Memorial. Tyler approached and took off his bowler hat and looked up. ATKINS, THOMAS; AXWORTHY, JOSHUA...BROWN, WILLIAM. He wondered how many Browns had been killed in that war on another continent. Halfway down the second column he read PLOUVIER, HECTOR.

"What would you say if I told you I fucked my Aunt Sammy?"

The guys listed here would have been in other regiments from his and Hector's, but they would have all gone through the same shit. People who hadn't been there had no idea.

Tyler thought of Hector's father, with, what did Rose say, thunder in his face, riding up on his horse and dismounting at the edge of the green grass and looking at the list of war dead. And his mother, the Frenchie, Marie, Tyler pictured her in a black dress and hat like the old country-women wore in France. And would Aunt Sammy come and look up here, as Tyler was looking, with a sense of fondness and loss? And what about that boy who, Rose said, lived with Aunt Sammy? Hector had never mentioned anything about no boy. How could he? He didn't know. The kid must be about six or seven now. He'd like to see him. He'd like to see Aunt Sammy.

Tyler turned away and put on his derby, tapping it on the crown with his good hand. Best leave things alone, don't go digging up any more. He pulled out his pipe and walked back by the river to the station. He'd most likely have a long wait for the train back south.

# EPILOGUE

"Do you have beer, madame?"

Mon Dieu! Celine looked across the bar counter of the estaminet at the tall man in the light blue uniform of the air force. The oddly handsome face was prematurely lined with the marks of war. Not too tall, not too handsome. My God! She was knocked all of a heap.

"Are you not feeling well, madame? Pardon me, but you look as though you are going to faint."

The young man's expression showed kindly concern. He was wearing pilot's wings and the ribbon of a medal for gallantry on his left breast. His French was as fluent as Hector's. He had placed his cap on the bar top and his hair was as fair as Hector's. The way he held his shoulders, slightly hunched... Holy Mary, it was enough to give anyone a turn.

"I'm all right, sir." Celine was breathing heavily and her hands trembled.

"That's all right then. You had me quite worried there."

"We have a little beer, not much. The Yanks came through last week and drank nearly all we had. The war, you know, sir. But I have a bottle I can let you have."

"Wizard."

He was standing at the corner of the bar where in the old estaminet that horrible bed was curtained off for her and Suzette to take turns on. When they'd rebuilt the place after the first world war she'd begged her father to remodel it altogether, but old M. Trou had been obstinate and the new bar was shaped exactly the same as the old one and in the very same place. No bed.

"Not to worry, madame, it's nearly over, the jolly old war." He translated his air force slang into French. "We've got old Jerry on the run now."

He had Hector's eyes, and he gave her a shy glance after he spoke as though half apologizing for anything he said. Celine opened a dusty bottle and poured his beer.

"This is on the house. We certainly owe you brave boys in the R.A.F. a lot. During all the years of the Boche occupation you were our only hope."

"Royal Canadian Air Force, madame. Now. I started in the R.A.F."

My God, it gets worse. My head's bursting. I think I shall scream if I get much more like this. Who is this charming man she would like to reach over and give a motherly hug to, this quite eerie phantom from across the ocean, this second coming of Hector?

"Someone at the Town Hall said perhaps you could help me. I'm looking for Hector Plouvier. A soldier in the last war. I say, madame, are you really all right?"

She took a firm hold of the counter while the officer looked at her anxiously. She turned carefully to the row of bottles behind her and poured herself two fingers of brandy.

"I'll join you in your drink, sir, if you don't mind. I had a spot of bad news this morning...about my cousin, and you know the way something like that nags at you."

"Certainly, madame. I do. Look, I'll trot along if I'm being a nuisance. Just knock this beer back and chocks away."

"No, no! I'm all right now, truly. Who did you say you were looking for?"

"A Canadian soldier called Hector Plouvier. Not him really, he's been dead for years, went for a burton in the last show, poor guy. No, it's his grave I'm trying to find and I'm having a deuce of a time getting a handle on it. Seems as though part of the cemetery was shelled or bombed in this war. Can't even leave the dead in peace, can they? I'm not saying the Hun did it deliberately. It may even have been our side, you never know. Anyway, I promised his parents I'd pay my respects to Uncle Hector if you follow what I mean."

Celine drained her drink at one go and poured another. She was nearly thirty years older than she had been at Chaubet when Hector had asked her if he could go back with her and her father and help in restoring the farm and the estaminet. She was dumbfounded. She had believed that it was all settled that he should stay with the Gabereau business and marry Madeleine. Now her hair was greying and her complexion had a yellow tinge, eyes pouched but she stood erect and most of the old whore flab had gone. She looked hard at the features of the visitor's face, as if not believing what she saw.

"He is, was, your uncle then? This Hector?"

"Well yes and no. It's rather complicated. I'm Flying Officer Leech by the way. Richard Leech."

"Enchanted. And I am Mme. Trou."

They shook hands with grave formality. Celine's hand trembled.

"My mother and I lived at his aunt's ranch house. I was brought up there. It's a long story. I'm told this guy Hector called her Aunt Sammy." He laughed. "Darned funny name for a lady when you think about it. She's a honey, I can tell you. I call her Aunt Sammy, too, I guess because he did. Course I never met this Hector, Uncle Hector I call him though he's not my uncle really, not even a cousin or anything. I must be boring you, madame."

"On the contrary. Please continue."

"You see my dad died in a fire before I was born."

"How sad for you."

"In a way, yes. But he didn't mean anything to me. How could he? Just a name, my father. Uncle Hector was my idol. Aunt Sammy would say, now don't cry, Richard. You've got to be a brave little soldier just like your Uncle Hector."

Hector had come back here after the war with Celine and her father, Suzette and Tina, Uncle Joe and his concertina, and what a mess it was, an ocean of mud and wire, and what years it took to put things back in shape. Hector had married her. After consultation with her father he changed his name to Trou and had a good laugh about that, but he believed it was politic to discard his old name once and for all for you never knew who might come snooping by. And rather than invent a new name, why not take his wife's.

He lightened up a lot, but only Celine was aware of the demon filled abysses of gloom he endured from time to time. I've got to stick it out, he would say, there is no atonement, no forgiveness. The villagers who came back to rebuild their homes along the river valley made no obvious gossip about the newly married Trous at the estaminet farm. They minded their own business. Celine's first husband, Big Red Jean may well have been killed in the war for she saw neither hide nor hair of him. Those of her former beaux who had survived were gallantly discreet. The lawyer with the orangery had died a natural death, she heard. One of Suzette's, not the father of Tina, started visiting and after a period of decorous courtship they married and moved off to another village. Celine did not think him much of a prize, for the poor wretch had lost one eye at Arras and the other one watered badly, but she was happy for her cousin.

"This nice lady at the Town Hall said there was a Hector Trou who lived here. And I thought what a coincidence! Hector's not a common name is it?"

"Yes. My husband was Hector. He...died last year."

"I guessed he might be related to you when you told me your name. I'm very sorry.... Look, madame, I'll go away if I'm upsetting you."

"No. Stay."

"Well then, just one more question. Did he speak English...was he, no he couldn't be, of course not. Pure fantasy. Please forget it, madame."

"Was he what?"

The officer made a self-deprecatory face.

"He wasn't a Canadian by any chance?"

"No, no, no. He came from round here, down the valley a bit. He was my husband, monsieur, so I ought to know. He spoke a little English. He learned it at school."

She and Hector had worked hard and done very well entre les deux guerres. Her father and Uncle Joe—his carbuncle never did really shrink—died in reasonable peace in due season and at least they were spared a second war. The apple orchard was replanted and the blossoms came again in the spring and green growth mantled the mud and corpses beneath it. She and Hector had no children. They would walk through the orchard on a summer evening and Celine once laughingly showed him the spot where a cavalryman had tried to seduce her. Hector never once mentioned Aunt Sammy.

During the second war, the German panzers had roared through the farm but they were so keen to get to Paris that Celine and Hector were fortunately left in a local backwater. They endured stoically the restraints and indignities of enemy occupation but in the matter of preserving their home and farm this time they were luckier. It was hateful enough, but if only things had stayed like that. Things never did. After the first shock and paralysis of the national defeat and disgrace men came knocking on the door, men from the maquis. Hector, who had never risen above the rank of private in his own Canadian army, became a local resistance leader. This is my big chance to wipe the slate clean, he said to Celine and she was never quite sure what he meant by that. By that time his French had merged into the local patois and with his two languages he was an ideal contact man with the British. His group became more and more daring.

They smuggled allied pilots through the underground escape route, attacked German lines of communication, and blew up ammunition dumps, not always without loss to themselves. Celine worried about him but often risked her own neck to help in the covert operations. She saw a new light in her husband's eyes. He seemed to have dug down and discovered unknown resources of purpose and vindication. "You've no idea of what this means to me," he told her. He dodged all the bullets, as he had done in the first war, until just before D-Day when he was captured by the Gestapo and tortured and finally shot by a firing squad in full view of the village. What was left of him was thrown off the back of an army truck in the village square.

☙ ❀ ❧

"Nick brought the mail up from Higgins Bend. There's a letter for you from Richard."

Bridget handed it to Angie, and the two grey haired women, still living together in the same ranch house, sat down to savour it, Angie first, Bridget trying to squint at it over her shoulder but her sight was not so good and she hated wearing eye-glasses. Angie opened the envelope, and as she was extracting Richard's letter a photograph fell out.

ೞ✾ಐ

Dear Mom: I guess you and the folks have heard—I'm not giving away big secrets so I won't get my ass in a sling—that this blankety blank war is just about over—though some of our army boys had a bad time in those darned Dutch canals. Must have been terrible for them—you'll be glad to know I've not been on a combat mission for ages. Funny thing—now I've got through it without a scratch—knock on wood—I shall miss the excitement. Back to the ranch soon, eh? No. No little English girl or French girl in tow.

Remember I promised you guys I'd try to find out what I could about Uncle Hector's grave. You'll be glad to know I've been doing my homework. When I was in Ottawa I managed to get a look at some old military maps, trench positions and so on, and got an idea of where U.H.'s regiment was during that big offensive way back in 1917—and yesterday I reckon I was just about there, right on the spot. I'd taken a few days local leave—the guys wanted to know if I was going to Paris—see what I give up for the folks back home? You can tell Annie Lou missing Paris was no big deal, mom. Ooh-la-la!

There's this estaminet, see—it was flattened by Jerry in the first war and my guess is that the estaminet was just about in the middle of that battle where U.H. got his. I want to draw a veil over some of horribleness and just mention that not every soldier is buried where the War Graves Commission says he is—just leave it at that and let me say I figure U.H. and a lot of other Canucks are buried not far from where I was—from the estaminet—even though there are no little white crosses.

But there's a bit of a weird story comes out of all this. The old lady at the estaminet—she's the owner called Celine Trou—took a shine for me. I'd gone into her bar to ask a few questions, mainly to get my bearings right and she looked at me as though she'd seen a ghost. Her husband was also called Hector and apparently I reminded her of him. He'd been in the Resistance, a local hero—she told me they'd written to her about him getting a French gong—Croix de Guerre—that's a darned big honour, mom. He was tortured and killed by the Gestapo not long after D-Day. Anyway the widow insists we go to see his grave—can you beat it—and I haven't the heart to refuse. She closes up the bar and puts on a black hat and shawl and we go out the back way through an apple orchard to the village cemetery. We come to this grave and there is a vase of fresh flowers on top of the little mound. The inscription on the headstone is simple. HECTOR TROU—then in smaller letters—beloved husband of Celine and some dates which I can't remember. I stand to attention and salute. Weird, ain't it?

Love to Aunt Sammy and the rest—and of course to you, dear old mom. Richard.

P.S. Mme. Trou insisted on giving me this photo of her husband. She said send it to your folks. You can't really make out much of him because of the beard.

CR✤SO

Aunt Sammy picked up the creased black and white snap from the floor. She could not bear to think of the indignity of his being shot like a dog by a firing squad. She could not bear to think of the unimaginable tortures he had endured.